A ONE WAY
TICKET
to DEAD

D.V. BERKOM

A ONE WAY TICKET TO DEAD
Copyright © 2014, 2016 All rights reserved.
By D.V. Berkom
2nd Edition
Published by

ISBN-978-0-9979708-3-8
ISBN-10: 0997970839

For Mark.
The best is yet to come..

1

I NEVER DREAMED I'd come back.

I shouldn't have.

Even though I told myself things were safer compared to when I'd passed through all those years ago, deep down I knew I was only kidding myself.

The deepening shadows brought scant relief from the blistering heat, although the lower the sun dipped on the horizon the more bearable it became. The sun set early in this part of the world. I took a deep drink from my water bottle and wiped the sweat from my face with the back of my hand.

And waited.

I'd changed my hair for the umpteenth time and wore brown-tinted contacts so I'd blend, but there's only so much a girl can do to change her appearance short of surgery. Thanks to Quinn and his lies, the men who had tried to kill me thought I was dead. For now. The ruse wouldn't last long, not if someone from the old days got curious about the new American woman in town.

No sense lingering longer than I had to. Find the stash if it was still there, then get the hell out of Mexico.

The tiny house on the even smaller lot looked like the owner had lost interest and decided to let nature take its course. Dirt-green vines strangled the walls as if they were trying to squeeze the last drop of moisture from the filthy stucco. The cracked and faded flower pots flanking the walkway grew dirt in profusion, their long-dead occupants a distant memory. Two lime trees in the side yard still shaded my target. The ground looked like it hadn't been disturbed in all the time I'd been gone.

If my luck held.

I'd spent the day and evening before casing the place, watching for signs of life. The house appeared abandoned. How much longer could I stay without arousing suspicion? More time than absolutely necessary in Los Otros made me nervous, and I itched to get the deed done.

My stomach growled as I walked back to the rental. With a loan from Luis, my contact in the Drug Enforcement Administration, I'd chosen an unassuming Nissan Versa with plenty of dings and scratches. I told him I needed to find someone before going back to the States now that Roberto Salazar was dead. At first Luis had argued, asking why I'd even consider staying in Mexico, but finally relented when I told him I owed my life to this person. Nothing he said would change my mind.

Memories of the old man who'd saved me from being gunned down in the street eleven years before flooded my mind. *Oggie.* Vincent Anaya's right-hand guy, Frank Lanzarotti, put a bullet in him as we left Oggie's house. I'd never forgiven him and felt grim satisfaction when

Frank had been shot. This final trip through cartel-country wasn't only about the money.

I got in the car and turned on the air while I ate the now-cold tamale I'd bought earlier. I could have gone back into town and gotten something else, but wanted to keep my visibility to a minimum. Old friends would not be a welcome diversion and I'd already risked discovery by staying the previous evening at a nearby hotel.

Hours later, after I'd moved the car twice and taken a fitful nap, I parked in the dirt-track alley behind the house and cut the lights. From behind, the abandoned house took on a miserable, thoroughly depressive mien. I could almost make out the dark windows and back door, all three of which appeared as though they hadn't been seen to in years. The backyard where Lana served me dinner so many lives ago was grown over with tenacious vegetation, the kind that could survive drought-ridden, remorseless summers.

What had finally prompted Lana to leave? I tried to imagine her happy, dragging her sadness and the fallout from the choices she'd made to wherever the wave of her life deposited her. All that came to mind were bottles of cheap tequila on a beat-up nightstand and dark, lonely sojourns with men who didn't care.

Bad choices put me in this backyard of a tiny, run-down two-bedroom *casa* at the end of an unpaved street in a one-horse Mexican town. I hoped this wasn't another of those.

Bad choices, I mean.

I popped the trunk and walked around to grab the pickaxe and shovel I'd purchased the day before, along with a large backpack. My idea was to work as quickly as possible until I'd unearthed the stash of gallon-sized plastic bags, backfill the hole and leave. I glanced through the rear window at the glowing clock on the dash: a quarter past three. The post office wouldn't be open for hours. I'd have a long wait.

I walked along the back of the house to the side yard, picking my way past rampant prickly pear and creosote and paused in the shadows to listen. The wind slid past me, circling my bare legs, churning the dirt at my feet into a dust devil that swirled and crested, and then disintegrated into the night. The breathy *hoo* of an owl nearby assured me I wouldn't work alone.

The three other homes on the street remained dark, signifying no one on the block suffered from insomnia, at least not tonight. The houses were far enough apart and on the opposite side of the unlit street from where I'd be working so it was reasonable to assume my efforts would go unnoticed. One of the three boasted a noisy swamp cooler that clanked in protest at the stifling night air, helping to further disguise my activities.

I proceeded to the lime trees and leaned the shovel against the house. The new pickaxe broke through the caliche easier than I remembered and soon the earth resembled a miniature plowed field. Afraid I'd damage the plastic bags or wake up light-sleeping neighbors I reined in my enthusiasm a few inches deep and switched to the spade.

Though not as noisy, the shovel took much longer to dig the remaining depth of the hole. About an hour later, when I still hadn't hit what I was looking for, worry crept in like a feral cat scrounging for food. *What if it's not here? What if Lana somehow found it, dug it up, and is now living large somewhere in South America?*

Well, then I'd have to figure out something else. If it was gone, I'd be shit out of luck. I straightened and took a deep breath, collecting my thoughts. Panicked and wired from dodging death that night so long ago, I thought I'd be back to retrieve the stash long before now. A faulty memory could be the reason I hadn't found it yet.

Or Lana was dancing the tango in Argentina.

Discarding the tango possibility, I stepped past the freshly dug hole to survey the yard. Closing my eyes, I thought back to that night, the memories resurrecting long-buried emotions. So many years of running, of looking over my shoulder, never being able to live a normal life.

So many friends lost.

Fallout from a bad choice made long ago. Payback, I supposed, for being stupid and young and attracted to shiny things. My fingers curled around the onyx jaguar figurine I wore around my neck. Now that Salazar was dead, I hoped my life could get more or less back to normal.

Then again, what the hell was normal?

I opened my eyes and took in the lime trees, the house, the surrounding vegetation. The yard had looked different back then. Well-tended. Then it hit me.

Unchecked catclaw choked the tree trunks, creating an optical illusion. I'd misjudged the distance of the stash from the base of the tree and had dug too far out. Once again working the pickaxe, I hacked away with new purpose at the base of the overgrown shrub until I cleared a space where I gauged the target should be.

Rinse, repeat. Switch to the shovel.

Focused on digging, I didn't realize I had company until it was too late.

"Hey," a voice demanded in slurred Spanish. "What're you doing?" The rank smell of cheap tequila accompanied the words. Slowly, I turned.

His features semi-distinct in the darkness, the man swayed on his feet, his thick torso and muscled arms reminiscent of a man who worked long hours lifting heavy things. I gave him a half-smile and tightened my grip on the shovel.

"My friend Lana asked me to stop by her house and pick something up for her. I noticed the vines were choking the tree." I glanced over my shoulder at the offending catclaw. "She'd be very upset if one of her trees died, so I thought I'd clear some of it away before I left." Not a great story, but the man was obviously drunk, so I didn't think I'd have to be too convincing.

With a puzzled expression, he swiveled unsteadily on his feet, glancing first down one side of the street, and then back the other way before returning his bleary gaze to me and the shovel. His expression morphed from perplexed to concerned, transitioning to a leer.

"You're a liar," he slurred as he lurched toward me. "No one lives here." He took another step closer. "You do somethin' nice for me, an' this'll jus' be our lil' secret, yes?" he stage-whispered, reaching for his fly. I hoisted the shovel over my head. I couldn't afford to wake the neighbors.

"One more step and you're going to have one hell of a headache come morning," I said, my voice low.

"Huh?" He gaped at the shovel in my hands, incomprehension clouding his face. Frowning, he wiped his hands down the front of his shirt, his confusion obvious. He closed his eyes for a moment but lost his balance and stumbled to one side, barely catching himself before taking a header onto the street.

"*Aye carumba*," he muttered, shaking his head. Obviously unhappy with the way things were turning out, he waved me away, mumbling incoherently to himself as he zigzagged a path down the street.

I lowered the shovel with a sigh. I'd have to work faster, in case he came to his senses and raised an alarm.

Forty-five minutes later the muted clang of metal against dirt changed to a dull thud. I cut in around the spot with the edge of the shovel and then scooped out the rest by hand, revealing a dirt-encrusted bundle. My heart beat faster as I slid the tip of the shovel underneath the plastic bag and pushed down on the handle, leveraging the first package out of its resting place.

Eight gallon-sized bags later, I stopped to take a breath. I leaned the shovel against the tree and knelt down. The outer bags had become stiff from the dry and the dirt and the heat, but remained intact. I grabbed one and opened it, removing the inner bag, which was surprisingly flexible. I flashed on how long it would take for plastic to degrade when it wasn't subjected to light, like in a landfill. Our civilization would be long gone before that ever happened. For now, I had immense gratitude for the durability of plastic.

I slid open the plastic zipper holding the bag closed and reached inside for a stack of bills. Money in hand, I flipped through the hundreds with my fingers, fanning my face.

Still there. Still intact.

Yes.

Once all eight bags were safely inside the backpack, I zipped it closed and stood, kicking some of the dirt back into the hole to make it look less obvious. Since the house had evidently been abandoned and my visitor had been quite drunk, I doubted anyone would take notice, at least long enough for me to disappear. I picked up my tools and the hefty pack and returned to the car, my heart light. With Salazar dead, even if the home had been on a cartel watch list, it wouldn't be now. They were tenacious, yes, but that would be too obsessive, even for cartel thugs. Besides, they thought I was dead.

I threw everything in the trunk and climbed into the driver's seat. One more errand and I'd be long gone.

Goodbye, Mexico. Hello, freedom.

2

ACCORDING TO THE sign on the window the post office in the back of the small grocery store opened at nine. The front door stood propped open to take advantage of the non-existent morning breeze. A woman in her early seventies wearing a T-shirt and khakis looked up from the ledger on the counter in front of her and smiled when I walked in. Gray hair framed a weathered face and her dark eyes snapped with energy.

"*Buenos dias, Señora,*" she said, her gaze skating to the large envelope in my hand.

"*Buenos dias,*" I replied with a smile as I neared the counter.

"May I help you?" She'd switched to English without skipping a beat.

"This is probably going to sound strange, but I'm looking for someone. A friend of a friend I knew a long time ago."

Her smile changed to one of polite interest. "Well, you came to the right place. I have lived here all of my life. In this town there are very few people I don't know."

"I hoped that would be the case." I glanced at her hand. No ring. She was about the right age. "Actually there are two. The first person's name is Ogden. He went by the nickname Oggie. I'm looking for his lady friend."

She stilled and the polite look switched to cool wariness. "I'm sorry, but I don't know anyone by that name."

"I met him several years ago and always meant to look him up if I ever got back this way. He said he had a good friend who worked at the post office here in town. Are you sure you've never heard of him?"

She narrowed her eyes slightly as though trying to gauge what kind of threat I might pose. After a couple of seconds she nodded, apparently coming to some sort of conclusion.

"He died last year."

"He—" I stopped short. "He died *last year?*" I must have looked shocked, as her expression changed to one of concern and she leaned toward me.

"Are you all right?"

I placed my hand on the edge of the counter. "Yes— of course. It's just that…" I took a deep breath. "If I may ask, how did he die?"

The corners of her mouth turned down, her eyes growing moist. "Cancer. He survived the diagnosis for two years, but it claimed him in the end." She glanced at me through tear-filled eyes. "He was a very dear friend."

"I'm so sorry. Please accept my condolences." My mind raced for an explanation. I'd heard the gunshot, saw Frank emerge from the small house wearing blood-spattered clothes, and had assumed the worst.

The woman frowned as she looked at me. "I'm sorry for asking, but you seem confused. Why?"

"No reason. I'm just sorry that I wasn't able to connect with him before…" I stopped mid-sentence and lifted my hands, palms up.

"Who is the other person you are looking for?"

Asking about Lana probably wouldn't be such a good idea since I'd just dug up her side yard. I shook my head. "Never mind. It's not important." I turned to leave but at the last minute remembered why I'd come. "Here," I said, handing the thick envelope across the counter. "I'd like you to have this. In Oggie's memory."

She glanced at the envelope and then at me, recognition arcing across her features. "You're Kate."

"Yes."

She nodded. "Oggie told me what happened. How he helped you get away from those animals only to have them find you at his *casa*. He never forgave himself for stopping at the house. 'If I'd just kept driving, they would never have caught her,' he'd say." Her fingers curled reflexively around a small gold cross on a chain at her neck. "He thought they killed you."

"He had to give his cat medicine or it would have died. The fault is mine for involving him." I closed my eyes for a moment, awash in memories of that awful day. "I thought he'd been murdered by the man who came after me."

She nodded. "The bullet didn't kill him. He was still conscious but pretended to be dead until the man left. It was a miracle of God I chose that day to deliver his mail and found him lying on the floor in a pool of his own blood. I bandaged him the best I could and took him to the doctor." She sighed at the memory. "We were both very lucky."

"We all were." The news brought a bittersweet end to my search. The guilt I'd harbored over his death lessened so that I could breathe again. Oggie's life hadn't been cut short for helping me. Then regret elbowed its way in and slapped me upside the head, telling me I should have come back sooner.

She glanced down at the envelope and slid it toward me. "You don't need to do this."

I slid it back. "Yes, I do."

Her eyes held mine for a moment before she nodded. "For Oggie."

"For Oggie." I turned and walked toward the door.

"They were here, you know." Her quiet voice echoed through the small store.

I stopped, turned back, afraid to breathe. "When?"

"Not long ago. Maybe one week. There were three of them, all dressed in black. *Narcos.*" She spit the word, crossing herself. "I told them what I knew, which was very little. Luckily, they believed me."

A week ago I'd been at a resort on the Riviera Maya, just outside of Tulum. *Don't freak out, Kate. Quinn only recently floated the rumor of your death. It's coincidence.*

Or not.

Time to leave.

3

THE PLANE TOUCHED down at Seattle-Tacoma International, the warm spring day a salve to my weariness. It was the kind of day that lulls you into believing the Pacific Northwest is the most incredible place on the planet, bar none. Before the incessant rain, and the gray, and the cold that seeps into you so deep it takes a trip to the tropics to thaw out. After sweating so long in dry-but-sweltering Sonora, the million different shades of green surrounded by copious amounts of salt water and cooler temperatures were a welcome relief.

I made reservations at a large hotel not far from Pike Place Market, preferring the anonymity of corporate luxury to a more intimate, boutique experience. The fact that it was close to a certain private investigator's offices may have had something to do with my choice.

I scanned the elegant lobby, searching for anyone out of place or showing an unwarranted interest in the thirty-something woman with shoulder-length brown hair carrying a large backpack and dragging a small roller case behind her. After hearing from Oggie's girlfriend about the three *narcos* dropping by, Kate's Paranoia Store was open for business and I couldn't help but buy the goods.

"Welcome to the Plaza on Pine. How may I help you?" The woman at the check-in counter smiled a professional welcome, her makeup flawless, the ironed creases in her blouse so sharp you could slice an overripe tomato without ooze.

With one more quick glance around the lobby, I dropped the backpack on the marble floor and smiled.

"Reservations for Kathryn Reid," I said, handing her my passport. Luis had chosen the name when he'd had his guy create the documents. Close enough to the real thing but still anonymous.

"Yes, Ms. Reid. I have you in room 1214." Crisp-shirt typed my information into the computer and then gave me another bright, corporate smile. "And how will you be paying today?"

"I'm afraid I lost my wallet recently and haven't received a replacement credit card yet. Would it be all right if I paid cash?"

Crisp-shirt's smile faltered ever-so-slightly but returned a micro-second later even brighter. "Of course. That will be eight hundred and ninety dollars."

I gave her a sharp look.

"We require a two hundred-dollar deposit for incidentals," she added, the pseudo-sympathetic smile gone as fast as it appeared.

I reached inside my bag, counted off nine hundred-dollar bills and slid them across the counter. She gave me ten dollars in change and then handed a key card to a young man who'd appeared at my side. "David will help you with your bags."

I smiled at the clean-cut kid in the forest-green blazer as he grabbed the handle of the roller case and reached for my other bag.

"I've got this," I said, hoisting the heavy backpack onto my shoulder. "Shall we?"

"The elevators are this way, Ms. Reid."

Once David had shown me around the one-bedroom suite and I gave him a tip, he left, closing the door behind him. I walked over to the desk and grabbed the wireless keyboard, returned to the loveseat and aimed the remote at the television. The Internet sprang to life on the screen. I reached inside my purse for a business card I'd stashed there and typed in the web address.

An understated, easy-to-navigate website with the title *Akiaq Investigations* in block letters across the top appeared on the screen. I clicked through to the *About* page and read what Sam had written about himself.

Akiaq Investigations: specializing in missing persons, corporate and criminal investigations, and insurance fraud. Results-driven and ethical. Former law enforcement.

Typical Sam. When we'd first met, getting him to say more than three words counted as a major victory. The email address at the bottom listed no names, only info at AkiaqInvestigations.com. I resisted the urge to send him a message, telling myself I was still on the fence about whether I should contact him.

Really, Kate? Why else did you come to Seattle?

If I did decide to contact him, and that was a big if, I preferred to see him face-to-face. I clicked off his website and onto the hotel's, and made an appointment for a massage and a facial, followed by a decent haircut. It wasn't like I was contemplating a visit to an old lover or anything.

Right.

Several hours later, after the spa treatments, a light dinner and a couple of margaritas, I made my way back to my room, feeling relaxed and lightheaded. In my semi-inebriated state, three margaritas sounded better than two so I picked up the phone and ordered another—this time a double. As I waited for room service, I pulled the bags out of the backpack and removed the stacks of bills, lining them up across the king-sized bed, curious to find out how much I'd recovered.

Each stack consisted of ten-thousand dollars in hundreds. I'd put twenty stacks, give or take, in each gallon-sized bag, for a total of one-point-six million. Not bad, considering I'd lost at least two-thirds of the money in my race across Mexico. That meant I'd stolen almost five million dollars from a Mexican drug cartel.

Yeah, I was lucky to be alive.

Room service delivered my margarita and I sat on the chair across from the bed, sipping my drink as I considered the money. I'd have to plan my expenditures if I wanted the cash to last. A million and a half didn't go as far as it used to. My splurge on this hotel would have to suffice for a long while.

The more I thought about the money, the more I wondered why Salazar and Anaya had continued to come after me. I could see the reasoning behind looking for me at first—I'd have been pissed off, too—but after the failed attempts to track me down, why keep trying? Eleven years is a long damn time to expend resources to find someone who'd stolen your money, especially when the amount constituted a tiny percentage of your annual revenue.

Yes, Roberto's pride had been wounded by my betrayal. Yes, a cartel boss lives and dies by his reputation for exacting revenge. But seriously, why waste so much time going after an insignificant player for so little return? Wouldn't it have been better to just let it go—consider it a bad debt and write it off, so to speak?

Except drug cartels didn't do business like normal people.

Never mind.

Must have been the tequila. I was thinking too much like a rational person. *Narcos* were anything but rational when it came to betrayal.

And money.

But it didn't matter anymore, not with Roberto Salazar dead. I'd been on the run for over ten years before the opportunity to fight back presented itself in the form of a group of commandos living deep in the Yucatán jungle. Salazar's death ignited a flicker of hope within me—hope for a normal, quiet life without having to look over my shoulder, wondering if someone wanted me dead.

I drained the margarita and set the glass on the table before I got up and walked unsteadily to the bed. Grabbing the bundle of cash closest to me, I unwrapped first one stack and then another, fanning the bills and scattering them across the bedspread like an expensive duvet.

The lyrics from an old Dire Straits song, "Money for Nothing", danced through my head.

Although the cash represented freedom, it also symbolized spilled blood and tragically disrupted lives. Oggie. Tristan. Sam. Cole.

Me.

When viewed from a distance, the fallout from that one colossally stupid mistake was breathtaking in its reach. I'd been young and naïve, unaware of how one choice could upset the balance of so many lives.

I knew now.

Tristan had been in the wrong place at the wrong time, and with the wrong woman. He'd stolen the money I'd managed to hang onto, yes, but he hadn't deserved to die. Cole—the man who'd been my best friend as well as my lover for the better part of the past year—didn't remember me after being shot in the head, and refused to become involved with a woman who might put his young daughters in danger. I didn't blame him. I wouldn't be with me, either.

I closed my eyes, took a deep breath, and let it go. Images of Sam with his dark, compassionate eyes and calm demeanor wove their way through my mind. My breathing calmed, the muscles in my shoulders released. I needed to see him, needed to know I had at least one friend.

Maybe if I asked for forgiveness the memories would fade.

I'd considered visiting my family in Minneapolis, but nixed the idea before it took hold. I'd go back someday when I'd put all that happened behind me. For now, Seattle seemed like a far friendlier place.

Maudlin from the three margaritas, I wiped angrily at the tears filling my eyes.

Get a hold of yourself, Kate. You've just got to start over. You can do this. You've done it a million times before.

I sat up straight, cleared my throat, and turned my attention back to the wad of money in my hand. I broke the paper band and held up the bills, letting them fall to the bed like so much confetti. A piece of paper the size of a business card fell out, landing on the bedspread. Curious, I picked it up and held it close, squinting at the small, neat letters hand-printed on the front. The first line was an indecipherable string of alpha-numeric characters.

The second listed a series of numbers separated by periods, similar to an IP address.

My curiosity piqued, I walked out to the sitting area and brought up the Internet to search the string of numbers on the card. Because my motor skills had taken a vacation, compliments of the tequila, it took a couple of tries before I got it right. My excitement rose as I waited for the computer to come back with the results. It wasn't every day that an eleven-year-old mystery fell into my lap.

Nothing significant came back. Disappointed, I searched the next nonsensical group of letters and symbols. Again, nothing.

Not yet ready to give up, I searched for information on how to use IP addresses to connect to webpages and came across a site that looked them up for you. I typed the number into the search box, and was rewarded with a link, which I clicked. A blank page with a small search box in the upper left-hand corner appeared. Intrigued, I entered the first line on the card but received an error message. I could feel a low-grade, throbbing headache coming on, beating time with my heart. Ignoring it, I typed the next line of characters into the dialog box.

The screen filled with photos that looked like they might be from someone's vacation: a famous street in Mexico City; a couple of beach scenes, complete with graceful palm trees with a hammock strung between them; a smiling vendor at a market stall; an old Spanish church.

Who would have a password for a webpage with pictures from a trip hidden in a stack of one hundred-dollar bills?

Oh, right. The information had been in a shipment belonging to Roberto Salazar.

When I'd left Roberto that terror-filled night, he'd already been one click shy of crazy town. The word paranoid couldn't begin to describe him—the video surveillance, the food tasters, the bodyguards. The only reason I'd been able to leave that night was because he'd been a little preoccupied.

Slitting the throat of your closest friend could do that to you.

And, being Roberto's girlfriend, I'd been given some leeway. Of course, when I got into the van idling in the driveway with a shipment of cash meant for Vincent Anaya and left the premises, the guy watching the monitors did sound the alarm. It just took Roberto a little longer to respond than usual.

Which gave me the perfect opportunity to escape.

At that moment, another dialog box popped open, warning me the computer I had logged on with was not the default address and that I needed to enter another password to continue. A digital timer to the left of the message counted down from :25.

I tried a couple of other alpha-numeric combinations, hoping I'd get lucky, but I didn't and the screen went blank. Exhausted from the trip and too much tequila, the pounding in my head grew more noticeable and I switched off the computer. *Screw it.* The site probably had something to do with Salazar's belief that his enemies would use anything against him, even vacation photos.

My curiosity gone and fatigue setting in, I walked back to the bedroom and lay on the bed, pushing the loose bills to the side to make room.

My last thought before falling asleep was of Sam.

4

I WOKE TO the jangle of the telephone next to my ear. The headache had devolved into a dull throb, and my tongue felt like I'd licked the floor at a tequila factory. With a groan, I pushed to a sitting position and took a deep breath, trying to clear my head.

Had to be the front desk. No one knew I was in Seattle, much less at the Plaza. I picked up the receiver and held it to my ear, closing my eyes against the morning sunshine blazing through the window.

"Good morning, Ms. Reid. This is Monica at the front desk."

I winced at Monica's chirpy tone. "Good morning," I managed. My voice had a raspy quality due to a desiccated tongue.

"You left instructions with Room Service last night to deliver your breakfast at eight o'clock. It's now eight-oh-five. The attendant left the tray outside your door when you didn't answer. I just wanted to make sure you still wanted your meal."

"I did? I mean, yes, of course. I must have been in the shower. Thanks." *Damned tequila.*

"My pleasure. Please let us know if there's anything else you require." Monica rang off and I set the phone back in its cradle.

I glanced at the hundreds lying loose on the bed. *What the hell had I been thinking?* On shaky legs, I staggered to the door to retrieve my breakfast tray, which I left on top of the coffee table in front of the loveseat. Then, wincing with each step, I made my way into the bathroom to guzzle a glass of water while I waited for the shower to warm up.

The steam from the shower helped my headache, and I stood under the soothing torrent for way too long. By the time I turned off the water, the worst of my hangover had disappeared, although my energy level had decided to take a siesta. I grabbed a towel and wrapped it around me as I walked back out to the living room.

I uncovered the plate of eggs and toast, took it off the tray, and set it on the table in front of the loveseat, along with a carafe of coffee and glass of freshly squeezed orange juice. As I slathered jam on the toast and inhaled the lukewarm eggs, my attention drifted toward the slip of paper I'd found in the packet of bills the night before.

Something told me I shouldn't pursue the mystery of the photographs and the unknown password. The information may have been eleven years old, but the website still existed. Who knew what kind of trouble I could get myself into if I were able to access the site again? Now that the tequila had worn off, I didn't want to have anything to do with Salazar, even if the pictures on the site were innocent trip photos.

Knowing Salazar, the photographs probably had something to do with where someone had been killed, or where a business front was located. A shiver traced up my spine at the thought of him and his far-reaching influence of fear and intimidation, even after his death.

Salazar is dead. Leave your past behind, Kate. Isn't that why you're here?

After I finished breakfast and set the dirty dishes outside the door, I corralled the money and opened the hotel safe, keeping a few hundred for the day. Unable to fit in the backpack, I removed the bills and stacked them neatly inside, and closed the door. I set the combination to my actual birthdate, which Luis hadn't used when he had my passport made.

The first item on my agenda was to find Akiaq Investigations. The website mentioned his office was located above a deli near Pike Place Market. If I couldn't find the physical address, I'd pick up a disposable phone and try calling the number on the card Sam had given me.

My last meeting with Sam had been brief—it was the night before I infiltrated Hugo Morales' compound after being thrown into the middle of a cartel war in the Yucatán. There'd been so much I wanted to tell him, but the timing sucked. He'd delivered an open invitation to come to Seattle, had tried to get me to leave Mexico with him, but I'd been on the cusp of something important I needed to finish.

I hoped he hadn't changed his mind.

I took the elevator to the lobby and walked through the main doors, turning left. If I remembered it right from a past visit, I'd find a Nordstrom Rack just a few blocks away. I intended to get myself some new clothes to go with the new me and there wasn't any sense in paying full pop.

An hour later, I emerged from The Rack wearing a pair of designer sunglasses, a sexy black skirt and matching camisole with a rockin' new pair of cherry-red sandals. I caught a glimpse of myself in the window and smiled.

The original Kate might have vanished into someone completely different, but I thought Sam would approve.

Since I needed to work up my courage in order to drop in on Sam, I took my time perusing the open stalls in the Market, chatting with the women who sold the enormous flower bouquets and taste-testing the different foods: Korean, Italian, Afghan, Thai. I'd forgotten how fun it was to walk through Pike Place and watch the tourists and vendors interact. The Fish Market still entertained passersby with their fish-throwing antics, and I couldn't help but laugh at the wide-eyed wonder of a pair of toddlers as they ran their chubby hands along the slippery salmon their father had just bought.

After an hour or so, I wound my way through the rabbit warren of interior shops, passing by an animatronic fortune-teller booth in front of a magic store. A favorite pastime when I was a kid, I walked up to the old-fashioned machine and slid the quarters into the slot. The turbaned mannequin with the eerie glass eyes waved her hands over the tarot cards spread out on a table in front of her for a few moments, her disembodied voice urging me to heed her words or pay the ultimate price. The mannequin came to an abrupt stop, and a card slid into the tray below her. I held the fortune up to the light and read the preprinted words.

Danger surrounds you. Be certain of your enemies, even more so of your friends. You will soon have reason to fear.

Startled, I glanced at the fortune-teller, lifelike eyes staring through the glass. A feeling of dread grew in my stomach, permeating the rest of me at an alarming rate.

"What the hell do you mean, *I will soon have reason to fear?*" I slammed my hand into the side of the booth, angry at the nerve of the stupid doll's fortune. Alarmed, a young couple hurried past me, giving me and the machine a wide berth.

Pascal, one of the commandos I'd worked with in the Yucatán and a shaman of sorts, told me I still had several bad spirits surrounding me—the ones that had plagued me for so long—but to remember I now had help. How was this anything even close to help?

I dug in my purse for more quarters, crammed them into the slot and jabbed the button. The gypsy card reader stared past me, unseeing and mute. My frustration grew, and I pressed my shoulder into the booth and pushed, trying to force the change to fall the rest of the way into the slot and activate the dummy.

It didn't work. Gasping from the effort, I turned and scanned the area for something I could use to stick into the coin slot and push the change down. A small crowd had gathered to watch the crazy woman trying to break into the fortune-teller machine. My face grew warm. I had to clamp my mouth closed to stop from saying something sarcastic and making things worse.

Take a deep breath, Kate. It's only a game. Don't take it seriously. You should probably leave now.

With as much dignity as I could summon, I gave the machine one last shove before stalking away.

5

I T TOOK THE better part of an hour to calm down. Obviously, I hadn't yet recovered from the events in the Yucatán.

Give yourself a break, Kate. You killed two men, one of whom was a man who'd been after you for over a decade. It's going to take time to get past that.

If I ever did.

I almost missed the unobtrusive white sign with black lettering leaning against a second-floor window. Located partway down an alley over a busy deli, Akiaq Investigations took advantage of a central location without the overhead of a major downtown Seattle address. A wood and glass door to the right of the deli opened onto a set of stairs leading up to Sam's office. I pressed the buzzer labeled *A. Investigations* and waited. Someone buzzed me in and I walked inside.

The steep stairs had me breathing heavily by the time I reached the top, and I wondered whether Sam's clients balked at the climb. The workout wouldn't have bothered him in the least, and I doubted he'd even considered it when he chose the location. A long-distance runner, Sam Akiaq didn't have an ounce of fat to spare and rarely broke a sweat.

I walked along the carpeted hallway, the new-paint smell hardly registering, and paused at the door with a plaque that read *Akiaq Investigations*. My heart hammered in my chest and I had to consciously relax my shoulders and take a deep breath before I knocked. The smell of pastrami from the deli below reminded me that I was hungry again.

"Come in."

At the sound of his voice, I opened the door and walked into a small waiting area. Two comfortable-looking, tangerine-colored chairs stood at opposite ends of a matching loveseat, flanked by a couple of metal and glass side tables. Sam sat at a glass desk behind a raised counter, looking through a file folder in front of him. He'd tied his long black hair back in a ponytail and wore a royal blue button-down dress shirt, sleeves rolled to his elbows, and untucked over a pair of form-fitting jeans. A small silver earring dangled from his left ear.

He looked up, the file still in his hands. His polite smile changed to one of surprise before he rose from his chair and stepped past the counter toward me. He stopped a few inches away, his dark eyes searching mine.

At a loss for words, I opened my mouth to say something, but he closed the distance between us, cupped my face in his hands, and lowered his mouth to my lips before I could speak. He smelled of cedar and spice and musk and I relaxed into the kiss, relishing his welcome.

He pulled back, his eyes never leaving mine, and smiled his slow, easy smile.

"Hello, Kate."

It was all I needed to hear.

"Obviously you made it through whatever Quinn dreamed up back in Mexico. Was it worth it?" Sam watched me as he took a swig of his iced tea.

We were sitting at an outside table at a vegetarian restaurant a couple of blocks down from Sam's office. Full-to-bursting baskets of colorful trailing petunias hung at intervals from the roof, giving the place a Babylonian garden-like feel. Shrugging, I picked at the sweet potato fries on the plate in front of me.

"Salazar's dead."

Sam tilted his head in acknowledgement and let the revelation slide by. He drained the iced tea and held his glass up for a refill. The waitress came over and took his glass, giving me the once-over. Apparently, he frequented the establishment and the waitress felt protective. Sam had a way about him. I'd have done the same.

"So tell me. What made you give up law enforcement in Alaska? I thought you liked it there," I said, ignoring the looks the other wait staff gave me.

Sam smiled his thanks as our waitress dropped off the refill. Once she'd gone, he turned his attention back to me.

"After they found Joe…" His voice trailed off and the sentence hung in the air between us. Joe, or Captain Miller, had been Sam's boss at the department. They'd found his mutilated body outside an abandoned cannery around the time Sam was shot—yet another of Angie McKenna's multitude of sins. He took a sip of his drink and cleared his throat. "The job just wasn't the same. Besides, I needed to keep an eye on things."

Startled, I glanced at him, unsure what he meant. "Things? What kind of things?" I knew he'd had a friend of his watch out for me while I'd been in Hawaii. Did he mean he'd been in the background all along? That could explain the five relatively uneventful years in my life after I left Oahu.

It was his turn to shrug. Silent Sam strikes again.

"How long ago did you quit the force?" I asked.

"After you left," he replied.

"After…you mean once you were released from the hospital?"

He nodded.

"And you moved to Seattle, when?"

"Not long after that. I have cousins who live in Ballard. They offered me a place to stay until I figured things out."

"And, you needed to find a way to make a living, so you became a private investigator." I finished the abbreviated version of his story. It made sense. He had contacts within the various law enforcement agencies. He'd been a good cop—they'd trust him.

"Yep."

"Did you by any chance ever make it to Arizona?"

His deep brown eyes showed nothing. I exhaled in frustration and sat back in my chair.

"You're not going to tell me, are you?"

"You're pretty smart for a white girl."

I rolled my eyes. "Well, if you did, I should probably thank you. So, thank you."

He waved my thanks away with a slight frown, and signaled the waitress for the check.

If he'd been watching over me in northern Arizona then he'd known all about my relationship with Cole. I studied him for a moment, considering what it must have cost him, seeing me with a new lover and not being able to let me know he was there. Then again, if he had been operating in the background, why hadn't he let me know? Cole and I didn't get together until I'd been in Durm for several years.

Sam held my gaze and, as if reading my mind, said, "You told *me* you didn't want me around."

I let go another frustrated sigh. "Because you could have been *killed*. I'd rather die lonely than be responsible for your death. Or anyone's, for that matter."

"Then explain Cole Anderson."

His expression told me I needed to tread carefully. Why did I get involved with another man? If anything, I should have contacted Sam before that happened, but I'd let my guard down. I hadn't contacted him because I didn't think Sam ever wanted to see me again. Not after what had happened.

The man almost died because of me.

I peeled off a piece of the label on my root beer. "I shouldn't have let it get as far as it did." I gazed out the window, remembering that horrible morning at the rest area no more than a couple of months ago when Angie shot Cole and left him for dead. "You see what happens when I get involved with someone? I probably shouldn't even be here." I leaned back and crossed my arms.

And now I'd gone and done it again. Hoped things could be different. The only part of the equation that had changed was that Salazar no longer posed a threat to me or to Sam. What if his death hadn't changed things enough? What if just by being here I put Sam in danger? Again?

I stood and picked up my purse, intending to leave. Sam grabbed my wrist. I checked at his touch and took a deep breath.

"Sit down, Kate."

I hesitated for a moment but then sat down when I realized I needed to be near him, at least for this brief moment in time. I'd leave in a few days, before the spirits had time to screw things up. Surely they'd give me that?

"Where are you staying?" he asked.

"The Plaza."

"Room?"

"1214."

Sam reached into his wallet, took out some bills and slid them onto the table. Then he got up, took my hand and led me out of the restaurant.

6

SAM HADN'T MELLOWED in the six years since we'd been together. Then again, neither had I. As soon as I closed and locked the door to my room, we went at each other like a couple of sex-starved teenagers, ripping each other's clothes off, barely making it two feet inside the front room.

Naked, we slid together, unable to remain apart. With his long black hair now loose from its tie, he resembled nothing so much as a dream lover, the hero on the cover of a torrid romance, his strong, broad shoulders and rippled stomach sculpted to perfection, with slim hips and long, lean runner's legs.

He cupped my face with his hands and smiled as he gazed into my eyes. I turned my head and took his fingers in my mouth, gently sucking each one. His breathing, already fast, quickened as he pushed me against the wall and lifted my leg to wrap around his hip. I leaned my head back and reveled in the feel of him, hard and insistent against me. Using his strong shoulders for support, I wrapped my other leg around him, urging him on. He moved into me, slowly at first, but then bore down with more force, pushing me hard against the wall. The momentum built and we moved together until I couldn't stem the tide any longer and cried out as I came. Sam slipped over the edge a moment later, groaning with the release.

We remained standing, my back pressed against the wall, as our heartbeats returned to normal. Lowering my feet to the floor, I gently brushed his hair from his face. Then I led him to the bedroom and we took turns discovering new territory. Lovemaking had always been natural with Sam. I hadn't felt this calm and secure since before that fateful decision to go on the run with Salazar's money eleven years ago.

Later, we lay in bed, his body encircling mine in a languorous embrace. I turned in his arms and traced his cheek with the tip of my finger, looking into the depths of his eyes. He nuzzled my neck and nipped at my earlobe, sending new chills vibrating along my spine.

"You haven't changed," he said, a wicked grin on his face.

I smiled back. "Neither have you."

We spent the afternoon making love. As the sun set over Puget Sound, I showed him the rooftop pool, where he taught me a beginner's butterfly stroke. Afterward, we had dinner in one of the hotel's restaurants and then went back to my room.

I poured two glasses of wine from a bottle we'd ordered at dinner but hadn't finished, and walked over to sit next to him on the loveseat. As I handed him a glass, he held up the slip of paper I'd found hidden in the stack of bills.

"Did you need this? It was on the couch."

I held my hand out but he turned the writing toward him to read.

"These numbers look like an IP address," he said.

I dropped my arm and didn't say anything right away, trying to decide how much I should tell him.

If you're serious about changing your life, you need to be honest with him, Kate. That's what you'd want.

"Remember the night in Alaska when I told you I'd taken money from Salazar so I could escape and that's why he came after me?"

Sam nodded, quiet.

"And remember when I said I'd lost most of it except for some I'd buried at a woman's home in Sonora?" Another nod. "On my way back from the Yucatán, I stopped there. The home looked abandoned so I waited until dark and dug up the money. That slip of paper was inside one of the stacks of bills."

Sam's eyebrows lifted a fraction as he took in the information. "You've already been online looking for this, haven't you?"

I nodded. "I'd had too much to drink and my curiosity got the better of me. I mean, it's an eleven-year-old mystery. Salazar's dead. What did I have to lose?"

"And?"

"It led to a website with somebody's vacation pictures."

"Salazar's?"

I shrugged. "Maybe. I'd only been on the page for a few seconds before a pop-up appeared asking for another password. Something about not accessing the site from the right location."

Sam sat forward.

"What?" I asked, anxiety spiking through me.

"You said Salazar's dead?"

I nodded. I didn't want to tell him I'd been the one to pull the trigger. His death was still too fresh in my mind.

"Then you shouldn't have anything to worry about. What you encountered is called a pingback, or a trackback. Someone programmed a second layer of safety into the site's access to make sure the information wouldn't get into the wrong hands. I wonder why the address and password were hidden in a stack of bills?"

"The van I stole was parked outside of Salazar's hacienda. Later I found out the shipment of cash inside had been slated to be delivered to Vincent Anaya. In effect, I'd stolen from both of them. Not one of my finer moments."

The memory of that night eleven years ago came back with a vengeance: the surreal scene of watching Roberto Salazar slit the throat of one of his most trusted friends, galvanizing my escape; the terror of possibly being found out and tortured or killed; and the short-lived relief as I caught a ride in the back of a farmer's pickup and watched the van I'd just abandoned disappear behind me in the dry Sonoran dust.

"It was probably something Salazar put into the shipment for Anaya," I said. "Although, I can't imagine why the webpage would have a password. It was just some travel photography—and not very good, either."

"The pictures could have information encrypted within the pixels."

I frowned at him, not making the connection. Then it clicked. "Like what Al Qaida did with those porn movies?" Sam nodded.

The terrorist group had embedded secret codes into something they believed no one would think to connect to Islamic extremists: pornography. The thought hadn't occurred to me, but it made sense. Thank goodness the website and password I'd found were over a decade old. I shrugged off an uneasy feeling, passing it off as old habits dying hard.

"What do you think I should do? I was going to throw the paper away." *Why hadn't I done it already? We wouldn't be having this conversation.*

"What about Luis? It's possible his people at the DEA would be able to make sense of the information."

I bit my lip. "I wasn't going to tell Luis I'd recovered the money. How would I explain finding the website?"

"You couldn't. Not unless you told them what you did. Or lied."

"I'm not comfortable with either of those options. I'm trying to change my life for the better, not continue with the same mess I started."

"You could have left the money in Mexico," Sam said, his voice quiet. I opened my mouth to reply but he raised his hand. "I'm just putting it out there. I'm in no position to judge your actions, Kate. You did what you thought best at the time. Sometimes we don't have enough information to understand the reason events happen the way they do." He placed the slip of paper on the table. "Do whatever you think best. But do it soon. I want to go back to bed."

I arched an eyebrow, deciding to forget the conversation and questions it raised for now, and climbed across the loveseat to straddle his hips. He slid his hands across my thighs and I untied the sash holding my robe together, letting it drop from my shoulders. Sam slid his hands up my body to gently cup my breasts. I sighed and pulled his head closer.

The bed forgotten, we moved together, all thought of Salazar and drug money and the DEA pushed deep into the recesses of my mind. Afterward, we found our way to the bedroom and fell asleep entangled in each other's arms, exhausted but happy.

"I'll meet you for dinner at Lemongrass around six." Sam paused at the door and pulled me to him, bruising my lips with a passionate kiss.

He broke away, a seductive smile on his face, and walked down the hallway while I worked to regain my composure. He looked over his shoulder and flashed me a wicked grin before disappearing into the elevator.

Smiling to myself, I went back into my room and closed the door. The remnants of breakfast littered the top of the linen-covered room service cart. Absently, I fingered the petals of the blood-red rose the hotel had included with our French toast and coffee.

I stretched my arms above my head and yawned. More relaxed than I'd been in weeks, I sauntered back into the bedroom to shower and change, glancing at the clock on the night stand. 6:45. The day stretched in front of me and for the first time in a long while I realized I had the gift of time. No work, no laundry, no escaping from psychotic drug lords.

After showering, I opened my suitcase and pulled out a fresh pair of jeans and a T-shirt. The weather station had predicted unseasonably warm temperatures for the day, but in Seattle that meant comfortable when compared to where I'd just been. I added the red sandals I'd bought the day before and then walked back out to the living area and brought up the internet to see what I might find to do in the Emerald City.

I was in luck—in a couple of hours I'd be able to try stand up paddleboard yoga in Shilshole Bay. I checked the bus schedule and found one that would drop me close by. Then I called to reserve my spot in the class.

As I hung up the phone, I thought that I could get used to having some actual free time. Maybe things would be different now that Salazar was dead. Maybe I'd be able to stay in Seattle a little longer than I thought.

A girl could always hope.

7

THE SHIMMERING LIGHT reflecting off of Elliot Bay told me it was getting late. I sat on the wall at the Harbor Steps a while longer, watching the shadows lengthen and people hurrying home from work before I headed back to the hotel to change for dinner. The day had been calm and pleasant and I'd found a new favorite pastime in paddleboard yoga.

Lost in thought, I took my time walking up First Avenue, past the Seattle Art Museum and the *Hammering Man*. The energy of the city lifted my spirits as did watching the tourists thronging the sidewalks. SUVs outnumbered the other vehicles on the street except for hybrids and electric cars. "Seattle Nice" was in full display as I waited at a stoplight. People smiled and drivers could only be called polite as they waited for pedestrians to cross.

I turned right on Pine and headed up the incline to the Plaza, past Macy's and Nordstrom's and the ubiquitous espresso shops and microbreweries. It felt good to be in a city where no one knew me or wanted me dead. The beautiful day mirrored my mood, the anticipation of having dinner with Sam icing on the cake.

I could get used to this.

As I neared the front door of the hotel, a woman dressed in black with a shock of white-blonde hair walked out of the building and turned right, heading away from me. Something about her seemed vaguely familiar and I slowed my pace. She stopped and her head snapped up. I stepped behind a large planter as she turned, the breath catching in my throat.

Angie.

I froze as several emotions cycled through me: fear, anger, disbelief.

Why is she here? Then, *It can't be coincidence.*

I closed my eyes and took a deep breath, willing myself to calm down. Several people waited at a bus stop nearby. If the bus arrived soon enough, maybe I'd be able to board without Angie catching sight of me.

My fists clenched to stop them from shaking, I waited a few beats before peeking around the container. She stood several yards away watching people pass by her on the sidewalk. Without warning, she turned. Too late, I ducked behind the planter but knew by the sinking feeling in my stomach she'd seen me.

"Excuse me, but do you have the time?" I asked an older kid passing by carrying a skateboard.

He pulled out his ear buds and looked at his phone. "Five ten," he replied.

His attention on the screen, he didn't notice me edge closer to him. I glanced at Angie. Her eyes narrowed. She turned her head to look behind her, and I grabbed the kid's arm and pulled him back down the sidewalk, away from the hotel.

"What the fuck, lady?"

"Just keep walking. You need to get out of here, now," I said in a low voice.

The kid's bicep tensed as he pulled away, his face a mask of confusion.

"The woman behind us is very dangerous. I don't want you in the crossfire—"

"Kate, darlin', I *thought* that was you, honey." Angie's cheery southern drawl held an underlying steeliness as she followed us down the sidewalk.

The kid threw his board to the ground and leapt astride. A split-second later he kicked off, racing to the bottom of the hill without a backward glance.

I sighed in relief.

Running would only trigger Angie's chase response. I'd be better off standing my ground. She wouldn't gun me down in the street, not with all the potential witnesses, right? And what the hell was she doing here, anyway? It couldn't be because of me.

As far as she knew, I was no longer among the living.

I turned to face her. A crowd had gathered, waiting for the bus.

"I heard you were dead." She stopped a foot from me, her smile fading. Her hand rested inside her bag.

"I am. Forget you saw me and no one's the wiser."

That made her laugh, although her tone told me she didn't find the idea all that humorous.

"Something funny?"

She nodded and her smile evaporated. "I should've known you weren't dead. Jesus. Did you really think you'd get away with it? All these years later?"

"Get away with what, exactly?" My sales technique had been honed through years of running. I just hoped Angie was in the mood to buy.

She rolled her eyes. "And I'll bet it's purely coincidence that you're here in Seattle. C'mon, darlin'. Hand over the access code." She held out her hand and wiggled her fingers.

"I don't know what you're talking about." I kept my gaze steady, afraid I'd telegraph my next move. *How did she know about the code?*

The pingback, Kate.

"Not goin' to cooperate? *Quelle surprise.* Well, I'm sure I can devise some way to get the information out of ya'll." She stepped toward me.

A city bus hissed to a stop at the curb next to us. The doors swung open and spilled riders onto the sidewalk. Without thinking, I cut behind the bus and darted into traffic. I caught sight of Angie out of the corner of my eye as she dodged cars in an attempt to follow me.

Adrenaline and the blare of car horns from pissed-off drivers spurred me on as I sprinted toward the other side of the street. I rebounded off the trunk of a sports car and narrowly missed becoming the hood ornament on a dark-brown van before I pushed into a flat-out run, dodging tourists and speed-walking office workers headed for the nearest Happy Hour.

Storefronts blurred into one another as I ran. Halfway down the block a door to my left opened and two men in business suits walked out of a restaurant. I swerved around them and ducked inside, pushing my way through the people waiting to be seated, heading further inside the semi-darkened room. When I reached the back of the restaurant, I pivoted in time to see Angie's white-blonde head bobbing up and down in the crowd near the front, searching for me.

Heart nearly exploding in my chest, I scanned the back wall for a bathroom but noticed instead two swinging doors leading to the kitchen. A tray filled with dirty dishes rested on a stand nearby. I covered the distance in two strides and hoisted it onto my right shoulder with both hands. Making sure the piled-high plates and bowls were between me and Angie's line of sight, I walked rapidly into the kitchen.

I set the tray down on the first counter I came to and stopped a waitress before she walked out the door.

"Is there another way out of here?"

Startled, she frowned. "You shouldn't be back here."

"I know, but there's this guy out there…" I let the sentence hang, hoping she'd get my drift. A knowing look reached her eyes, and she nodded toward the back.

"The rear entrance opens onto an alley."

"Thanks." I raced through the kitchen, dodging surprised sous chefs, busboys, and waiters before reaching the exit.

I burst through the screen door, scanned left and right and chose left, racing to the end of the alley. A large commercial garbage bin squatted on the asphalt to my right, but I knew it would be the first place she'd look. I sprinted to the end of the alley, turned left and kept running.

I had to call Sam, let him know Angie was here, but I hadn't bought a phone yet. I needed to make it back to the hotel without Angie's knowledge. I guessed it had been no more than fifteen or twenty minutes since I asked the skateboarder the time. Sam was due at the restaurant at six, which gave me just enough time to get to the room and grab my suitcase and backpack.

Continually looking over my shoulder to make sure Angie wasn't behind me, I took the quickest route back to the Plaza and rode the elevator to the twelfth floor. She shouldn't be able to find me that quickly. The Plaza never gave out guest information.

It took less than ten minutes to change my clothes, pack my things, and stuff the money into the pack. Zipping it closed, I double-checked the room in case I'd missed anything. I hadn't. I dug Sam's card out of my purse, picked up the telephone and punched in his number. It went directly to voicemail.

"Sam. It's Kate. The pingback's still active. Angie's been to the hotel and knows I'm here. She's wearing black and has white-blonde hair. Be careful. I'm sure she'll recognize you if she sees you. I'll meet you at the restaurant. If it's not safe, I'll find a way to call you." I hung up and went to the door, leaning against it to listen.

Not hearing anything, I eased the door open and peered into the hallway. Empty. I slipped on a canvas hat I'd picked up as an afterthought in Mexico and moved quietly out of the room, closing the door behind me. I turned right instead of left and headed for the emergency stairwell.

With both bags in hand, I descended to the level marked P-1 and eased the door open, edging out of the stairwell when I didn't see anyone. The overhead lights glowed sodium yellow as I moved quickly between cars, the clack of the wheels on my roller bag echoing through the shadow-filled parking garage.

I walked up the ramp and stopped at the entrance, checking the street for Angie or anyone else suspicious. Blinking against the late afternoon sunlight, I reached into my purse for my sunglasses and put them on before moving out onto the sidewalk. The glasses and hat wouldn't be enough. I'd have to change my walk, the way I stood, everything.

Again.

8

HALF A BLOCK from the hotel, I ducked inside Foxxy Roxy's Entertainment Emporium, hoping to buy a wig. The woman at the front looked up from her smart phone and smiled.

"Well hello there, gorgeous. What can Foxxy Roxy's do for you today?" Tall and thin and wearing a retro mini dress, her jet-black hair fell straight to her broad shoulders. Along with a pair of enormous hoop earrings and a chunky necklace, she rocked some of the longest fake eyelashes I'd ever seen.

"I need a change," I said, as I approached the counter. To my right, among the displays of dildos, feather boas, party costumes, and Pocket Pals, stood a massive wall o' wigs, with every length, style, and color imaginable. Pink, peacock green, even striped—Foxxy Roxy's had it all.

"You came to the right place, honey. Let me see..." She tilted her head to the side and pursed her lips. "Have you tried a short black bob? You know, like the flappers from the twenties? With the shape of your face, it would look fantastic." She moved to the wall and, using a long-handled grabber tool, took down the wig in question and handed it to me.

I let the backpack slide to the floor and pulled on the wig, tucking my hair under the elastic band. The woman pushed a mirror across the counter and turned it toward me so that I could look at my reflection. The short, dark hair did the trick. Even Sam would have a hard time recognizing me.

"I'll take it," I said, and reached into the top pocket of the backpack for the cash.

As I waited for my change I glanced at the clerk's nametag which read, "Hi! My name is Michael. How may I help you?" and noticed for the first time her pronounced Adam's apple and the hint of a five o'clock shadow.

I did come to the right place. Apparently, I'm not the only one trying to hide.

After Michael cut off the price tag, I thanked her, wished her luck, and walked out the door, rolling my suitcase onto the busy sidewalk, a little less nervous with my new disguise.

Several people were waiting for a table when I arrived at the restaurant. I scanned the room to see if Sam might already be there, but didn't see him. I noticed an upper level that looked like it might have a bar and stopped a waiter walking by.

"Is there somewhere I can stash this? I need to go upstairs to see if my friend is here," I asked, smiling. The waiter glanced at the case and frowned. Thank goodness it was small.

"Of course."

As I handed him the case he said, "It'll just be over here behind the bar area."

"Thank you," I replied.

I made my way up the stairs to the second level and had a seat at a table by the railing with a view of the front door. A waitress appeared and I ordered an iced tea. Ten minutes later, Sam walked in. I waved until he recognized me and headed for the stairs.

"I got your message," he said, as he took the seat across the table. "Nice wig. Always thought you'd look good with black hair." He leaned forward, elbows on the table. "Do we know where Angie is now?"

"Not sure. I managed to out-maneuver her. I assume she'll watch the hotel entrance, but I've already been back and got everything." I took a sip of tea. The glass shook, and I set it on the table. "I'm going to have to leave again. She'll find you. If she does, she'll use you to get to me." Now that she knew I was alive and assumed I had the code, what would she do next? Uncertainty clawed its way up my spine as the repercussions slammed home.

"Does she know you accessed the site?"

"I denied it, but I'm sure she didn't believe me. She has to know. Who else would have access so many years later? Especially now that Salazar's dead."

"The real question is, who hired her, if not Salazar?"

I knew the answer to that one. "Vincent Anaya. Remember I told you I found out later that the money I stole had been on its way to Anaya?"

"And Anaya's still alive?"

"Yeah. The last time I saw him he tried to kill me, Viet Cong-style."

Sam frowned and cocked his head to the side. "He what?"

"Never mind. What's important is that as far as I know he remains among the living, although Luis tells me he's been relatively inactive. He usually let Salazar handle the business side of things."

"Those must be some kind of vacation photos if he's willing to get back on the DEA's radar."

The waitress stopped at the table and Sam ordered a club soda with lime. When she left, he leaned across the table and put his hand over mine.

"You're not alone, Kate. I'm here. You need to decide what to do with the card."

"You think I should take it to Luis, don't you?"

Sam held my gaze. "It's not my decision. Only you can choose which way to go from here."

He was right. I needed to go to Luis. I didn't have to tell him how I came across the website.

"Can I use your phone?"

"Sure."

Sam handed his phone over, and I punched in Luis' number from memory. The call went to voicemail. Didn't anyone pick up a live call anymore?

"Luis. It's Kate. I need to speak with you. It's important. I'll try again later." I ended the call and handed the phone back.

"My information doesn't display on caller I.D. He may not have picked up because of that."

"He'll answer next time."

"You can stay with me. Angie doesn't know I live in Seattle," Sam said.

"Not yet, she doesn't." I sat back in my chair, watching my plan to stay in Washington with Sam evaporate. "I'll take you up on your offer tonight, but I can't stay longer than that." I closed my eyes and took a deep breath. No matter how hard I tried, I always brought trouble. There'd always be someone waiting to rip my life to shreds or hurt someone I loved. "I'm sorry, Sam. I thought this was over."

"You can stay. If not at my place, then I'll give my cousins a call. They've got a little apartment in their backyard you can use until we figure things out."

"But Angie—"

"How's she going to know? She has no idea I'm here. And even if she did, she doesn't know who my cousins are."

"She can follow you. We'll be looking over our shoulders, waiting for her to find us." No longer hungry, I pushed back from the table. "Even if I give Luis the information, it won't stop her. She's not one to leave a loose end. I'm a loose end. So are you."

"Kate. Listen to me. I think you should try to calm down. Look at things logically, rather than just react. Yes, Angie pinpointed the Plaza because of the pingback, but she wasn't able to locate the room. It's next to impossible with the number of computers in the hotel. Besides, you're no longer there." Sam watched me for a moment, quiet. "You're not responsible for me, Kate. I choose my own path. I don't fear death."

"You may not, but I do. Not mine. Yours. Although," I added, watching the doorway, expecting to see Angie walk in. "I'd prefer to stick around a little while longer, myself. Try to live a safe, quiet life."

"You canceled that option when you took the money from Salazar."

My face grew warm, and I bit back a retort. *That's it, Kate. Alienate one of the only friends you have in the world.* I took a deep breath and slowly exhaled.

"You're right. I made a mistake. But that was many years ago and believe me, I've paid." He was right, of course. I had to take responsibility for my past actions, even though I'd been young and stupid when I made the choice. Real life didn't work that way. Do-overs were rare.

"What if I gave her the code? From what I saw, it's just vacation photos, probably only important to Anaya." The idea had some merit, but a niggling feeling in the back of my mind kept telling me there was more to it than that.

"Not until you know what the webpage and pictures signify. What if it includes sensitive information, like the names of informants? Some may still be active. You'd put their lives in danger."

"I hadn't thought of that."

The waitress came by and asked whether we wanted to order. Even though I was in no mood to eat, I ordered the Buddha rolls and a green papaya salad. Sam ordered duck. The food came a little while later, and I ate with an eye on the doorway, hardly tasting anything.

When we finished, I walked down the stairs while Sam kept watch over the entrance. I retrieved my suitcase from behind the bar, shouldered the backpack, and joined Sam at the door. After a quick check for Angie, we walked out into the mild evening air, accompanied by the accordion rumble of city traffic.

He'd parked in a nearby garage and we hurried around the corner, our heads down. Seattle was a big city, and the restaurant was far enough away from the hotel that Angie would have to have psychic powers to be able to track me there.

Or a really good guess.

Either way, I drew a sigh of relief when I shut and locked the passenger door on Sam's nondescript SUV and we drove out of downtown Seattle.

9

THE NEXT MORNING dawned with a brilliant blue sky and no clouds. Sam fixed fried eggs and salmon for breakfast. Afterward, we took our coffee to the patio to soak in the peaceful start to the day.

Deceptive.

I leaned back and closed my eyes, trying to quiet the voices in my head screaming at me to leave now before Sam became a casualty. During the night when sleep wouldn't come, I'd given the situation a lot of thought. The best I could come up with was to give the code to Luis and skip town. If I left today, went somewhere completely different, paid cash for everything, I should be able to stay a step ahead of Angie, at least for a while. Once Anaya realized the information had been compromised, it was possible that he'd call her off.

Possible. Not probable.

It all depended on how determined Anaya was to get to me. If he'd been after me because of the website, then handing it over to the DEA would give him something else to focus on. I doubted it was the money. One-point-six was pocket change to a man like Vincent Anaya.

"What's the plan?" Sam asked.

"I'm going to give the information to Luis."

His chin tipped up. "Ah." He frowned into his coffee. "You'll stay with my cousins?"

"No."

Sam fell silent and sipped his coffee. I set my cup down on the table between us.

"I won't put you in danger, Sam. I'll go somewhere away from here, pay cash for everything. She won't be able to track me." Same-old, same-old, except that I had money now. I could disappear, at least for a while.

"You've made up your mind."

"Yes."

Without saying a word, Sam rose from his chair, and walked into the house. He returned a few minutes later and handed me his phone.

"Call him."

I took the phone and tapped in the numbers. It rang three times before Luis picked up.

"Luis Gonzales."

"It's Kate. I—"

"About time you called." His voice had an edge I didn't normally associate with calm, easy-going Luis.

"What?" I asked, my fist curling around the handset.

"Somebody kidnapped Cole's kids."

The breath left my body as my abdominal muscles did the cha-cha. "Somebody" could only mean one person. *Anaya has Lauren and Abby.* The words jammed in my throat and I couldn't speak. Cold sweat trickled down the side of my face as fear for Cole's daughters sprinted through me.

"Cole called me early this morning, Kate. Someone broke into his home through a back window and took the girls. They left a note telling him to find you or they'd kill the kids. They also told him not to tell anyone except you."

"Oh, my God." I collapsed into my chair and tried to breathe. Sam leaned forward, a concerned look on his face.

Cole was Sheriff Cole Anderson, the man I'd been involved with while living in the small town of Durm, Arizona. Anaya and my ex, Roberto Salazar, the monster I'd killed in the Yucatán jungle, had hired Angie to kidnap me and bring me to Mexico. She'd shot and seriously wounded Cole when he tried to protect me. The damage from the bullet erased a portion of his memory and he didn't recall the last couple of years.

More accurately, he didn't remember me.

"What the hell's going on, Kate? How do they even know you're alive?"

I took a deep breath and exhaled slowly. "I discovered a website with some vacation photos on it, but I got a pop-up that said I had accessed the page from an unknown source, and I needed to enter another password in order to continue. I didn't have the second password."

"A trackback? How'd you come across the website in the first place?"

"That's not important. What's important is that I did."

"It's very important, Kate." Luis' voice took on a steel-like quality. "That doesn't tell me how they knew it was you."

"I was in my hotel room when I triggered the pingback. The next day, Angie showed up."

"And she saw you." Luis was silent for a moment before he continued. "Where are you now?"

"I'm with Sam."

"In Seattle?"

"Yes."

"What are you planning to do?"

"I'm leaving. Today."

"Stay with Sam. He can protect you."

"He can also be killed."

"He's a professional, Kate. He knows Angie. Stay with him. I don't want you out there without any kind of support."

I swallowed my objections and waited.

"Is that why you called and left a message last night?" he asked.

"I was going to give you the information."

"Was? You mean you are, right?"

The website was the only leverage I had, both with the DEA and Anaya. Not only that, but a cartel informant from several years before might still be operational. Luis' boss had determined there'd been a plant in either the DEA or the Mexican government agency with whom they worked, but hadn't been able to identify the leak.

"Kate? I can't help you if you don't help me."

"The note said not to contact anyone else."

"Cole didn't know how else to find you. Besides, he's law enforcement. This is what we do."

Of course Cole would call in the DEA, the FBI, Homeland Security, whoever and whatever could help him. *They had his kids.*

"How long do you think it will take to hack the second password?"

"Not long. A couple of hours," he said.

"And Anaya won't know you're doing it, right?"

"You mean disable the pingback? That shouldn't be a problem."

"How about the photographs? Can you figure out what's hidden in them?"

"I'll make it a priority, Kate."

The way I saw it, I didn't have much choice. I couldn't make an exchange alone without putting Cole's kids, or myself, in danger. Once Angie and Anaya got what they wanted, they wouldn't think twice about killing me. They might let the kids go—or, they might not. Having the FBI and the DEA working toward Lauren and Abby's release would have far better odds than me going it alone.

"Kate, the FBI's been notified. They're mobilizing. We're waiting on you."

"Hold on." I hesitated. What if the informant who leaked Eduardo's whereabouts was still active and working for the DEA? Then they'd give or sell the information to Anaya, who wouldn't need the kids anymore. I didn't trust Anaya to let Abby and Lauren go. The possibility that he might have plans to sell them once he got what he wanted sent shivers up my spine.

"You said the FBI's mobilizing. I want to give the information directly to the FBI."

There was a brief pause at the other end. "Is this because of what happened to Eduardo?"

"Yes."

"We've been over this before. I've worked with these people for years. I like to think I'd know if they were plants."

"I don't care if you think I'm being paranoid, Luis. I want a secure way to get this information to whoever's heading up the investigation at the FBI."

"Fine. I'm going to give you the address of a secure chat room they've set up for this operation. You'll be able to send a private message to Agent Landers, who's taking the lead on this. Ask Sam if he's got encryption software installed on his computer."

I went back outside and asked. Sam nodded.

"He says yes."

"Good. Follow his instructions to send the address and access code. That way we'll be covered on both ends."

I wrote down the address and recited it back to him.

"That's it. I assume you don't have a phone if you're calling on Sam's."

"Not yet."

"Get one. Then call me back with the number. I'll relay it to Landers."

"But you're helping, right?" My throat constricted at the thought of Luis not being involved.

"Yeah, of course. My guys have been supplying names, addresses, phone numbers, VINs, whatever we have on Anaya's and Angie's known associates." Luis paused for a second before continuing. "Don't worry. We'll get them back."

"We have to." I disconnected, my emotions reeling—lurching from fear for the kids to anger at Anaya and Angie, to self-loathing for visiting more trouble on Cole and his family. Sam put his hand on my arm. His warmth brought me back to reality.

"What did he say?"

"They took Cole's kids."

"Cole Anderson?"

Nodding, I stared at the yard, unseeing, thoughts swirling through my mind. The old, familiar rage mixed with feelings of impotence and futility yanked at me, threatening to swallow me whole and overshadow any good sense I might have.

A yellow and black butterfly fluttered past, briefly capturing my attention as it perched on a spike of lavender near the fence. It stayed for a moment before attempting to lift off but for some reason was unable to fly. I leaned forward to see what stopped it and noticed a lacy web glinting in the sunlight, bridging the gap between flowers.

I crossed the distance to the lavender and gently released the butterfly from the spider's web as its eight-legged architect beat a hasty retreat under a leaf. The butterfly's wings trembled once before it took flight from my hand and floated away in the breeze. I turned and walked back to join Sam.

"They took his children." The words exited with a snap through gritted teeth, as I paced the length of the patio and back, too keyed up to sit still. The pain of my fingernails digging into my palms broke through the panic. *Think, Kate. Freaking out isn't an option.*

"You're sending the information to Luis as an encrypted file?"

I shook my head. "The FBI. I'm too paranoid to let him have it. There's the possibility an informant may still be active in the DEA. Luis and his team will continue to provide whatever information they can, but the actual operation will be coordinated by the FBI." I glanced at Sam. "The message said not to involve anyone else. If Angie or Anaya find out the FBI or the DEA's involved…" I continued to pace, trying to work off the anxiety, but knowing it was here to stay.

"It's going to work out, Kate. The kids will be safe."

I hoped Sam was right.

10

AS SOON AS I sent the encrypted information to Agent Landers, Sam drove me to a nearby convenience store, and I picked up two disposable phones. One number went to Luis to pass on to the FBI, but only Sam knew the other one. I made sure to purchase two different models: bright red for Sam, black for the FBI.

A girl can't be too careful with her phone numbers.

After much discussion with Sam, I relented and agreed to stay at his cousin's detached apartment in Ballard. Even though I wanted to be with him, I refused to stay with Sam at his place in case Angie discovered he was living in Seattle. Threatening to kill Cole's kids would have been enough leverage for normal kidnappers. As I knew only too well, Angie and Anaya weren't normal. Besides, I'd be leaving town as soon as I knew where the exchange would take place, and it would just be that much harder to leave if I were staying with Sam.

Sam pulled into the driveway of an older, well-kept home in an established neighborhood. We got out of the car and Sam hoisted the pack with the money over his shoulder while I grabbed my suitcase from the back. A man who looked to be in his fifties with short salt-and-pepper hair came out of the house and strode toward us, vitality radiating off him. I immediately liked the guy.

"John, this is Kate, the woman I told you about. Kate, this is my cousin, John Oscar." Sam nodded at the older man. I held out my hand.

"Thank you for allowing me to stay here, John."

John nodded as he pumped my hand vigorously. "Any friend of Sam's is a friend of mine. Welcome." He turned to Sam. "Any word on the woman?"

Sam shook his head. "No sign of her. We weren't followed, and there's nothing obvious connecting me with you, so if she does find out I live in Seattle there shouldn't be any problems."

John shrugged. "If there are, I'm not worried. I doubt she's had much call to deal with a native Alaskan." The twinkle in John's eyes made me smile.

We followed him around the side of the house—a big, turn-of-the-century hulk of a place, its severe lines softened by mature rhododendrons and hydrangeas, filled in with a smattering of lush hostas and sword ferns. In the back, John stopped next to what looked like a detached garage. He took out a ring with several keys on it and unlocked the side door, swung it open and stepped aside, motioning for us to enter.

The garage had been renovated into a spacious, furnished apartment. To my left, a large center island with cupboards separated the full kitchen from the high-ceilinged living room. A multi-hued rug covered most of the wood-plank floor, along with a large leather couch and recliner, two side tables, and a wall-mounted television. Three doors spoked off the main living area;

two of them led to bedrooms with a full bath in between. A small desk with a laptop computer took up part of one wall.

"This is perfect, John. Thank you," I said.

"I'll let you two get situated. Come on into the house when you're settled. Martha's got a couple of dungies cooking. You don't want to miss that." If I had a choice between a gourmet dinner with all the trimmings and eating myself sick on Dungeness crab, I'd park myself in the sand, boil 'em up and devour every last one without taking a breath.

John left and Sam took my bag into one of the bedrooms. I followed and stuffed the backpack in the closet. I'd have to figure out a safer place to keep it—lugging it around didn't foster peace of mind.

The small bedroom consisted of a queen-sized bed with a table on each side, two thrift-store lamps, one of which looked like it had been made out of a big chunk of white marble, the other mauve ceramic. An LED alarm clock and a silver frame with a black and white picture of an older woman rested on a wooden chest of drawers across the room against one wall.

"You'll be safe here, at least until Luis or the FBI contacts you." Sam's eyes held mine for a moment before he glanced around the room. "Towels are in the bathroom, and you'll find shampoo and soap in the shower." He reached behind him and brought out a nine millimeter, which he handed to me. "Keep this with you at all times. You can give it back to me later."

"You're not staying?" I asked, unable to keep the disappointment from my voice.

"I'll stay for lunch, but I've got a full caseload I need to clear. I'm sorry. I would if I could. Besides," he said, sweeping my hair back off my shoulder, "We'd never get any sleep if I stayed, and we're going to need it."

"We?"

"You don't think you're going to do this by yourself, right?"

A ripple of relief skipped down my back at his words. "You mean you're coming along?"

Sam smiled and leaned in so his lips were inches from my ear. "To serve and protect, Kate."

It turned out that Martha and John had boiled up more than a couple of crabs for the meal. Along with organic produce from Martha's garden, fresh salmon, oysters, and something delicious called geoduck that tasted a lot like clams graced the picnic table in the backyard. I warmed to Martha's earth mother vibe as she chatted about organic gardening and battling slugs in the Northwest. Softly feminine, her mellow demeanor stood as a direct counterpoint to John's wired-and-fired bulldog of a personality. Watching the two of them together reminded me of my folks.

Three more of Sam's cousins joined us for the meal: Becky and George, both in their late thirties and upwardly mobile, and their son, Trevor. Trevor was fourteen and had just come back from an extended stay with family in Alaska. His tale of coming nose-to-nose with a dumpster bear brought back fond memories and we all shared our Alaskan bear stories. John and Sam each had the most encounters, by far.

The best part of the meal was listening to John regale us with what he called "Tales from the Tundra". Martha, John, and Sam had grown up in a rural area a few miles apart in two separate villages in Northwestern Alaska and had experienced a similar upbringing. I learned more about Sam's early life, prior to the day the village shaman chose Sam to be his apprentice. Before that, his life sounded adventurous. Both John and Sam grew up as subsistence hunters. Hunting, fishing, and trapping took the place of the local grocery. Martha and the other village women would preserve the fish, seal, moose, and caribou by smoking the meat over the fire for days and then supplement their diets by collecting berries and other plants, digging for razor clams, and tending a garden. Their reverence for the natural world was impressive and I couldn't help wishing that more people felt the same way.

After we cleaned up the dishes and put the food away, Martha asked if I'd like to go for a walk around the neighborhood with her and Becky. I said I did, and we left the men to their fish stories. The temperature had risen to a balmy eighty degrees and the gorgeous blue sky had only the occasional scudding white cloud for company—perfect weather for Seattle. I inhaled the scent of warm cedar and fresh-cut grass.

"How long have you known Sam?" Martha asked a few minutes into the walk. She smiled as she said it, but I detected a hint of protectiveness in her tone.

"We met in Alaska a little over six years ago. He'd been hired to protect me."

"From what?"

"I made a stupid mistake when I was in my twenties. As a result bad people came after me. Alaska seemed like a good place to run. It wasn't." Memories crawled through my mind of hiding in a snowy field, watching one of Angie's thugs gun down the private investigator she had hired to find me, and I shook my head to clear it. I refused to allow the scene where she shot Sam to make an appearance.

Martha nodded. "Ah. You are the one." She turned to Becky and explained. "You remember when Sam almost died and the chief of police he worked for was murdered?" Becky nodded. Martha went on. "Kate is the woman he saved."

Startled, I stopped walking. Martha noticed I was no longer beside her and she turned.

"What?" she asked, a puzzled frown on her face.

"Nothing. It's just that I'm used to hearing the event spun in a more negative way. You sound as though you don't judge me." I caught up to the two women, and we continued our walk. "I realize everything's my fault and he'd be better off without me in his life. I've tried to tell Sam that from the beginning, but he insists on helping me."

"Sam is a good man." Martha fell silent for a moment. "We don't always know why things happen, Kate. The spirits put events in motion for a reason. Sam did not die. He very easily could have, but such was not his fate. Assigning blame is counterproductive. For all we know, there is a grand plan behind all of this. Yes, people have lost their lives, but in my culture death is not the worst thing that can happen."

Hot tears pricked my eyelids as her words made their way deep into the prison that had become my heart, unlocking the metal doors guilt and remorse had created. Here was a woman I'd never met telling me in so many words not to be so hard on myself for the choices I had made, stupid though they might have been. Forgiveness had been in short supply these past eleven years, especially my own.

"Two children are in grave danger and it's my fault, again." The tears had breached the dam and I wiped my now-wet cheeks with the back of my hand.

Both women stopped as Martha pulled a tissue out of her pocket. Gratefully, I accepted it and wiped my eyes as I took a shaky breath.

"Remember what I said. Who are we to question events?"

I blew my nose and nodded as I wadded up the tissue and put it in my pocket.

"Thank you, Martha," I said in a quiet voice. She took my hand in hers and we made our way back to the house.

11

LATE THE NEXT morning Trevor showed up at my door with a huge grin on his face and handed me a mesh bag and a shovel. I cocked my head and smiled as I took the items from him.

"And I get to do what, exactly, with these?"

He flushed pink and shrugged, still grinning. "Sam said you'd want to come clamming with us. This is your shovel and a bag to put the clams in."

"He did, did he? Well, he was probably right." I hadn't slept much the night before. Stark images of Cole's kids tied up and held at gunpoint by Anaya's goons floated in and out of my dreams. I'd jumped at every creak and groan in the apartment. Time away from my thoughts would do me good while I waited for Luis to call.

"Here's your shellfish license." He handed me an official-looking paper in a green plastic holder. "You can catch dungies, too."

"Great. When do I need to be ready?"

"John wants to leave in half an hour. Wear your swimming suit, if you have one."

After Trevor left, I changed into my bathing suit and some shorts, and slipped on a pair of flip flops. I grabbed a small backpack from the main room and, after checking to make sure it was fully loaded, slid the gun Sam had given to me in the front pocket, along with the two cell phones.

I'd resigned myself to the idea that I'd always need to carry some form of protection. Salazar's death hadn't changed that.

What *had* changed with my killing him? Someone was still after me, still wanted me dead. People I cared about were still in grave danger. I still needed to run.

That's a lot of stills.

With a deep sigh, I shrugged on the pack and walked out the door, making sure to lock everything up tight. Maybe getting outdoors and digging for clams would take my mind off of things enough to relax, at least a little.

Sure.

We took John's SUV. An older model four-wheel-drive with room for six and a thin film of dust and dirt covering the outside, it was the perfect vehicle for clamming, fishing, or anything else you could dream up that involved mucking about in boats or tide flats. All carpeting had been removed to make cleanup a breeze. John drove while Martha rode shotgun, Becky and George took the middle seats, and Trevor and I sat together in the back.

"Do you think you'll ever go back to Alaska to live?" I asked Trevor.

He nodded. "My uncle invited me to work as a deck hand on his fishing boat next summer."

"Dangerous work, but good money, right?" I said. George turned his head slightly so he could hear our conversation.

Trevor glanced at his father and shrugged. "It's not any more dangerous than working construction. And the money's better."

"If you catch anything," George added.

"Uncle Joe always catches his limit."

George snorted and shook his head. Becky nudged him and he grew quiet.

I leaned over and whispered, "Dad's worried about you, huh?"

Trevor cut a look at me and smiled as he nodded.

"He's your dad. He's always going to be worried. That's a good thing."

"I guess."

I patted his knee and turned to look out the window at the lush scenery flowing by. One thing I could say about Washington State: it knew how to grow trees. Great, tall, telephone-pole-sized ones. The SUV slowed as John maneuvered into line to wait for the ferry to begin loading.

"I'm going to get coffee. Any takers?" Becky asked.

"I'll go with you, Becky," I said, and followed her out the door.

As we headed across the parking lot toward the espresso stand, the little hairs on the back of my neck stood on end, and I experienced that old, familiar feeling of being watched. I scanned the cars waiting in line, but sunshine glinted off the windshields, making it difficult to see inside. Eleven years of running, trying to stay a step ahead of pissed-off drug lords and crafty assassins had instilled in me a finely-tuned paranoia, the likes of which rivaled Roberto Salazar's. I'd learned to pay attention, even if nothing was there.

Better safe than sorry.

Becky glanced at me, a slight frown on her face.

"Are you all right, Kate?"

"Sure. Why?"

She shrugged. "No reason. You seem preoccupied and more than a little alert."

"I'm probably just worried about Sam." I knew as soon as I said it, I shouldn't have. Becky stopped and looked at me.

"Why would you be worried about Sam?"

Obviously, John hadn't mentioned to her why I was staying in their converted garage, although Martha knew.

"I always worry about him," I said. *Well, that was a lame answer.*

Becky's look said she didn't buy it. "Why would you be worried about Sam?" she repeated, her mouth set in a firm line.

I took a deep breath. "Because someone's after me, and I'm afraid they'll find out Sam's living in Seattle, which could put him in danger. Again."

Becky nodded. "I wondered why you weren't staying at his place." She continued walking. "Doesn't staying at John and Martha's put them in danger?"

"Sam doesn't think so, or he wouldn't have suggested it. Even if the person looking for me finds out he's in Seattle, they don't have any way to connect John and Martha to him."

"Couldn't they follow him to their house?"

I'd thought that, too. "Sam assures me he can shake any tail they put on him. Besides, he doesn't plan to go back to the house until it's time for me to leave."

"Where are you headed then?"

"I can't really say."

"Is Sam going with you?"

"Yes." My stomach twisted into a knot at the look on her face. "Look, it wasn't my idea for him to come along, but I can't lie to you—I'm glad he is. What I've got to do scares the hell out of me, and having Sam along helps me feel like things are a little less hopeless. Yes, it's selfish, but Sam's a grownup. He can make his own choices." The ferocity with which I said the words surprised even me. Becky put her hand on my arm.

"I'm sorry, Kate. I didn't mean for you to take it like that. It's okay to ask for help, you know. I know Sam wouldn't do this if he didn't think it was safe. He's not one to take unnecessary risks."

I nodded and took a deep breath to try to bring my blood pressure down to a more manageable level. A few minutes later, we reached the espresso stand. Becky ordered a vanilla latte, and I ordered a regular coffee with cream. As we waited for our order, I got the feeling once again that someone was watching.

This time the feeling stayed with me.

12

THE SUN HAD just begun to dip toward the horizon as we bagged our limit of clams. Known as one of the most breathtaking bodies of water in western Washington, Hood Canal was home to a multitude of seals, otters, fish, and shellfish. The long stretch of oyster- and clam-packed beach we'd been digging belonged to Becky and George's good friends, the Richards.

The day and the water had been warm, the clams plentiful, and the jokes between the cousins and old friends fast and furious. The beach boasted a dock and several kayaks, and it didn't take much persuading to get me into one of them. Trevor and George gave me some pointers on how to get the most out of kayaking and then took me to a pretty little cove not far from the dock.

When we returned, George and Becky's friends had set up a table near the dock, now close to collapsing from the weight of salads, desserts, and drinks, while the clams boiled off to the side in a deep, stainless pot on a propane-fired burner. Martha handed me a glass of white wine and clinked hers against mine.

"Pretty spectacular place, isn't it?" she said, as we watched an eagle swoop down to the water and capture a fish in its claws before flying off toward its nest.

"Incredible." *I could get used to this.* If only the bad spirits following me would take a long walk off a short pier.

Martha eyed me as she sipped her wine. "Ever think about staying?"

"If I could be sure of Sam's safety, I'd do it in a heartbeat." I closed my eyes, savoring the peace in this slice of a moment. "But, until the problem I'm involved in is resolved, it can't happen."

"Well, just keep us in mind, Kate. The Northwest seeps into your bones and doesn't let you go. And, it's a damned fine place to live."

I smiled as Martha moved over to give John a hand dipping the cooked clams into bowls.

"Hey there, beautiful."

I turned at the sound of Sam's voice and smiled. He wrapped his arm around my waist and pulled me in for a kiss.

"Heard anything yet?" he asked, leaning over to give Martha a hug as she walked by and handed him a bottled water.

I shook my head. "Nobody's called. How was your day?"

"Busy. But I'm about finished buttoning up the last of the cases," he said, sitting on the dock. "I was out most of the morning, but filed a bunch of paperwork this afternoon."

"I wondered where you were." Trevor walked over to join us, a can of soda in his hand.

"Did you try to call me?" Sam asked.

"Worse. I stopped by around nine thirty, but when you weren't there, I took the bus over to John's."

"Come and get it," John yelled.

We headed over to the table to grab a plate. As I reached for some corn on the cob, one of the cell phones in my purse rang. Sam and I glanced at each other before I dug out the black phone and walked to the opposite side of the dock to answer.

"Kate Jones."

"Hey, Kate. Luis here."

"Any news?"

"Yeah. Your friends just now contacted Cole to set up the trade. You need to get to Durm ASAP. It's taking place the day after tomorrow, and the FBI wants to brief you before you go in."

I tried to swallow, but my mouth had gone dry.

"I'll be on a flight first thing in the morning. I'm bringing Sam." I looked over at the group and realized he was keeping an eye on me as he ate. My shoulders relaxed a notch.

"Good. I need to warn you, you'll have to meet with Cole. He insists."

"They're his kids, Luis. It's understandable." My shoulders inched back up in a familiar defensive posture. I wasn't looking forward to seeing Cole.

"Maybe, but there's a fine line between helping and hindering an operation. He may be a professional, but he's a demanding son of a bitch."

I stopped myself short of delivering a snappy retort. I'd be a son of a bitch, too, if my family was involved, but Luis had only been trying to warn me and didn't deserve a snippy reply. I'd have to watch my anger. The stress of my imminent meeting with Cole and my fear for the kid's safety was making me short-tempered.

"Thanks for the head's up, Luis. I'll keep that in mind."

"Call me when you land."

"I will. Thanks."

I ended the call and slid the phone into my pocket as I walked back to the group, panic beginning its slow crawl up from my gut. *Don't worry about it, Kate. It'll all be over soon.*

The beach party wound down about ten. By the time we made it back to John's and said goodbye to George and Becky, it was past midnight. Trevor offered to stay the night in order to help John prep the house for painting the next day. I'd booked our flight to Phoenix on Sam's phone earlier that evening, and he planned to pick me up in the morning, since he still needed to pack. I thanked John and Martha for the great day, said goodnight to Trevor, and walked out back to the apartment.

I slid the deadbolt home on the front door and dropped my bag on the kitchen counter. The day's activities had done a good job of taking my mind off my impending meeting with the FBI, Cole, and Anaya's thugs, but after the phone call from Luis my mood had turned somber, and I had a hard time not thinking dark thoughts.

There were so many ways the trade could go wrong. Was Anaya monster enough that he'd order Lauren and Abby killed without a second thought? Would Angie do what he asked?

I closed my eyes and took a deep breath. I didn't know how to answer either of those questions. Anaya normally wouldn't blink when it came to tying up loose ends, but I didn't know if that callousness extended to children. He'd take himself out of the equation, stay removed from the act of killing. I doubted he'd go through with it if he had to be the one to pull the trigger. Distance made the situation less visceral, less personal. Even Angie would probably have someone else do the job.

It was possible I was giving them both too much credit in order to assuage my fears, but when I'd been trapped in Salazar's world, there'd been no talk of killing innocent children. At the same time, if a rival became a problem, I had no doubt that their children would be fair game for kidnapping, at least.

I had to break it down to a manageable level or I'd have a hard time pushing through my fear for the kids. If the fear won, I wouldn't do anybody any good. I ran through dozens of scenarios, taking each to their logical conclusion, and kept coming up with the same answer every time: I had to make sure Cole's kids were safe.

End of story.

13

MY EYES SNAPPED open as I tried to figure out what had woken me. I slid to a sitting position and listened.

No sounds came from outside the bedroom, but that didn't mean anything. After being on the run for so many years I didn't ignore things like waking up in the middle of the night.

I reached under my pillow for the gun and realized I'd left it in the bag on the kitchen counter—something I never would have done if I hadn't been so tired. I crept out of bed and made my way toward the door, aware of the fact that if anyone had broken in, they could be wearing night vision goggles, which would put me at a distinct disadvantage.

How could anyone even find this place? You're just being paranoid, Kate.

Then I remembered the feeling of being watched at the ferry earlier that day.

I eased the door open and peeked through, straining to listen. It might have been my imagination, but I thought I heard someone breathing. Not the kind of panting I struggled to suppress along with my galloping heart, but a slow, measured inhale and exhale, the kind a professional might make.

The thought occurred to me that I had an advantage, however small, because I knew they were in the apartment, whereas they had no idea I was awake and aware. I tiptoed back to the bed and felt for the lamp. Following the cord, I eased the plug from the outlet and grabbed hold of the base with both hands, lifted it off the nightstand, and turned it upside down as I raised it to batting height.

Scarcely breathing now, I crossed the room and stood behind the door. I'd feel stupid if I was wrong and there wasn't anyone in the apartment, but I'd learned never to worry about stupid if dead might be the only other option.

I attempted to calm myself while I waited, hoping to quiet the annoying sound of blood pumping through my ears. Sweat trickled down the sides of my face as I held the lamp like Miguel Cabrera setting up to hit a homer.

About the time fatigue hit my arms, the door moved. At first I credited my overactive imagination, but the door kept inching open.

No windows had been left open, so it couldn't have been the wind, and I remembered closing and locking the door.

Not wanting to broadcast my position, I fought the urge to move. A dark silhouette partially emerged on the other side. I waited until he was halfway into the room before I threw myself against the door and slammed him into the door jamb. A gun went off but the shot went wide. I took a step back and swung the butt end of the lamp into what I hoped was a head.

The base connected with a satisfying thud. The prowler groaned and slumped against the wall, followed by the sound of an object clattering to the floor. I stepped from behind the door and, keeping my eyes on the inert form, reached down to scoop up the gun and aimed it at the body. I was about to flip on the overhead light to see whose head I'd just bashed in when I heard a scuffle outside the apartment. Seconds later, two more gunshots echoed through the apartment.

Heart in my throat, I backed into the room and away from the intruder, his loud snores assuring me I hadn't killed him.

A concussion, maybe, but not death.

The front door crashed open and someone ran across the living room. Just as I took a step behind the door, John burst into the room, breathing heavily, a Louisville Slugger in his hands. Martha followed right behind him holding what looked like a .38. John flipped on the light and took in the scene: the guy on the floor next to the chipped lamp base and me with a gun.

"Holy Christ. Who the hell is that?" Still brandishing the bat, he stepped over the body. Blinking against the light, Martha kept her gun leveled at the man on the floor. Her hands shook.

"I think we need to call the police," I replied, scanning the room for something I could use to tie him.

John nodded and pulled his phone out of his bathrobe pocket. "Martha dropped the guy outside."

"I think I killed him," she said, her voice unsteady. A shudder ran through her.

"Are there any more?" I asked.

"Not that we could see—" Martha said. "John was in the bathroom when he noticed someone sneaking into the backyard. We came up behind him, real quiet. He had a gun—" Her voice trailed off.

John nodded. "The guy didn't know what hit him."

"Good thing you had the thirty-eight." I crossed the room and disconnected the cord from the phone, and returned to the man on the floor. Dressed in black, he had a light-brown, military-style haircut and camouflage paint on his face. A trickle of blood from where he'd collided with the lamp had stained its way down the side of his head and onto his neck, giving him a macabre look. With Martha's help, we pushed him away from the wall so I could wrap the cord around his wrists.

John paced the room as he waited for the call to the police to connect. "How'd they figure out you were here?"

"I'd like to know that myself."

"What the—" He narrowed his eyes and leaned down to look more closely at the man's arm. "See that?" he said, pulling back his sleeve to reveal the tattoo of a bulldog with the words *Semper Fi* underneath. "Marine." He shook his head and then turned to me. "I thought some Mexican drug lord and his assassin were after you."

"They are. Angie's been known to use local talent."

"He'd better damn well be a *former* Marine," he muttered as he stepped away to speak to emergency services.

Martha lowered her gun, conflicting emotions arcing across her features.

"I'm so sorry, Martha. I didn't think they'd find me here," I said, my attempt at a heartfelt apology landing with a thud between us. Martha nodded, took a deep breath. In the background, John gave the operator the address and explained the situation.

"I'd better check on Trevor." Martha turned to leave.

In a flash I knew how they'd found me.

I needed to call Sam.

"Wait," John said, pocketing the phone as he followed her. "There might be more."

The police arrived a short time later, their lights flashing. I gave them my statement and the man's gun, while they cuffed the gunman who was still alive and hauled him away on a stretcher. They bagged the one Martha shot and took him away, too. He had a similar tattoo on his forearm as the other man. I had a hard time reconciling what I knew about Marines and their immense pride and honor with the two men who'd been sent to kill me.

Sam showed up soon after. It turned out the first gunman had cut a window pane on the front door and unlocked the deadbolt by reaching inside. They found the section of glass on the ground outside the apartment. That must have been what woke me up. The other gunman had probably acted as a lookout.

Sam made me a cup of tea and sat down beside me on the couch. I sipped at the scalding liquid, trying to choose my words.

"I think Trevor led him here," I said. Blunt, but effective.

"But how would Angie know I was here?" Sam asked. "There's no way they could have found me that quickly."

"Your business is listed on the Internet under your last name. It wouldn't be that hard."

"Why would they look for me? It doesn't make sense. For all they knew, I still lived in Alaska."

"Remember when I told you about Eduardo being murdered after he helped me escape from Salazar?"

Sam nodded.

"Even though he'd been put into the Witness Protection program and the U.S. Marshals were taking him to an undisclosed location, they *still* got to him. They found his severed head a few miles south of Nogales, in the desert." I shook my head at the memory. "Back then I was convinced there was a leak, but no one could figure out if it was in the Mexican government or the DEA." I turned and looked at Sam. "What if the leak's in Luis' office?"

"But it's been ten years. Why wouldn't the informant have told Salazar or Anaya your location? You've kept in contact with Luis all this time."

"They followed me to Alaska, and to Arizona."

"Good point." Sam fell silent. "But things were relatively quiet for years after you testified."

"Both Salazar and Anaya were in prison."

"They'd have been able to track you from inside. It's not like everything stops once a person's incarcerated. Especially in Mexico."

"True enough, but I didn't tell Luis exactly where I was in Alaska until a few years later, when I witnessed the PI's murder. It's a big state."

"But he knew you moved to Durm, right?"

"Not right away, no. I was always a little cagey about my location, and he never asked me outright."

"So you think that when Trevor came looking for me, a gunman was watching my office and decided to follow him here?"

"Yes." Acid churned in my stomach at the idea that any of Sam's family could have been hurt, or worse. "I have to leave." I looked at Sam's wrist, trying to see his watch. "What time is it?"

Sam glanced down. "A little after two."

"I should check into a hotel for a few hours, try to rest." Sleep wouldn't be in the cards for the remainder of the night—that much I knew—but at least I could try to relax.

"Let's go." He rose from the couch and extended his hand. I set my cup on the table and let him pull me up.

It was going to be a short, sleepless night.

14

W E TOUCHED DOWN in Phoenix later that morning, rented a car and were in Durm by a quarter to three. I called Luis on the way and he met us outside of town at a diner that'd partied hard in the twentieth century and wasn't wearing the twenty-first very well.

I slid into the cracked, red vinyl booth and ordered a cup of coffee and a slice of apple pie with cheddar cheese on top. There was something comforting about eating pie in a diner. Sam had ice water and a chef salad, and Luis ordered a bacon cheeseburger. I picked at his French fries while he briefed me.

"Agent Landers is the lead on the operation. She's got twenty years with the Bureau, the last five working kidnappings, most of them children. This is her first involving a cartel boss."

"Technically Anaya isn't a boss anymore. He sold out, remember?"

Luis smirked. "Looks like he's getting back in business. At any rate, my guys have been feeding her team all the information fit to print: known associates, vehicles, phone numbers, last known addresses, cousins, uncles, BFFs, pets, you name it. The last piece of the puzzle is you."

"Did you find anything on the website?"

Luis nodded. "One of the photographs revealed several GPS coordinates hidden within the pixels—three of which were known to us. Super labs, for lack of a better description. Huge drug operations churning out methamphetamine. We dismantled one of them a few years back. Thanks to you, the information should make a nice dent in business, as long as we're careful who we share it with."

"That's it? Why would Anaya be so hot to get the information? Wouldn't Salazar have shared the locations with him?"

"We think Salazar had been gaming Anaya for years—skimming off the top of whatever business he did with him, while at the same time keeping the labs a secret in case things went south in their relationship."

"Sounds like Salazar. He was king of the backup plan." Thanks to his massive paranoia, he constantly worked to stay a step ahead of the competition and the assassins they hired. "These super labs—just how much do they bring in?"

"You'd never believe it."

"Try me."

"Let's just say it's more cash than you could spend in a dozen lifetimes."

"Did you find anything else in the other photos?" Sam asked.

"Yeah. The second one had a bunch of names we never heard of along with dollar amounts and what we think were drop sites. Paying off employees or informants, we're not sure which. We'll have to look at them more closely. The information's over ten years old, so I'd guess a lot of them are dead or gone by now. I had one of my guys float a couple of the names to handpicked informants. So far nothing's turned up. The other photographs appear to be clean."

"And you're sure whoever accessed the website was able to do it without activating the trackback?" I asked.

"FBI says yes. They've been forthcoming with the information, and they don't want to endanger the kids."

"Of course." My default was to always question assumptions. I'd been wrong too many times to take anything at face value.

"Tell me about the gunmen." Luis took a big bite of his bacon cheeseburger and looked at me expectantly.

"The one who came after me was middle-aged. Both of them had military buzz cuts," I said. "Also, both had a United States Marine Corps tattoo—a bulldog with the words *Semper Fi* under it. Any ideas why they'd send in someone from the Marines? Are they trying to throw off the authorities?"

"Probably ex-Marines. I doubt they're active. They'd have limited say in where they're sent. Deployment would render them useless." Luis swallowed and took a drink of his cola. "The cartels are tapping prison inmates in the US as associates when they get out and they're recruiting ex-military, too. It's like a fucking job fair out there."

"Seriously?"

"Yeah." Luis shook his head. "They're pulling the same shit here as they do in Mexico. The cartels pay a hundred times better for combat experience compared to what these guys get from the military. Find someone who has a dishonorable discharge, some kind of beef with the government, and they're ripe for the picking."

"Like the Mexican police," I said. "Tax-free income, more than the government pays. So what if you have to look the other way. If you don't comply, they're experts at changing your mind." When it came to money, all bets were off, especially when your new employer threatened your family.

"These guys aren't just 'looking the other way,' Kate. They're hired killers—getting fifty, sixty grand a head, doing for the cartels what they did for Uncle Sam."

"Makes it easy to carry out a hit in the States," Sam added. "Am I right when I say cartel influence is increasing in this country?"

Luis took another sip of his drink. "Let's just say right now I'd hate to be a cop at a major transportation hub like Chicago."

Sam sat back in the booth, absorbing the information. Uncomfortable with the idea of cartel members lurking at every port in America, I decided to change the subject.

"What do I need to do for tomorrow?" I asked.

"As it stands right now, Anaya's people are supposed to contact Cole and give him the location where you'll pick up a phone. The caller insisted they speak only to you regarding the exchange. When they call, they will tell you where and when the meet is supposed to go down. Once you have that information, you'll get into your car and drive there. We, meaning the FBI, myself, and a handful of other agents, will be watching everything. There'll be a tracker on your car."

"What if they know you're there?"

"They won't."

"Did you ever find that leak?"

Luis shifted in his chair, shook his head. "No."

"Ah. I see." My voice caught as memories of Eduardo swept over me. I cleared my throat and turned to Sam.

"My bet's the leak is or was in the DEA—Luis' boss, Chance, tended to play his cards close to his vest with the Mexican government back then."

"I've known my guys for at least five years, some of them a hell of a lot longer than that," Luis said, getting a little hot. "There hasn't been a wedding or a birthday party I've missed, or an anniversary or funeral. Only a few handpicked people on my team know about this operation, Kate. I made sure to include agents I'd trust. We're closer than most families, so don't worry. I'm ninety-nine-point-nine percent sure it isn't one of them."

By the look on Luis' face, he believed what he'd said. The pesky little point-one percent had me worried.

"Ready to meet with Cole?"

I took a deep breath and nodded.

Might as well get it over with.

15

I WASN'T LOOKING forward to seeing Cole again, and not only because he no longer remembered me. It's not every day you get to confront the woman who was the reason your children were kidnapped.

Another thing I hadn't allowed myself to think about until Sam and I reached Durm: Cole might not remember the past year and a half, but I did. We'd begun to build a relationship, forged from a mutual attraction, and from having faced dangerous circumstances together. I likened it to how fellow soldiers or cops and their partners developed a special bond. Once you go through something intense like that with another person, you can't help being connected on some level.

He'd been there for me when John Sterling, the corrupt DEA agent, got out of prison and came to Durm gunning for me, and he'd been there to pick up the pieces when I became the target of a deranged banker and his psychotic enforcer.

Not to mention the cruise to the Caribbean.

Cole got to know Vincent Anaya when the cruise ship we were on came under attack by Anaya's hired pirates. I was one of three people kidnapped off the ship and brought to Anaya's little hideaway island deep in the Caribbean. When I explained how I'd lost the money I'd stolen from him, Anaya tried to kill me using unusual methods designed to deliver excruciating pain to the victim. In the end, I escaped with Cole's help.

The three of us finished our meal and then left separately, with Sam and I leaving first in case someone decided to follow us. It wasn't far to the rendezvous point, but the minutes felt like hours. We didn't say much to each other on the way, and I wondered how he would react when I met with Cole. Knowing Sam, he wouldn't let on how he was feeling, to me or anyone else. The man was a paragon of stoicism. It was hard to get used to. At least with anger you knew where you stood.

We arrived at the abandoned quarry twenty minutes later. Cole leaned against an unmarked SUV, arms crossed, sunglasses on, his lips pressed together. It looked like the hair on one side of his head had been shaved, but was now growing back. My heart leapt when I saw him, which shouldn't have been surprising. Guilt, love, and a big helping of grief gnawed at me, telling me I had some deep soul-searching to do if I ever got out of this thing alive. I glanced at Sam, but as expected, his face betrayed no emotion.

Nothing like feeling more guilt for putting Sam through this. Maybe it was time to swear off relationships.

Right, Kate. That had worked so well in the past.

We pulled alongside the SUV, and Sam turned off the engine.

"You want to talk to him alone?" Sam asked.

"Do you mind?"

"No."

I opened the car door and got out. I didn't blame him for not wanting to be caught in the crossfire when Cole lit into me. Cole lifted his chin in acknowledgement, and I braced for the onslaught.

"Kate, right?"

Oh God. It hadn't occurred to me that he wouldn't know me on sight. The breath whooshed from my lungs, and I put my hand on the hood of the car, disoriented.

"Yeah. Look, I—"

Cole cut me short, yanking his sunglasses off. "I don't want to hear your apologies. I want to get this thing over with as soon as possible and get my kids back."

The lines on his face were new, with the few days' growth of beard barely camouflaging his obvious exhaustion. And his eyes—those beautiful, dark blue eyes that had once meant safety and love to me now held such worry and pain that I almost cried. My emotions swung wildly between confused and joyful, conflicted and sad. Joy that he could walk and talk with nothing worse than a lapse in memory, confused because for some reason I expected him to remember me, conflicted because my feelings for him matched those I had for Sam, and sad because none of it mattered.

What did matter was getting Lauren and Abby back safely.

Afraid he'd let loose the anger I could feel radiating off him, I remained quiet. When I didn't say anything, he let out a frustrated sigh.

"Why can't I remember you?" he asked, his tone sharp, pleading.

Startled, I glanced at him and got a faint hint of what it must be like for him to have no memory of the last year of his life. Deeply buried emotions welled up inside of me and I stepped toward him.

"I wish I knew. I wish you could remember how much I cared for you and for Lauren and Abby. Not that it would make any of this better." My words trailed off as I stared into the distance. A red-tailed hawk drifted in lazy circles through the sky, hunting for its next meal.

"You're right. It doesn't."

I looked in his eyes. "I'm sorry, Cole. I know that isn't enough, will never be enough, but I don't know what to say to make any of this better." I raised my hands, palms up, not knowing how to bridge the gap between us or if it would even be possible.

He glanced down and cleared his throat, then looked up at the hawk, now spiraling closer.

"I know," he said, his voice tight. He turned away from the bird's trajectory. "I came here wanting to hate you, to tell you how much trouble you've caused me and my family and that I wish you would disappear, but I can't." His eyes filled with frustration. "When I look at you, something pulls at me, something familiar, but I can't put my finger on it. The past year is a complete blank." He glanced at the sky and shook his head. "I have to get my girls back."

"We will, Cole." I put my hand on his arm. There was no spark of recognition, but he didn't seem as angry.

I'd take it.

We both turned as Luis pulled up next to the SUV and got out. A dark colored four-door sedan followed close behind. A woman, on the upper side of thirty with shoulder-length black hair and wearing a dark blue suit, got out of the passenger side of the car. A much younger man in an ill-fitting brown ensemble that must have come straight off the rack at the Men's Wearhouse exited the driver's side. I motioned for Sam to join us. He did and I introduced him to Cole. They shook hands.

"Agent Landers, this is Kate Jones and Sam Akiaq," Luis said.

"Pleasure. Here's the deal," Agent Landers began. "One of Anaya's people is supposed to call Cole's cell phone within the hour. Cole, you pick up the call, tell whoever is on the other end that Kate's in town. I doubt they'll stay on the line very long, but in case they do, I've installed software that will give us the best shot at determining their location. Before you hang up I want you to request proof of life. They may or may not give it to you. The main thing is to keep them on the line as long as you can."

"What then?" I asked.

"They will give Cole the location of the phone they want you to use. I assume they'll have installed their own tracking software and will monitor your every move. It's imperative that you don't say anything to us over the mic at that point. More than likely they'll have installed a listening device along with the tracker."

"I'll be wearing a wire?" News to me. I glanced at Luis, who cut a look at Agent Landers.

"We're all good with Kate wired for sound, right?" she asked, glancing at the group.

Luis cleared his throat. "I don't think—"

"It's fine," I interjected, giving Luis a look that said, *I'm okay with this. Pick another battle.* He clamped his lips together.

Apparently satisfied, Agent Landers gave a curt nod and returned to business.

"As I was saying, Kate, don't speak into the mic. The only time I want to hear your voice is if you're answering them or need us to be there, now. If that's the case, I want you to say the word *superficial* loud and clear. That'll be our cue to move." She looked around at the group, singling each of us out with her gaze. "I know I don't need to remind you that there are children's lives at stake. There's no room for error. We must be precise in our execution or things will get ugly, fast."

"You can count on me." I thought back to when I had to face Hugo Morales, head of a powerful drug cartel in the Yucatán, little more than two months ago. Terrified he'd find out I'd been working for a group dedicated to taking him and his kind down, I knew I had a good chance of getting killed or worse. Even so, I hadn't been wired then.

But Lauren's and Abby's lives weren't at stake, either.

"Good." Landers nodded her approval. "We'll be with you every step of the way, Kate. If we determine that either the children's or your safety has been compromised, we'll move in immediately."

"Thanks." Why did I not feel better? Landers' cool authority and handle on the situation should have helped, at least a little. I chalked it up to a heavy case of nerves.

"Are we good?" Landers glanced around the group again. Satisfied, she pulled Luis off to the side for a quiet conversation.

"And now we wait," Cole said.

"Yep." I looked for the hawk, but it had disappeared. There were so many things I wanted to say to Cole but knew I'd never get the chance. It was a selfish thought, really. If I unloaded everything I was feeling, then I'd be freer, lighter, and Cole would end up being bogged down by my confessions, as would Sam. Better not to say anything.

Half an hour went by. My right eye developed an annoying twitch, and Cole kept rubbing his face. Sam walked over to talk to Agent Landers, leaving me with Cole and Luis.

"Waiting is the hardest part of any operation," Luis said as he leaned against the car. "So, other than amnesia, any side effects from the head wound?" he asked Cole.

"Like I told Kate earlier, I've got some weakness on my left side. Occasional blurry vision. Nothing too terrible."

"You were one lucky man."

Cole nodded, looked down. "Yeah."

A minute later, Cole's cell rang. Everyone snapped to as he picked up the phone and put the call on speaker mode.

"Cole Anderson."

"Take me off speaker, now."

Angie's voice crackled through the phone and the group's tension spiked. Cole hit the button, doing as she said.

"Where are—" he started, and clamped his mouth shut. "Yes, she's in town. Wait—" His hand shook slightly as he felt his shirt, and then reached in his back pocket for his billfold. Landers handed him her pen as he took out a slip of paper.

"I have a pen," he said, cradling the phone underneath his chin. He scribbled on the paper and repeated it back to her, his tone strained. "Forest Service Road Fifteen, six miles from the turnoff. Metal fence, juniper, large stump. Ten o'clock tomorrow morning. She'll be there. Yes, alone and unarmed." He listened for a moment, then said, "I need to talk to my kids."

His face flushed red.

"Goddammit—*I need to know if my kids are all right*—" He jerked the phone away from his ear, and slammed his fist into the hood of the SUV. "She hung up. She fucking *hung up.*"

Without thinking, I closed the distance between us and put my arms around him. His shoulders sagged as he dropped his head to my shoulder with a ragged sigh. I held on, speaking to him in a low voice, telling him it was going to be all right, that we were going to get his kids back, that they'd be fine. He bought it, for a moment.

Until he didn't.

"No—" With a violent shrug, he pushed me away. I released my hold and took a step back.

He rounded on me, his face filled with impotent fury. "They've got my kids. *My kids.* You know what that's like? Do you?" He narrowed his eyes as I involuntarily stepped backward. "Of course you don't. You have no children. That would make life too complicated, wouldn't it?"

I stood my ground as he raged. *Let it out, Cole. You need this. I can take whatever you give.*

He turned his attention to Sam. "You'd better watch your ass, buddy. She leaves death and destruction in her wake. No one is safe." Recognition lit his eyes. "You're the cop that got shot in Alaska, aren't you? How'd that work out for ya? Come back to see if she could finish the job?"

Surprised, I glanced at Luis, wondering if he'd mentioned what had happened to Sam. Luis closed his eyes. Cole zeroed in on our silent exchange.

"Yeah, Luis told me all about how everyone you know ends up either dead or sucking on some tube in the ER."

Luis shook his head as he stepped forward. "That's not what I—"

"Well, it's the goddamned truth, isn't it? Nothing she does can undo the terror my children are feeling and the memories they'll live with if they even survive…" Cole's voice cracked, and he took a shaky breath. His face held a mixture of rage and deep pain and even though his anger was directed at me my heart still ached for him.

Sam had come to stand by my side as the rant escalated, and now moved past me toward Cole. I grabbed his arm, trying to hold him back. Other than an icy stare, a slight tic near his jaw was the only evidence of his anger. I'd never seen Sam react to the slightest provocation until today. They glared at each other as Cole curled his hands into fists. I held my breath.

Minutes ticked by before the storm abated. Cole managed to wrestle his emotions into submission, and he once again became in-control Sheriff Anderson of Hohokam County. Everyone in the group breathed a collective sigh of relief. Sam stood down.

"Ready to go?" Sam asked in a low voice, keeping an eye on Cole.

Agent Landers handed me a card with a phone number and address written in ink.

"Be at this address tomorrow morning at eight thirty. We'll wire you and your car before you go." She pointed at Sam. "You need to stay at the hotel. The fewer people, the better."

Chastened, Sam nodded.

"The phone number is for you to call for updates," she said to me. "I'll give you the rest of the instructions tomorrow. Get a good night's sleep. We'll see you in the morning." She and the other agent walked back to their car, got in, and left in a cloud of quarry dust.

Luis stood next to his car, watching them leave. "Cole—" he said to Cole's back. Cole turned. "Let's go get a beer. I'm buying."

Cole thought for a moment, and nodded. "Sure." He pushed past me and got in his SUV, then gunned the engine as he turned around, waiting for Luis near the quarry entrance.

Luis glanced in our direction. "You two going to be all right for the evening? I mean, you got a place to stay and everything?"

"Yeah. We're good. Thanks, Luis." I gave him a nod.

"Okay then. See you tomorrow." He got into his car and the two of them drove away, dusty rooster tails trailing behind them.

The sun had just begun to set, casting an orange glow on the rocks surrounding the quarry. I looked up as another red-tailed hawk—or maybe the same one—appeared, circling slowly in the air, belying the intensity and violence of a raptor on the hunt.

"You okay?" Sam asked.

"Yeah. Of course."

"What do you mean, 'of course'?" he asked.

"I mean of course. I totally deserved what Cole said and more. I think I got lucky, to tell you the truth."

Sam sighed and shook his head.

"Listen, Kate. You didn't know Anaya would go this far. Hell, you didn't know what you were doing when you activated the trackback. Yeah, maybe you shouldn't have dug up the money, but it's done. I realize Cole's in an untenable position, but you don't deserve to be treated like his whipping post. He was out of line."

"It's over, Sam. He needed to vent and I was handy. I am also the reason his kids were kidnapped, so yeah, I deserved whatever he gave. But, thanks. I appreciate what you're saying." We were standing side-by-side at this point. I nudged him and gave him a little smile. "You hungry?"

"I could eat."

"Good, because this may be my last meal on the planet, and I want to go out with a plate of blue corn enchiladas with adobo sauce and a double margarita at Pepe's."

Sam narrowed his eyes. "This is not your last night on the planet, but you know the area so we go where you want. Pepe's it is."

16

PEPE'S WAS CROWDED, the smell of fresh tortillas and peppers adding to the cozy atmosphere. We got a table on the back patio and ordered drinks: club soda with a twist for Sam, double margarita on the rocks for me. After the waitress had taken our order, I reached across the table for his hand. He watched as I traced the line along the middle of his palm, ending at his wrist.

"Your lifeline is long, Sam. If I were to guess, I'd say you'll live well into your nineties, maybe even longer." I stared at the crisscrossing lines on his hand, wishing I could see some indication of what would happen in his future.

"Do you read palms?" he asked.

I smiled. "No. But I'm eerily accurate when it comes to how long it will be before someone gets laid."

"Oh, you are, are you?" He grabbed my hands and flipped them over, perusing my palms.

"Do you read?" I asked.

"Of course. I wouldn't be much of a shaman's apprentice if I wasn't able to see—"

He cut the sentence short.

"What?" My heart skipped as thoughts of impending doom crowded out whatever I'd been thinking.

The wisp of a frown crossed his features as he shook his head. "Nothing," he said, his expression clearing. "Ah, yes. I see a night of passion with a dark-eyed stranger who can think of nothing else but your naked body beneath his."

"Stop it, Sam. You saw something, didn't you?"

He smiled a slow, lazy smile. "I just told you what I saw. Sex, and lots of it."

I pulled my hand back and searched the lines on my palms. I'd had mine read a couple of times with varying degrees of accuracy, and I was still kind of on the fence about its merits. Although, if my experiences over the years with bad spirits were any indication, I wasn't about to discount something having to do with forces I couldn't see.

"Well, then, we should probably make reservations for the night," I said.

He took out his phone and searched available rooms. We chose the Sol Inn, a small hotel not far from the restaurant but out of the way. The safer I felt, the more chance I'd get some rest.

After dinner we made the short drive to the hotel. The room smelled of fresh roses from a bouquet left by the manager on the small table in front of the couch, along with a bottle of red wine and two glasses. A gas fireplace took up part of one wall, with a queen-sized bed across from it. Sam flipped a switch and the fireplace flickered on, taking off the evening chill. I kicked off my shoes and sat on the couch, tucking my legs underneath me.

"Wine?" Sam asked, reaching for the opener.

"No, thanks. One of Pepe's margaritas is plenty for me." Although the idea of trying to forget about tomorrow had appeal, my instincts were to stay as coherent as possible. I refused to think about what would happen if I made any mistakes.

Sam stood behind me and kneaded my neck and shoulders. I closed my eyes and melted into the massage, thankful I didn't have to spend the night alone. Sleeping would be hard enough.

"We don't need to make love tonight. I was just trying to get your mind off tomorrow," Sam murmured.

I smiled and lifted the hair off my neck so he had clear access.

"Keep this up and you won't have a choice."

He leaned in and planted kisses along the back of my neck, sending chills down my back. I blocked images of Cole, the kids, Salazar, and Angie from my mind and concentrated on my physical senses as Sam did his damnedest to help me forget.

"Too bad we can't bottle you. We'd be rich," I said.

Sam chuckled as he came around to the front and sat on the couch. With nimble fingers he unbuttoned my shirt and took it off, followed by my bra.

At that point, I felt the tide turn from being fearful about the next day and depressed because of the scene earlier that afternoon with Cole, to a single-minded desire to get Sam naked and feel his smooth, hard body next to mine. Thank God, because I sure as hell didn't want to spend the entire night worried.

There'd be plenty of time for that.

After tossing for a couple of hours and getting no sleep, I eased out of bed. Careful not to wake Sam, I crept across the room to the rocking chair next to the window. The moon hung halfway up in the clear night sky, and I stared long and hard at it, working through next-day scenarios and wrestling with my feelings for both Sam and Cole.

Even though I knew no future existed for me with Cole and his girls, my feelings for him stubbornly refused to go away. I glanced at Sam's sleeping form and knew in my heart that if things went right the next day and we succeeded in rescuing the kids, I would leave Arizona behind for good. There was no reason for me to stay and make everyone's life more complicated. Besides, you can't leave what you don't have.

But did I want to complicate Sam's life? I doubted the FBI or DEA would get their hands on Vincent Anaya, since he rarely participated in jobs his minions could accomplish. Now that he knew I was alive and had obviously accessed the money, would he continue to hunt me down in the name of revenge?

Probably.

Revenge ended up being a cartel boss' only friend. If he was indeed getting back into the life as Luis suggested, then I guessed his insistence on turning over a new leaf had gone up in smoke when the Feds destroyed his Caribbean island. I never could wrap my mind around a kinder, gentler, more spiritual Anaya. My last run-in with him in the Caribbean cemented my original theory of his having a bad case of psycho.

The best outcome tomorrow would be to rescue the girls, capture Angie and whoever else was involved, and extract Anaya's location from one of his people. If the

FBI and/or the DEA succeeded in capturing him, I could breathe again.

Until then, I'd have to watch my back and that of anyone I was connected to. Granted, having only one cartel boss after you was a heck of a lot better than two, but it was still a freaking cartel boss.

I leaned my head back on the rocker and closed my eyes. Maybe someday my life would make sense. If I survived tomorrow's trade, then maybe I could find a job in Seattle, rent a place, have a normal life with Sam where we went out to dinner every now and again, spent the weekend at a bed and breakfast, did all those normal things couples do.

Nice thought.

Not very realistic.

Sure, Anaya might not get the information on the names and the super labs that he so desperately wanted, but it would in no way diminish the power or reach he already had. And, he now knew where Sam lived and that I'd been staying at his cousin's place.

Sam would be in danger, like Cole's girls were. If Anaya wanted to find me, all he'd have to do was threaten to hurt Sam. The realization that Sam wouldn't be safe as long as Anaya went free hit me hard. The only way this would end was if Anaya no longer needed to find me.

The only way that could happen would be if Anaya was dead or I gave myself up to him.

Not much of a choice, since killing him wasn't on the easy menu.

My eyes burned, and I'd grown cold sitting by the window. With one last look at the glimmering moon I made my way back to bed and slid next to Sam's warm body. He turned in his sleep and wrapped his arm around me, helping me to feel a small measure of safety. I counted myself incredibly fortunate that I'd had two wonderful men in my life who could make me feel safe, and who respected my strengths and overlooked my weaknesses. How that had happened was a mystery to me.

I also knew I couldn't expect anyone to live their lives on the run like I had.

With a deep sigh, I closed my eyes and breathed in Sam's scent. The familiar combination of cedar and spice filled my head, leaving me feeling protected, at least for now.

A girl can dream.

17

AT EIGHT THIRTY sharp, I pulled into the drive of the address Agent Landers had given me the night before. The place turned out to be an older home just outside of town. A guy dressed in jeans and a T-shirt came around the side and waved me through to the back.

The driveway led past the home to a two-car garage. I slowed to a stop when another guy, dressed in khakis, walked up to my window.

"Pull in and park," he said, indicating the detached garage. "Leave the keys. Go inside the house through the back door. Agent Landers is waiting for you."

I parked the Charger and walked over to the house and up the stairs onto the redwood deck. Landers appeared at the back door and held it open, stepping aside as I entered the bright, sunny kitchen.

"Right on time," she said, looking at her watch. She nodded toward a younger woman standing next to the stove. "Agent Howard here will take you back and get you set up."

"This way," Agent Howard said, and motioned for me to follow her.

We walked through the small living room and down a hallway that led to two bedrooms with a bath in between. She turned right into the first bedroom and shut the door after me.

"I'm going to need you to take off your shirt."

I pulled off my T-shirt and laid it on the bed. She opened the closet and handed me a cream-colored, short-sleeved button-down shirt.

"Here. Put this on. The second button is a wireless transmitter."

"Good color choice." I put on the shirt and tucked it into my jeans. "Anything brighter makes me a better target."

"We'll be able to pick up anything you say," she said, ignoring my quip. "If the danger to yourself or the children escalates during the meeting, remember to use the word *superficial* in a sentence and we'll move in."

The thought of trying to come up with a sentence under the intense pressure and scrutiny of whoever was going to be at the meet threw me. "I'd better come up with something right now. My brain tends to blank out when I'm nervous, and I guarantee I'll be nervous." Especially with the girls' lives at stake. And my own.

"As long as it doesn't tip them off that we're on our way."

"Oh, forget it. I'll improvise. I probably won't have to use it, anyway, right?"

"That's the plan."

Agent Howard opened the door and led me back into the kitchen, where Agent Landers was speaking into a small receiver.

"Yeah, I can hear you fine, Ted." She turned toward us when we walked into the room. "Your car's wired for both audio and GPS tracking. Whatever happens, we'll be able to hear."

"Great." I took a deep breath and slowly let it out. The reality of what I was about to do slammed home, and my hands started to shake. "What's next?" I asked, shoving my hands into my pockets. "I assume I'll be giving them something at least resembling the information, yes?"

Agent Landers picked up a card lying on the counter beside her and handed it to me.

"It's the same card that I found in the money," I said, looking it over. "Or if it's not, it's a darn good copy."

"It's the original. We don't know if Anaya and his informant used a specific type of paper and figured it would be prudent to use the actual card."

"Good point." I tucked the card into the back pocket of my jeans. "So we're giving him the information."

Agent Landers nodded. "It's the safest bet to get the kids back. The DEA has the names and addresses from the website. In essence the information is useless to Anaya, but golden for us. As soon as he or his associates try to access one of the super labs on the list, the Mexican government will be there to arrest them—with a DEA assist, of course."

"Sounds like a good plan. Although in my experience good plans often go wrong."

Landers nodded. "We've left very little to chance, Kate, but we're prepared to improvise if needed."

"Thanks. I've just got a case of nerves. Going into a meet blind tends to do that to a person."

One of the agents walked in the door and handed Landers the keys to the Charger.

"Car's ready," he said before heading back outside.

"Shall we?" Agent Landers went first, and I followed her to the garage. When we reached the dark blue car she turned and handed me the keys. "We'll be a couple of minutes out, tops."

"Okay." I got into the Charger and turned the key in the ignition. Landers leaned on the car door. "I'm going to buy your team dinner after all this is over," I said.

Landers nodded. "We'll all go out to celebrate—you, me, Sam, Cole, and the kids, but it'll be on me, okay?"

"It's a deal." I backed down the driveway and headed out of town, toward Forest Service Road 15.

That was one dinner date I was determined to keep.

18

TURN LEFT AT the next intersection." The car's GPS had the soothing tone of a woman who knew her directions—a good thing, since I wasn't familiar with the area. I turned left and followed the road for several miles, scanning for landmarks indicating where I would find the phone.

After I'd driven quite a bit further than I thought I should have and hadn't seen anything resembling a tall juniper next to a stump or a metal fence along the side of the road, the panic returned with a vengeance.

Think, Kate. Did you see a marker telling you this was the correct road? I couldn't remember.

Shit. I took a wrong turn. I'm going to be late. I skidded to a stop in a cloud of dust, spun the car around, and headed back to the main road, glaring at the GPS.

"Turn left at the intersection and continue for seven—" I smacked the GPS and cut the annoying voice short.

I turned right and punched the accelerator to the floor, rocketing past disinterested range cattle grazing on the sparse vegetation, counting the minutes until the green metal stake with white lettering signifying Forest Service Road 15 appeared at the next intersection. Downshifting, I skidded around the corner, the Charger fishtailing in the dust.

Five minutes later I slowed the car as I passed a lone juniper with the stump of another tree next to it. A rusty metal fence that led nowhere snaked past them both. I parked the car and got out as soon as I spotted the phone lying on the stump.

After checking the area for telltale indicators of cartel presence, like spent bullet casings or a barrel of acid, I skirted the ditch to reach the phone, leaning against the juniper in the sparse shade to wait.

The day was clear and the temperature comfortable. Like many places in northern Arizona, the dry ground sported even drier twigs and leaves, and the slender trees offered little shade. High in the branches of one, a raven barked. The wind soughed through the arid landscape, rustling the tufts of grass dotting the ground. A small stream trickled nearby, the only source of moisture in an otherwise sunbaked world.

I wondered how Anaya's thugs were treating Lauren and Abby, hoping the girls weren't too scared but knowing that wasn't realistic. Cole's kids were sweet. Innocent. Angie had been the one to call Cole, and I assumed she'd be acting as Anaya's point woman on this. If so, the girls might have a chance of coming out of this relatively unscathed.

Yeah, and I was probably giving her way too much credit.

A shiver ran up my spine at the thought of Anaya's gunmen laying a hand on either of them. Sweet little Abby—the first time I met her, I hadn't exactly been dressed for the occasion. Neither Cole nor I expected them to come home that night. She'd shown me the bathing suit she *had* to wear in her daddy's hot tub since he didn't let her go in the water without one, like I had. Older sister Lauren resembled her mother, minus Mom's icy personality, and even though only ten, the possibility that one of Anaya's men might hurt her…

Stop thinking like that, Kate. It won't do any good.

I shook off the dark thought and concentrated on how I could help make this trade work well enough that the girls would go free and no one got hurt. Remaining calm would be job one.

The nine millimeter Sam loaned me pressed into my stomach. Yes, Angie had specified I was to be unarmed, but at the moment I needed the feeling of safety it afforded me. Out here in the middle of nowhere I'd be an easy target in case one of Anaya's guys got smart and assumed I had the information on me. Then Anaya wouldn't have to deal with keeping the girls healthy and could do whatever he wanted with them.

And I'd be dead.

More than likely this little detour was a ploy to see if I was working with the FBI or DEA. I was sure Anaya didn't enjoy involving Cole in any of this. That being said, he certainly picked the right incentive to flush me out into the open.

A dragonfly flew past me, and I watched it flit and hover, tracing a square path in the air. When the phone rang it startled me so much I fumbled as I bent to pick it up and almost dropped the thing on the ground. I took a deep breath and pushed the button to answer.

"This is Kate."

"Well, it surely is nice to hear your voice, sugar. It's been ages."

I gritted my teeth at Angie's soft laughter. My fingers curled into a fist as the memory returned in vibrant detail of Salazar, Sterling, and Angie at Salazar's hacienda when I'd been kidnapped two months before.

Yeah, I probably shouldn't have tried to kill her.

"Where am I going?" I asked, my voice sharp.

"Now, darlin', is that any way to treat the woman who can give the order to kill those precious kids? Hmm?"

Deep breath, Kate. She's only trying to bait you.

"Where am I going, Angie?"

"*Tsk. Tsk.* You are just no fun anymore, are you?" she said with a dramatic sigh. "I guess you'll just have to get back in that sporty little blue vehicle of yours and turn right at the end of the service road. Follow that for ten miles, and I'll give you another call. Ta-ta for now, sweetie."

The line went dead.

As I walked back to the car I mumbled the directions for the FBI, making it sound like I was talking to myself, since the phone was more than likely bugged. She knew the color of the car, so they were watching me. I just hoped it hadn't been for long.

I turned right at the end of the road and continued until the odometer indicated ten miles. Given the flat terrain and lack of trees, Agent Landers and her team would have a hard time following me without being seen. It was possible they were monitoring me from the air, but I'd been keeping an eye out, and I hadn't seen any aircraft nearby. Although, I probably wouldn't have noticed a drone.

Nothing marked the spot—no mile marker, no big rock, nothing. Just a rusty, barbed-wire fence stapled to desiccated, ash-colored posts and fields of ragweed and purslane, punctuated by clumps of Mormon tea and a smattering of dusty buffalo gourd.

Desolate.

A few minutes later the phone rang.

"You follow instructions well, darlin'."

"I came alone like you asked. Where are the girls?"

"Three miles down you'll come to another intersection. Head east. About two miles later you'll come across an abandoned homestead with a bunch of piñyon pines. You'll know it's the right one by the old windmill to the south."

"The girls are there?"

No answer.

"Hello?"

Frustrated, I punched the end call button and threw the phone onto the passenger seat.

"Shit. Shit. *Shit.*" I gritted my teeth and shook the steering wheel, doing my best to pull it off the column. Lucky for me it didn't budge. After a couple of deep breaths, I started the car and drove on.

As I approached the ranch from the west, I kept my eyes trained on the abandoned buildings, looking for signs of Angie, or the girls, or…something. The closer I got, the less inhabited it appeared.

The ancient windmill spun lethargic circles in the light breeze, keeping an even more aged barn company, its roof collapsed inward like an old man's rheumatic chest. Dark shadows marked the buildings closest to me, giving the place an even bleaker appearance. I turned into the weed-choked driveway, hyper-alert, my hand closing around the gun.

I circled the weathered structure in search of the entrance. A derelict wooden porch slid into view with shadowy, glass-starved windows and mismatched shutters, hanging on by a disconsolate nail. The front door leaned against the jamb, jutting halfway out of the building, as though being associated might not be worth the effort.

This is where he's keeping the kids? I stopped the car and put it in park, opened the door and got out.

The breeze ruffled my hair as I walked slowly toward the house. No signs of life were evident except the frantic fluttering of my heart.

"Hello?" I called, unable to contain my anxiety. "Angie? Let's get this over with."

My nerves frayed, I stopped and waited, hearing only the wind through the gaps in the side boards and the occasional, uneven screech of the metal windmill.

A faint sound, like that of a distressed animal, came from behind me and I whirled around. I held my breath and waited until I heard it again.

The barn.

Tired of the game Angie was playing and determined to finish, I slid the gun out and threaded my way through waist-high weeds. Near the barn I heard the noise again. I edged closer and peered in.

My eyes took their time adjusting as I gazed through the gaping hole that used to be the barn doors but couldn't make out much in the dim light. Dust motes danced in the sparse sunbeams blazing through gaps in the walls. Alert for movement, I stepped through the opening—and froze.

At the far end of the barn a sliver of sunlight streamed through a fissure in the roof, illuminating a disemboweled coyote and three bloody jackrabbits.

I stared at the gory scene before me, dread pooling in my stomach. Each of the bloodstained animals hung by a rope tied to a crossbeam. All four had a handwritten note attached: one rabbit was labeled *Abby,* another said *Lauren,* and the last one read *FBI.* The coyote's moniker read *Kate.*

19

THE COYOTE JERKED its head and whimpered, obviously still alive. Startled, my heart leapt to my throat. Recovering, I raised the gun and fired, putting an end to its misery. All three rabbits were dead but just barely—their bodies were still warm. Whoever had done this hadn't been gone long.

"*Superficial,*" I said into the air, my voice echoing through the emptiness. "I'm alone and they left a message."

I stepped back and glanced at my feet. The ground where I stood had a dark cast. I bent to touch the damp dirt as my gut twisted, and brought my hand to my nose. *More blood.*

Where are the girls?

A short time later, Agent Landers and her team pulled into the driveway. The more I thought about the message, the more worried I became.

"What happened?" Landers stopped short at the sight of the hanging corpses. "Is this how you found them?"

"Yeah. I haven't touched anything, except for putting a bullet in the coyote."

She turned to study the bodies. "Anything other than the names on the cards?"

"Not that I saw. I haven't looked much further than this." I indicated the large bloodstain at my feet.

"Another animal?"

"I don't know," I said. The implication hung in the air between us.

Agent Landers's expression never changed. She was a hard woman to read.

A man wearing a black T-shirt with *FBI* in white lettering on the back tugged on a pair of gloves as he walked over to the carcasses. An agent with a digital camera joined him.

"What did they tell you over the phone?" Landers asked, studying the scene. "Was there any indication they knew about the surveillance?"

"I've been wracking my brain, but I can't think of anything I said or they said that makes any sense. Things were going fine. Somehow they knew."

"We had no indication the surveillance team had been detected. In fact, we were extra cautious due to the delicate nature of the operation." She put her hands on her hips and blew out a disgusted sigh. Her gaze took in the dark patch on the ground. "Damn."

A commotion erupted near the front of the barn, and we both turned in time to see Cole burst through the door. One of Landers's agents tried to grab him, but he shrugged him off. He strode toward us, his face dark with fury.

"Where are they?" His expression morphed from anger to shock as he took in the scene. "My god," he said, his stride faltering. "What happened?"

"We're trying to determine that now. You need to remove yourself from the scene, Cole. Go back outside." Landers' voice sliced through the air.

Cole ignored her and walked up to the dead animals, pausing as he looked at each one. When he got to the last one, he hung his head and stood as still as the death facing him.

Tears stung my eyes, and I wiped angrily at them. *Keep it together, Kate. The bloodstain means nothing. The girls are still safe. Anaya doesn't have his information yet.*

"Did you see them?" he asked, his back to me.

"The girls weren't here, Cole. I don't know if they ever were."

He turned to face me, his expression a carefully controlled mask. His glance dropped to the dark stain near my feet.

"What is that?"

"We don't know. They need to get samples."

Cole nodded. The mask slipped as multiple emotions warred for dominance in his face. Every twitch made my heart ache.

"I'll do whatever it takes to get them back, Cole. They must have figured out that the FBI was keeping tabs on me."

"You don't even know they're alive," he said, his voice a dull monotone.

"They're alive."

His gaze snapped up to mine. I winced at the obvious accusation in his stare. "How can you know that?"

"I know Anaya doesn't have the information he wanted. If he kills the girls, then I will never give it up and he knows that."

"But if he knows you've been working with the FBI, then he also knows the information's been compromised."

"Not necessarily. There are still the other photographs. Just because the FBI didn't find anything worthwhile doesn't mean there isn't something there. If Anaya had no use for Lauren and Abby he'd have left them here." *And they'd be dead*, I thought, although I would never voice that to Cole. "There has to be something left to trade—something that he believes no one will know how to decipher."

Cole stepped clear as one of the FBI agents stooped to take a sample of the bloodied ground.

"Her phone's ringing." The urgency in the agent's voice carried across the empty space.

Confused, I felt my empty front pocket. I'd left Angie's phone on the passenger seat. I jumped to my feet and raced through the barn, making it out to the car in time to rip open the door, grab the phone, and see the words *missed call* on the screen. Cole caught up to me first, followed by Agent Landers.

"Missed it," I said, trying to catch my breath.

Landers held her finger to her lips, and turned and signaled to the rest of the team standing nearby for silence.

"They'll call back," she mouthed. Landers's calm certainty proved prescient. The phone rang less than a minute later. A collective tension enveloped the group.

I took a deep breath and answered.

"This is Kate."

"Did you get my message, Kate darlin'? I hope it wasn't too obtuse for you."

I took a deep breath before replying. "Yes, I got it. Graphic."

Angie sighed. "I *know*, right? A tad dramatic for my taste, but Bobby thought it would give you just the right amount of motivation to let you know the seriousness of the situation." Angie paused a moment before she continued, her voice low. "Vincent surely does know how to pick them, hmm? Apparently, you and Bob have met before. By the way, he says to tell you hello and to thank you for the good time." She paused before continuing. "Really, Kate. I thought you had at least a semblance of good taste. The man is not only ugly as sin, but he has the *worst* halitosis I've ever had the misfortune to encounter."

Bob. I had to think for a minute before the memory surfaced. Toothless Bob? Seriously? The guy from Anaya's yacht? Bile rose in my throat.

"If he lays a hand on either of those kids—" I choked. Cole tensed beside me.

"Well then, you just play by the rules and your lovely sheriff will get his kids back in one piece, Anaya will get what he wants, and you—" Angie chuckled. "You'll get what you deserve."

"Fine. What do you want me to do?"

"First of all, you need to get rid of your entourage." Angie's tone hardened. "Do it in the next five minutes, or Bob's going to start cutting off some tiny little fingers."

I struggled to keep from screaming into the phone. She'd ended the call, anyway. I opened the car door, got in, and turned the key.

"What are you doing? What did she say?" Cole demanded, his voice low and controlled. He gripped the edge of the door until his knuckles blanched white.

I didn't answer as I gunned the engine. I glanced at Agent Landers and barely shook my head. Understanding lit her eyes and she nodded. She took a step back.

"Step away from the car, Cole," she murmured.

Cole's eyes widened when he realized I was leaving. Panic and anger mixed with disbelief pulsed across his face.

Landers signaled two of her agents to come forward, and they gripped Cole's arms.

"No—my kids—she can't just leave—" He struggled against the constraint, anger morphing into white hot rage as he fought not being able to go to his children.

"Cole—listen to me," Landers said to him, trying to get his attention. "She has to go. *You have to let her go.*"

"There's another way. There has to be—" He glared at Landers, his chest heaving.

"Let her go. It's the only option we have right now." She looked meaningfully at the car and back to him, obviously trying to remind him of the tracking device without giving it away to Anaya's people.

He closed his eyes and took a deep breath, the color draining from his face. Then he nodded and stopped struggling. The agents walked him away from the car.

I put the Charger into gear, resisting the urge to look in the rearview mirror as I drove past the dilapidated ranch house to the gravel road and turned left.

I drove for a good fifteen minutes before the phone rang again.

"Now what," I said, barely able to conceal the anger in my voice.

"When you get to the main road, head north three miles, then pull over and park at the scenic vista." The man's voice didn't sound familiar. Apparently Angie had more important things to do than talk to me.

I assumed someone would be there to pick me up and take me to wherever Angie was. Great. Switching cars meant no more GPS tracking by the FBI. All I had now was the radio transmitter in the button on my shirt. Sure, I was nervous about Landers and the FBI following me, but I also didn't want all possibility of a rescue operation to go down the tubes, either. At the very least I wanted them to be able to recover the bodies.

Yeah, that's positive thinking, Kate.

Twenty minutes later, the main highway rolled into view. I turned left and headed north, afraid to think about anything except driving. Three miles later, I pulled into the scenic viewpoint and parked.

I got out of the car and walked to the edge of the empty parking area, near the traffic barrier. The scene before me would have taken anyone's breath away: a deep, wooded canyon sliced in half by a glinting silver river carving a deep gash through the valley. Two golden eagles glided effortlessly on a thermal, each caught in the never-ending hunt for food. I closed my eyes and willed my life to be different.

If only it were that easy.

I opened my eyes and slid the card with the website address and password out of my pocket and studied the information, memorizing it. Then I tore it to pieces and scattered it to the wind.

No sense making it easy for them.

A short time later, a nondescript navy blue Tahoe pulled into the vista point and parked in a cloud of dust. I waited, unsure if it was my ride or another traveler stopping to check out the view.

The passenger side window rolled down and a man wearing aviator sunglasses and no sense of humor motioned for me to approach. I locked the car so some passerby wouldn't find the gun. I didn't have much choice—I had to leave it. No doubt Anaya's thugs would be looking for weapons as well as a transmitter. I hoped the device on my shirt was hard to detect.

Ignoring the fluttering in my stomach, I walked over to the SUV. The door opened and the man with the sunglasses got out.

"Over here." His gruff demeanor didn't give me the warm fuzzies.

I moved closer. He grabbed my arm and turned me so I faced away from him. With businesslike precision he pushed my arms out to the side and patted me down. "Turn."

I did and he checked my front. When he got to a particularly private area, I tilted my head.

"Don't I get dinner first?"

He didn't skip a beat and continued to pat me down without answering. He slid the burner phone out of my front pocket and tossed it into the Tahoe. Apparently satisfied, he stepped back and motioned for me to get in. As I stepped past him, he pulled my hands behind me and looped a plastic zip tie around them, cinching it tight.

The interior of the SUV smelled like stale cigarettes, competing men's colognes, and chewing tobacco. I glanced toward the front and sure enough, a beer can rested in the console's cup holder with the telltale remnants of somebody's bad aim.

The thug who patted me down sat next to me and stared straight ahead. The driver wasn't any more talkative. I peered into the front at the empty seat on the right and got a glimpse of an MP5 machinegun.

I slid back, my hands already turning numb from the zip tie, hoping I hadn't just made a very bad mistake.

20

WE DROVE AWAY from the scenic viewpoint and headed south. The guy next to me produced a black balaclava and pulled it over my head. I could feel my shoulders relax as some of the tension I'd been harboring dissipated. If they bothered obscuring my vision, it was possible they didn't plan to kill me.

Maybe.

Sometime later the Tahoe turned left and then right. The sound of the road changed from asphalt to gravel as stones pinged off the undercarriage of the SUV. I concentrated on my happy place and not on the probability I was heading into a viper's nest with Abby and Lauren still in danger.

We bounced along the gravel road for a few miles and then hit a deep pothole, jarring my head into my spine. Good thing I had my seatbelt on or I might have ended up on top of my chatty friend.

The vehicle came to a stop. The driver's door opened. My door opened next, and the driver snatched off the balaclava. I blinked against the bright sunlight and looked around.

We'd parked in a small clearing surrounded by pines, next to a two-story home near a swiftly flowing river. Largely comprised of glass and metal, the front of the structure consisted almost entirely of windows with an expansive redwood deck that took up most of the front yard.

"Out," the driver said.

I slid off the seat and awaited further instruction. He cocked his head toward the house.

"Walk."

I followed the two men through the back door into a laundry room with a full-sized washer and dryer. Stacked white cupboards lined the walls. The driver shut the door and the men removed their shoes. Chatty stared pointedly at my boots.

"Seriously?"

He reached for his gun.

Taking the hint, I kicked off first one boot and then the other, but kept my socks on. Chatty pushed me ahead of him into the main part of the house. The driver followed and went wide once we were through the doorway, covering us from several feet away.

The place looked like a photo spread from *Architectural Digest*, with soaring ceilings and a huge, river-rock fireplace on one wall, a tricked-out gourmet kitchen on the other. Both had a gorgeous view of the surrounding woodlands and river. A white, mid-century modern sofa and matching chairs faced a kidney-shaped coffee table. The fire in the fireplace gave it a nice, homey feel.

Except for the whole *we're going to murder you* vibe.

Angie glanced up as we entered the room. Seated on the sofa with a magazine in her lap, at first glance she looked like the perfect match to the place. Her platinum-blonde bob accented her angular cheekbones and flawless makeup, but the strain of the past few days was evident, showing up as puffy eyes in a haggard face. Always the fashion plate, her ensemble consisted of a herringbone shell paired with black cigarette pants, tasteful gold earrings and matching gold cuff, with a perfect strand of gleaming white pearls coiled loosely around her neck. In my opinion, the shoulder holster kind of ruined the look.

"I see you've arrived in one piece." She looked past me as she tossed the magazine onto the table in front of her. "Did she give ya'll any trouble?" she asked Chatty.

"No. No weapons, no wire."

She nodded. "Good. Come on over here, Kate. Let's have a look at you."

I crossed the room and stopped where she could see me. Chatty Boy followed, his gun never wavering from a direct shot to my skull. He tossed the phone he'd taken from my pocket onto the couch. Angie ignored it.

"Where are Abby and Lauren?" I asked, trying to keep my voice level. It was hard, what with the sound of blood rushing through my ears.

"Uh-uh. That's not the way this works, darlin'. First, give me the information."

"I have it, but not on me."

A flicker of anger swept across her face and then disappeared. She sighed. I could've sworn I saw her left eye twitch.

"Look, hon. This can go easy or hard, your choice. No information, no kids. It's that simple. The fact that your sheriff boyfriend called in the posse is reason enough to kill you and the little darlin's. Count yourself lucky Anaya decided otherwise."

"I need to know the kids are okay. After what Bob did to those animals—"

"Did I hear my name, *puta?*"

I narrowed my eyes as Toothless Bob walked into the room, a man with a bone to pick the size of Mexico. After Anaya's guys kidnapped me while on a cruise the previous winter, Toothless was my first and last guard on Anaya's yacht. Apparently, he was still pissed off about my role in his buddies' finding him hogtied with a bed sheet and locked inside a room. The tables had turned, and not in my favor.

"Bob, old buddy," I said, slapping a smile on my face. "How you been?"

Bob scowled and advanced toward me, a lethal glint in his eye. A hot cloud of sour beer, body odor, and stale garlic assaulted my nostrils.

"Still challenged in the hygiene department, I see," I murmured, taking shallow breaths.

Toothless' face flushed red as he moved to close the gap between us, surprisingly fast for his fitness level. Scrambling, I backed away until I hit the couch with nowhere to go.

Okay, that may have been stupid.

"I'm sure you two have a lot to catch up on, but let's not get ahead of ourselves." Angie wedged herself between me and Bob before he could wrap his hands around my throat. "Your little reunion will have to wait. We have more important business to attend to. Right, Bob?" she said, a warning look on her face.

It was possible Bob growled, but in the end he backed down.

I peeled myself off the couch and took a deep breath to slow the hammering in my chest.

"Show me that the kids are all right, and I'll tell you how to find the information. It's that simple," I said, surprised I sounded brave.

Angie opened her mouth to say something but I continued, hoping to delay the torture I assumed was next on the menu.

"Look. For all I know, you don't even have the kids. Anaya could have sold them as soon as they were abducted. Proof of life was never verified." I watched Angie's face carefully, hoping for some kind of a tell. She crossed her arms, but her expression remained impassive. By the look on her face, she was calculating the time and effort it would take to torture the information out of me.

"Fine." She gave a curt nod to Bob. "Go get them."

With a dark glance in my direction, he left the room. The air cleared noticeably.

"I'm curious," Angie said, turning her attention to me. "What on earth possessed you to go back for the money? You must have realized you wouldn't get very far."

"You'd never have known if I hadn't had one too many margaritas and tried to access the website. You said yourself you thought I was dead."

"Damned tequila." Angie shook her head. "Does it every time. I swore off the stuff years ago."

The surreal conversation wasn't lost on me. In front of me stood the woman responsible for immense heartache in my life, and yes, I wanted to hurt her in the worst possible way. But here we were, chatting like old friends. I didn't believe for a minute that our little exchange would buy me any more time than what she'd planned in the first place, but I figured antagonizing her would likely move the clock forward and I'd be dead a whole lot sooner.

And that was exactly where this train looked like it was headed: my death. Once Anaya had the information, what would stop him from having me killed? I could only hope that he hadn't developed a taste for murdering innocent children.

You knew this would happen, Kate. It's why you're here. Sam will get the money; Cole will get his kids back.

Maybe.

21

A SNIFFLING SOUND came from somewhere near the back of the house. I tensed, my attention riveted to the hallway, finding it hard to breathe, afraid of what kind of shape the girls were in. I silently made every deal I could think of with any and all gods for them to be okay. Moments later, Lauren appeared with Abby close behind. Bob had a hand on each as he steered them into the living room.

I let out a sigh as relief washed over me. Neither of them looked like they'd been hurt, but they were scared. Abby recognized me first and gasped.

"Kate—" She broke free of Toothless' grip and ran to me, tears coursing down her cheeks. Lauren followed and I dropped to one knee, wishing my hands weren't tied behind me so I could give them each a bear hug. They wrapped their arms tight around me and sobbed, clinging to me like wet leaves. I kissed them and murmured that everything would be okay, that their father loved them very much.

That I loved them very much.

"Where have you been?" Lauren asked, her bottom lip trembling. "Daddy lost his memory and doesn't remember anything about last year. We've been trying to make him remember, but it hasn't worked."

It broke my heart to see Lauren working so hard to fight back tears. She was trying to be the brave big sister so Abby wouldn't be afraid.

"Are you two okay? Have they treated you well?"

Fresh tears came, but they both quickly nodded their heads. A glance at Angie and Bob told me they'd coached the girls. I made eye contact with Lauren but couldn't get a good read on her. Between sobs, Abby kept repeating, "Take us home now, Kate. Please?"

"Okay. That's enough." Angie clapped her hands and the girls tensed, immediately quiet. "Take them back."

Bob grabbed them both and pushed them toward the hallway. Abby's wailing could have been heard in the next county as he dragged the girls from the room. I fought the overwhelming urge to follow, as I fought the rage boiling inside of me toward Vincent Anaya and Angie. With a chest so tight I could scarcely breathe and self-control at the breaking point, I climbed to my feet and watched as they disappeared into the back of the house.

"You better not have harmed one hair, Angie—"

"Or what?" Angie scoffed. "You're not in the position to demand anything."

I bit back a retort and took a deep breath, trying to calm down. "You're right."

"Your turn," she said.

"You've got to promise me you'll make sure Vincent lets them go." I winced as my voice cracked. "Please."

Angie's expression didn't flicker. "Sure, hon. Come on, now. I haven't got all day." Chatty Boy pushed the gun barrel against my head.

I swallowed and closed my eyes. Cold sweat trickled down my back. This was it. I'd be dead as soon as Anaya verified the information. And the girls...

What would happen if I stalled for time? I could give them the wrong password. Certainly, it would delay things. But what would it gain?

Just give it to her, Kate.

"The website—"

Chatty's radio squelched, interrupting my answer.

"We got company," said a disembodied voice.

At the urgency in the caller's voice Angie's attention snapped to the radio. Everyone tensed as she grabbed hers off the table. "Report," she said, her voice sharp.

"A line of black coming at you with a bird in the air. ETA fifteen minutes," came the reply.

"*Shit.*" Angie narrowed her eyes and glared at me. "How are they tracking you?" The words came out in a hiss as she stepped closer, her gaze sliding over me.

I didn't have to feign surprise. "I'm not wired, Angie. The car was, but not me. I'd never endanger the girls."

Toothless ran back into the room, gun drawn.

"Get the car and head north," Angie said to the driver, her voice deceptively calm. "Follow him," she said to Chatty Boy.

"You sure? What about her?" he asked.

"*Move,*" she snapped.

He holstered his gun and followed the driver out the door.

"Bob—grab the kids. We're leaving," she ordered. He nodded and raced down the hall.

Her attention on Bob, I lowered my head and slammed into her, shoulder first. Caught off guard, she sprawled backward onto the coffee table, sending the magazine flying. Quick to recover, her head popped up as she reached for her gun. A split-second later she sat up, aimed, and fired. Three shots in rapid succession ripped through the air as I dove behind the couch.

The bullets hit the back cushion but didn't exit. I rolled into a crouch, not knowing which direction she'd come from next.

"Time to go, Kate." Angie's voice cut through the room.

Her measured footsteps echoed through the room as she made her way toward me from the other side of the couch. I slid on my ass along the wood floor and slipped around the far end of the sofa, tucking my feet in as Angie rounded the corner.

"I don't have all day." Angie sighed in disgust. "If you think I'm leaving you here, you're out of your mind."

I remained silent, not wanting to give my exact position away.

"Now, Kate." She crossed the expanse of floor behind the couch and raced around the edge before I could change position. Her face pinched with frustration, she aimed her gun at my head.

"Get. Up." Her chest rose and fell in a futile attempt to control her anger. When I didn't respond, she reached down, grabbed hold of my hair, and wrenched my head backward.

"If you shoot me, you're as good as dead, Angie," I said through gritted teeth, flinching at the searing pain along my scalp. "Anaya will not be happy when you tell him you didn't get the information." I willed myself to stay calm. *She isn't going to shoot me. She can't.*

"Angie. We gotta go," Toothless shouted from somewhere down the hallway.

Angie narrowed her eyes as she hesitated.

"*Now.*"

Seething, she lowered her gun.

"Don't think this is over, darlin'," she said, her Southern drawl more pronounced than ever. "I'm going to enjoy making you suffer." With a vicious shove, she released her grip on my hair, ran to the hallway, and disappeared.

The blood rushed through my ears, blocking the sound of their exit. Once I'd calmed down enough to listen, I heard only silence. No distant doors slammed, and I didn't hear Abby or Lauren. After a moment of adrenaline-fueled waiting, I scrambled to my feet and sprinted through the living room and down the hallway where Angie and Toothless had gone. Both bedrooms and the bathroom were empty. The door at the end of the hall was ajar. Anxiety rising, I pushed it open with my foot and glanced out at an empty bay, the garage door wide open. Heart in my throat, I raced outside, hoping to catch a glimpse of what they used to get away. Nothing moved except for the river nearby.

My panic growing, I sprinted through the house, checking each room I came to, but knew in my heart they were gone. *I've lost them.* Tears of frustration fought their way to the surface, and I clamped down on the chaotic emotions.

Not now, Kate.

My plan to trade myself for the girls had failed. There'd be no way Anaya would trust me now. It didn't matter that I had no idea I was being followed. I steadied myself against the wall as despair descended, feeding on the oxygen of my fear.

It's over. The girls are gone. This was your chance to save them. The only thing left is an all-out manhunt for Angie and Toothless. Hopelessness inched its way up my spine as I thought about what Anaya would do when and if they cornered him. The girls would be the ones to pay.

Unless.

Think, Kate. You're still alive, and he still doesn't have the information. He has to believe he can get it.

He knew I wouldn't give him the password or website address if he killed the girls. His arrogance was such that he could conceivably assume the game wasn't over.

Yet.

I shook off the anguish and moved through the rest of the house looking for anything Angie and her henchmen might have missed in their mad dash to escape that might help Landers find the kids. There was nothing. The second floor looked as though it hadn't been used. I ran down the stairs, back to the laundry room.

Once I'd slid my boots on, with my back to the door I grabbed the knob with both hands, pulling it wide enough to wedge my foot between it and the jamb. Hopping on one foot, I pivoted and shoved my elbow into the opening. The distant *thwap-thwap* of a helicopter echoed through the valley.

Guns drawn, agents in dark clothing bearing the letters FBI and DEA crawled through the trees, flanking the home. I hesitated before stepping outside to make sure I wouldn't be shot.

"I'm unarmed," I yelled, hoping the agents could hear me above the din of the helicopter's blades.

I edged out the door, expecting at any moment to hear the crack of a rifle or feel the burn of a bullet, but none came. One of the agents gestured to the rest and ran toward me.

"They've got the kids. I don't know what kind of vehicle they're in," I shouted. He nodded and brought his hand to his earpiece as he said something into his mic. In a matter of seconds, several agents changed course and spread out through the woods. The agent motioned for me to turn around and then cut through the zip tie, freeing my hands.

"Thank you," I said, rubbing my wrists.

"Go with Harris," he said, nodding toward a man in an FBI T-shirt who had joined us. I followed Harris as he led me away from the house and over to where Agent Landers paced near one of the vehicles, talking into a radio. The helicopter roared past, skimming the trees, cleared the home and sped south.

"They've got the kids," she said. She released the com button on the mic and turned toward me. "How many were there?"

"Angie and one other gunman have the kids. Two more drove north, acting as a decoy." My earlier revelation that the girls were still valuable dissipated like so much fog on a warm summer day. There was no telling how Anaya would react to Angie failing to obtain the information.

And my escape.

"We got the two heading north. Did you see which way the others went?" Agent Landers asked.

I shook my head. Acid burned in my stomach at the business-as-usual look on Lander's face. Even though I realized she had to retain her professionalism no matter the circumstances, my emotions got the better of me. This wasn't just an operation.

I crossed my arms and turned away. Landers moved in front of me, blocking my path, her gaze locked onto mine.

"Something on your mind?" she asked, matching my crossed arms with her own.

"Yeah." I felt my face flush with anger. "It could have worked. She let me see the girls. I was about to give them the information when her lookout radioed your position." I squeezed my eyes shut, attempting to obliterate the picture of Bob dragging the sobbing girls away down the hall. It didn't work. I opened them and stared back at Landers. "Then it all went to shit."

The despair in my voice must have hit a nerve. Lander's expression softened.

"I've requested roadblocks. The chopper's searching. We'll find them, Kate."

But I was more afraid now than when we started.

22

WE LET THEM get away." Cole slammed his fist on the counter.

"We'll find them." Agent Lander's measured tone sounded reassuring.

The two gunmen had been placed in custody. We'd waited at the cabin for word that they found Angie and the girls, but it never came. We were now back at the house where they'd wired both the car and me earlier that morning.

"How did the girls look when you saw them?" Cole asked.

"As far as I could tell, they were unharmed. Pretty scared, as you'd expect. No signs of abuse, though. I think they're taking care of them, which is good. If they intended to kill them, I doubt they'd be so careful."

"Exactly." Agent Landers nodded. "We should be able to get something useful out of the two gunmen."

"If they know anything," Cole said. Anger radiated off him, putting us all on edge. I'd never seen him fight himself so hard.

"They knew where Angie kept the girls. They might know more," Landers said.

Cole turned to me. "You say they were unharmed. How do you know that, exactly?" He leaned forward, his fists clenched. "Were their clothes wrinkled? Did they look tired? What do you mean, 'they looked scared'? What did they say, exactly?" His rapid-fire questions peppered the air between us like scattershot.

"They both wore nightgowns, so I couldn't see every inch of them, but they were able to run," I replied. "And they hugged me." The raw emotion in his eyes as he registered what I said broke my heart.

"Which one of them ran to you first? Lauren or Abby?"

"Abby."

"What did they say?" he asked again. "Verbatim."

"They wanted to know where you were. That you'd lost your memory and they'd been trying—" My voice faltered. I took a deep breath and continued. "They said they'd been trying to make you remember last year, but it hadn't worked."

Cole leaned his head back and closed his eyes. The weariness in his stance spoke of the strain he was under. I stood quietly waiting for more questions, but none came. Lowering his head he looked at the floor, his expression grim.

"How did you track me when I had to leave the car?" I asked, changing the subject.

Agent Landers glanced at my shirt. "Your button. And a team in the air."

"I thought it was just for transmitting audio."

"Among other things. When we located the car, we knew we didn't have a lot of time to find you and the girls. Good thing they didn't make you strip."

"Yeah."

I'd already made an uneasy peace with how things played out. Agent Landers had done a good job of talking me down, telling me she thought they were still alive. Anaya hadn't gotten what he wanted. Angie's taking the kids alive as well as her not killing me emphasized the importance of the information I had. It wasn't over yet.

At least, that's how Landers saw it.

She had a point. It wouldn't have taken much to hunt me down in that living room and put a bullet in my brain.

"The question is, why are they continuing to keep the girls—" I almost said *alive* but thought better of it. "They have to know I already gave the information to you. There has to be something else."

"They're his bargaining chip," Landers replied. "There's more, or he wouldn't be doing what he's doing. I've checked with our techs, and they haven't found anything in the other photographs yet. They'll keep trying. I'm sure we'll find a back door eventually."

"Would it be possible for someone to drop me off at the car so I can drive it back?"

"I already took care of that."

I turned as Sam walked in the door. He headed straight toward me, giving me the once-over, his face taut with concern. As soon as he realized I hadn't sustained any significant damage, his expression relaxed, the earlier intensity replaced by calm, steady Sam. He walked past Cole and Agent Landers to where I stood and put his arm around me. Cole watched him, a look on his face I couldn't read, before he shifted his attention to Landers.

"What do we do now?" Cole asked. He appeared calm but had a slight tic near his left eye.

"We wait. It's their move," she answered, and looked at me. "Kate, where's the burner phone they gave you?"

"They took it."

"That means when they're ready, they'll contact Cole again," Landers said. She neglected to add that they probably thought I wouldn't be around to use it after meeting with Angie. She turned to Sam. "Take Kate back to the hotel and wait for my call."

I started to protest, but Landers stopped me.

"There's no need for you two to stay." Her gaze flicked to Cole, and back to me. I got her meaning—my presence only antagonized him.

Sam and I left a few minutes later and by the time we'd reached the rental car, the adrenaline coursing through me had bottomed out, leaving a bad case of weary in its place.

"That's got to be it," I said, leaning my head back in the seat. "As far as we know, Anaya didn't have Angie or Bob kill the kids, which tells me there's got to be something about those other photographs the FBI didn't pick up on yet—something more valuable to Anaya than super labs and a list of names, and something he's sure they won't find. The only reason he's keeping Abby and Lauren alive is because I've got the information he needs to access the website. He knows I won't let them die if I can help it. The minute he thinks otherwise is the minute they're gone."

"I agree," Sam said. "The longer he's got them, the lower their chance of survival." He shook his head. "This operation needs to be smaller, with less involvement by the agencies."

Startled, I glanced at him. "Did I really just hear you say that?"

He nodded. "The smaller the team, the faster it can maneuver, take advantage of shifting circumstances. Now that Anaya knows you're dealing with the FBI and the DEA, he's a more dangerous adversary."

I sighed. "I know. What concerns me most is that Angie didn't show the least bit of concern for the girls. That means she sees them as expendable, which puts an end to the faint hope I had that she'd be more protective. How stupid was I to imagine that just because someone is female, she would care about two scared kids? After all, she *is* an assassin."

Sam started the car and pulled away from the curb. "You said they didn't show any signs of physical harm."

I nodded. "But how long will that last? Besides, there are ways of hurting people that aren't obvious." I closed my eyes, refusing to go down that road. There had to be a way to get them back alive.

No call came that evening. I finally went to bed after midnight but kept waking up, having dreamed of Lauren and Abby with tears streaming down their faces, of Cole staring at me with accusing eyes, of Vincent Anaya laughing and calling me a fool.

The next morning, after a quick shower, we left the hotel and drove to a little hole in the wall restaurant that served good, hearty breakfasts. In no mood to eat, instead I drank coffee and picked at my pancakes and eggs. Sam remained relatively quiet, as usual.

We'd just paid the bill and were leaving the restaurant when my cell phone rang. I dug it out of my bag, heart in my throat.

"This is Kate."

"Agent Landers. We just received word that two American children matching Lauren and Abby's description have been spotted." She paused.

"And?" I prompted.

"And," she paused again. "They're in Mexico."

I froze. *Mexico?*

"They *what*? How do you know it was them?"

"Their pictures have been shared extensively across law enforcement channels. The information came from one of the DEA's paid informants outside of Nogales. A twin engine Cessna recently landed at a private airstrip the informant monitors for a local landowner. The passengers included two children wearing pajamas, the pilot, and a well-dressed woman with white blonde hair. They transferred to another small plane and took off."

"Anaya used to maintain a mountain hideaway east of Hermosillo," I said, my anxiety rising. "Even then, the place was considered impossible to breach. If that's where he's taken them, I guarantee getting them back is going to be tricky. The man isn't known for being understated in his security measures."

"Can you locate the compound?"

"I'm not sure," I lied. I wasn't willing to give Agent Landers everything I knew just yet. I wasn't convinced her way would work with Anaya. I needed time to think. "What does this mean, operation-wise?"

"This means more people get involved. The CIA will take the lead. We'll need to notify the State Department, who will then notify the Mexican government, which in turn will bring a shit storm down on Anaya and his operation."

"Why would Anaya risk that? I can't believe he'd intentionally put himself in the crosshairs of so much law enforcement. Not unless he had a plan." And not unless the information he wanted was crucial to him. I thought back to when he'd been cornered by authorities on his island in the Caribbean. He'd been willing to destroy everything in order to survive.

"It's possible he's not even in Mexico. That he's orchestrating everything from somewhere else," Landers continued.

"He's from Nicaragua," I offered.

"Well then, I think that's probably a safe bet."

"If that's the case, you'd better rethink the shit storm," I warned. "Anaya's not the kind of guy to just roll over because he's a government target. His ego's big enough that he'll believe he can sidestep any attempts on his life. What worries me most is that if you back him into a corner, the girls' lives won't be worth a damn."

"There aren't many options. I assume if and when Anaya's people call they're going to demand you come to them—ostensibly to make a trade, which I don't think we should even consider, at this stage."

"If it's the only way—"

"It's not. And it's far too dangerous. The DEA and ICE already have relationships with people in the region who can assist."

"Is Luis there?" I wouldn't get anywhere arguing with Landers.

"He is. Hold on a minute."

A few seconds later, Luis' voice came through.

"Kate," he said.

"Can you talk somewhere private? I'd rather Agent Landers doesn't hear your side of the conversation."

"Sure."

There was a pause on his end. I drummed my fingers on my leg as I waited. Luis came back on the line.

"Okay. Shoot."

"Remember a couple of months ago when you sent Sam down to the Yucatán to bring me back?" I asked.

"Yeah. Your commando friends didn't make it easy to find you."

"About those commando friends. What do you think of me contacting them and asking for their help? Anaya's ex-cartel, so I think Quinn and his men would be all for taking his operation out, especially if children are involved."

"I don't think that's a good idea, Kate. Those guys don't do anything for free."

"It wouldn't have to be for free. Doesn't the DEA have access to funds to pay informants?"

"They wouldn't be informants, but yeah." He paused for a moment. "Let me see what I can do."

"Thanks, Luis."

"I'm also going to have my guy in Valladolid try to contact them. No sense in you endangering your life, too, if Quinn and his guys are willing to do the dirty work."

"Check with the owner of the Hotel Maya in Tabai. His name is Ernesto. He might know how to get a hold of him."

We ended the call, and I filled Sam in on what Luis and Agent Landers had told me. Sam leaned against the car, his arms crossed.

"You're not going?" he asked.

"I won't if Luis can find a way to contact Quinn. Believe me, I have no desire to go back to Mexico. Not now, not ever."

"Glad to hear it."

"But if my not going puts the girls in more danger, then I will. You get that, right?"

"Yeah. You go and I'm coming along. You get *that*, right?"

I narrowed my eyes at him. "I suppose it wouldn't do any good to try and talk you out of it."

He shook his head, a serious look on his face.
"No. It wouldn't."

23

THE CONNECTION LUIS used before to find Quinn and his group was unable to make contact and suggested the commandos had gone to ground. Rumors were rampant, detailing how Hugo Morales, the leader of the local drug cartel, had infiltrated Quinn's group more deeply than originally thought and they had to take strong measures, including relocating the camp.

By the time I'd been introduced to Quinn and his group, Morales had placed one informant inside the commando's camp—a man named Frederick—who was now dead. I didn't like to think about Frederick, or One Shot, as he was called, even though he wouldn't be a problem anymore. I'd grown to like the man and had been caught off guard when his betrayal came to light.

Then, Ernesto from the Hotel Maya told Luis' agent he didn't know anyone named Quinn.

So much for that idea. Other efforts at tracking the group didn't pan out, either. I'd had a feeling it would be difficult, if not impossible. Quinn and his men knew how to disappear. In their line of work the ability was imperative. Time continued to run out for the girls, and in a private phone call to Luis, I offered to make the trip back to cartel country.

Not my first choice.

That evening, when Luis asked me why I thought I'd be able to locate Quinn and his men when his operative couldn't, I reminded him Ernesto knew who I was, that I had been vetted by Quinn, and that we'd spoken before, however briefly.

"Fine," Luis had said with a sigh. "If things turn out the way I think they're going to, you'll be headed there anyway. If you find him, let him know the op's funded— anything he wants, he gets."

"Who's bankrolling it—you guys? The CIA?"

"That's not important. Just make sure he knows he's got resources."

I didn't press him. I figured the less I knew the better. At least I had something to offer Quinn and his men if I did find them.

"If you leave on the redeye tonight, you can be in Tabai by morning. You've got forty-eight hours. If you can't locate them by then, we're going with Plan B."

"What's Plan B?" I asked.

"Sorry, Kate. That's on a need-to-know basis."

Apparently, I didn't need to know.

"Get a few hours of rest, if you can. A pair of tickets will be waiting for you at Sky Harbor," he continued. "I'll have a commuter plane here to fly you to the airport at oh-one hundred."

"Thanks, Luis, but we need to bring the rental back anyway. With the way Sam drives, we'll be in Phoenix in plenty of time."

Worried about a possible informant in Luis' office, I made my own reservation for the nonstop flight to Cancun. Back at the hotel, I waited until Sam fell asleep before I eased out of bed, slipped into my clothes, and grabbed the small overnight case I'd packed earlier. I hadn't told him I was leaving and hadn't let on to Luis that Sam wouldn't be with me. Better to deal with that little omission once I'd made it into Mexico. I was done being a problem for the people I loved. It was time for me to fix things.

I slipped out the door without waking Sam. I'd left a handwritten message next to the coffee pot imploring him to understand why I needed to go alone, adding how much I cared for him and how I hoped to see him again. The key to a safety deposit box with the money inside as well as the name of the bank where it was located lay next to the note. I kept a duplicate key with me.

Not wanting him to follow me if he happened to wake up early, I drove our rental to the airport and made my flight with thirty minutes to spare. I'd turned off the red phone for the trip, knowing that after he'd read the note, Sam would call and try to talk me out of leaving. I needed to be out of country before that happened.

I tried napping on the flight and managed a couple of hours. We touched down at Cancun International at eight in the morning. As soon as I walked off the plane, the swamp-like heat and humidity pummeled me like I was walking through a carwash, sapping my strength. I repeatedly peeled my sodden T-shirt away from my damp body as I waited outside to catch the shuttle for my rental car. This time I'd chosen a four-wheel drive SUV with darkened windows.

When in Rome…

An hour later, I hit Highway 180 and headed west. Once in the SUV, I turned on the air conditioning full blast and flipped the vents toward me. My body thought it was in the Arctic. Not acclimating would only make things worse, but I wasn't in the mood to care.

Two and a half hours later, I drove through the tidy streets of Tabai, along the tree-lined boulevards past the church where Salazar's men had tried to gun me down, and parked in the shade next to the Hotel Maya. I slipped on a pair of big sunglasses and a floppy hat and made sure my hair was completely covered by the wig I'd bought in Seattle. This was Morales country, and I didn't need unwanted attention, especially from the local cartel.

I walked into the lobby and approached the counter. The clerk had her back to me but turned when I cleared my throat to get her attention. With her black hair pulled into a severe bun and a colorful scarf tied neatly around her neck, she looked the same as she had the last time I'd rented a room there. She'd refused to rouse Ernesto that evening since it was oh-dark-thirty, and I'd had to wait until morning to see him, putting Quinn, his men, and my life in jeopardy. Since this time it was late in the afternoon, I hoped I'd missed her shift and would be able to speak to Ernesto right away.

"Good afternoon. May I help you?" she asked, smiling. A smear of red lipstick marred one of her front teeth.

"Good afternoon. I'm looking for Ernesto. Is he available?"

"He only just left a few moments ago. May I give him a message?"

"Do you know where he's gone? It's important I speak with him."

She narrowed her eyes and tilted her head.

"I know you, yes?"

I nodded. "Yes. I rented a room here a couple of months ago."

Recognition lit her face and was immediately replaced by suspicion. Her eyes cut to the door.

"You are the woman they were looking for." Her flat tone said she wasn't exactly thrilled to see me.

"I need to speak with Ernesto. It's a matter of some urgency." Polite banter wouldn't cut it this time. "Children's lives are in danger. If you don't tell me where he is, then you will have the death of two innocents on your soul."

Apparently I'd struck a chord. With a pinched expression, she picked up the phone and made a call.

"Ernesto? Clara. There's someone here to see you, the…woman from earlier this summer. She says it's urgent." She paused for a moment, and said, "I will tell her." She ended the call and placed the phone on the counter.

"He says to meet him in ten minutes at the laundry down the street." She pointed out the door to the right. "Please be sure no one sees you enter the building. There is an alley behind the hotel you can use that leads to the back door."

"Thank you, Clara. You've been very helpful."

As I turned to leave, I caught a glimpse of a rosary in her hand. She closed her eyes and began to move her lips. I hoped she prayed for Lauren and Abby.

Couldn't hurt.

I followed the hallway past several first-floor rooms to the alley behind the hotel and headed for the laundry. The building was easy to find from the fragrant detergent smell wafting through the back door, and I walked in. Startled, the woman attendant glanced at me in surprise but returned a friendly smile when I said hello. I made my way past a pair of busy washing machines and dryers, and several plastic bags filled with clothes, stopping a few feet from the window to wait for Ernesto.

The smell of laundry detergent and fabric softener coupled with the mouth-watering aroma of tamales and enchiladas from the restaurant next door brought me back to when I'd first come to Mexico. After all that had happened between then and now, my opinions of the country and her people had become confusing and complicated—much like my feelings for Sam and Cole. Back then, I'd fallen in love with the land and the culture, but those memories were from long ago. Things had changed.

I had changed.

I dropped some pesos in the soda machine next to the counter and selected a Fanta, downing half of it in one swallow. The heat from the washers and dryers, combined with the suffocating humidity, made the place more like a sauna than a laundry and I stood as close to the single electric fan on the counter as I could manage. Perspiration oozed from places I didn't realize could sweat as I watched the attendant expertly fold each order and wrap it carefully in plastic.

About the time I started to get worried that Ernesto wouldn't show, he walked in the door, brisk and efficient. Motioning for me to follow he strode past, headed toward the back of the laundry, and walked into an office tucked away in the far corner. The attendant kept her eyes averted and continued with her work as I walked by.

The tiny office smelled of stale cigarettes and bleach, and boasted a small desk piled high with invoices, receipts, and a well-used calculator. Ernesto took the chair behind the desk and motioned to the chair opposite. I remained standing.

"I see you are not dead." Ernesto was anything but cheerful as he wiped the sweat from his forehead with a crumpled napkin.

"No, and it's largely due to your suggestion to hide in the *cenote* outside of town. Thank you, Ernesto. I owe you my life."

He nodded, his expression softening a bit. "To what do I owe this unexpected visit?"

"I appreciate your seeing me on such short notice. I realize you are a very busy man, but I am in need of your services. It's a matter of life or death."

The look on Ernesto's face softened further, taking on an almost paternal quality. He leaned forward in his chair, resting his arms on the desk in front of him. "How may I help you?"

"The last time we met you were able to convey a message to our mutual friend." I paused, trying to gauge his openness to my inquiry. He remained impassive. "I need to find him. Time is of the essence. Two children's lives are in danger, and he holds the key to their rescue."

Ernesto frowned and shook his head. "Only yesterday a man I'd never seen before came by the hotel looking for our mutual friend. I told him nothing, not only because I did not know who he was, but also because our friend left me no way to contact him."

My expression must have changed to one of dismay because Ernesto quickly continued.

"Do not despair, Señora. There may be some avenue we have not yet explored." He rummaged through the papers on his desk until he found a small black book, which he opened. He thumbed through the pages, stopping about midway through, and picked up his cell phone. Moments later, speaking rapid-fire Spanish into the receiver, he told the person on the other end that he needed to see him immediately. He ended the call and turned his attention to the pile of paperwork in front of him. He sighed and glanced at me.

"Do you have a car?"

24

BACK IN MY rental, I followed Ernesto as he drove his gold-colored Lexus a few kilometers out of town on a gravel road. He turned left onto a dirt path barely wide enough for our vehicles and wove through dense jungle.

We stopped at what appeared to be an abandoned shack tucked away among the philodendrons and pica-pica, comprised of cinderblock and rusty corrugated metal surrounded by waist-high weeds. Ancient, greasy truck parts lay strewn along a narrow, tamped-down trail choked with vines of morning glory and tropical grape leading to what might have once been used as a front door. A poisonwood tree grew not far from the structure, the black tar of dried sap staining its bark.

I parked next to the Lexus and got out, wishing I had a gun.

Ernesto proceeded up the trail, stopped a few yards back from the front door and whistled. Nothing moved except for a couple of flycatchers that flitted by. Ernesto whistled again. A few minutes later, the corrugated metal door opened with a tortured creak, a sliver of dark shadow visible inside.

Ernesto motioned for me to follow as he made his way down the path, stepping over a corroded battery and empty cans of *Dos Equis*.

I followed him into the dark interior and waited for my eyes to adjust. Several different odors vied for attention in the stifling hot room, not the least of which was the unmistakable and overpowering bouquet of marijuana. Sweat from wearing the hot wig trickled down my neck as I tried to ignore the oppressive atmosphere.

As my vision sharpened, I noticed the outline of a metal cot covered with a thin mattress and pillow. Next to the bed stood a small table with a folding chair shoved up against it. Several wooden boxes, stacked one on top of the other, balanced precariously in the corner. A glass hurricane lamp and a half-eaten mango rested on the table. Next to it, a black plastic ashtray with *The Spot* printed on the rim held a partially-smoked joint.

Something moved to my left, and I turned as a pit bull of a man sporting a shaved head, a goatee, and jungle fatigues emerged from the shadows. I stepped backward and out of his way as he brushed past me, trailing the stale smell of tequila sweat in his wake.

In a brash American accent he said, "Ernesto, my man. How you been?" He clapped Ernesto on the back and almost sent him flying across the room.

Ernesto regained his footing and straightened his collar. "This woman is in need of assistance."

Pit Bull turned and squinted in my direction, as though noticing me for the first time.

"Who the hell is she?" he asked, his eyes glinting in the low light.

Ernesto cleared his throat. "She is a friend of Q's and needs to get in contact with him as soon as possible."

"I'm Kate—"

"No names, *comprendes*? I didn't get to where I am today by knowing names." He waved his hand, indicating the tiny shack and its bare furnishings. With a loud belch, he dropped onto the cot and cracked his knuckles, never taking his eyes off me. I tensed, not sure what this guy had to do with finding Quinn and his men.

"I have done all that I can do," Ernesto said. "I wish you good luck in finding your friend." With a nod at Pit Bull, he turned and walked out of the shack. I watched him leave, acutely aware of my lack of firearm. Pit Bull put off a random and seriously unhinged vibe that I didn't want to get to know better. Hopefully Ernesto wouldn't have left me alone with him unless he could be trusted.

Then again, how well did I know Ernesto?

Pit Bull's gaze never wavered, even when Ernesto left. I shifted on one leg, uncomfortable with his scrutiny.

"Mind if I have a seat?" I asked.

As if an afterthought, Pit Bull's stare floated to the chair by the desk.

"Knock yourself out," he muttered.

I slid the chair close to the bed and sat down. He didn't move. I took a deep breath and exhaled slowly. "You have family back in the States? Kids?"

Pit Bull cocked his head, the ghost of a smile on his face. "Don't try that bullshit on me, missy. I've been interrogated by the best of 'em and you ain't even close. Your wuss-assed attempt at pushing my psychological buttons ain't gonna help you here."

That was out of left field. "Look, I was only trying to determine if you'd have any sympathy for the fact that there are two little girls who are frightened beyond belief and don't have a lot of time to live if I don't find them."

"How old?"

"Ten and six."

"They yours?"

"No."

He grunted as a frown drifted across his face. "Then whose are they, and why the fuck do you care?"

"I know the kids. Their father and I used to be together."

"Still doesn't tell me why you care, or why I should."

"It's my fault they're in Mexico. A man who's been looking for me for a long time kidnapped them, knowing I'd do everything I could to get them back."

Pit Bull eyed me, a bemused look on his face. "Didja leave him? Dudes down here—" He shook his head. "They get wicked loco when their woman dumps their ass. Messes with their manhood or some shit." When I didn't respond, he added, "Then what, you steal something?"

I held his gaze but didn't reply. He watched me for a couple of seconds longer and grinned.

"Well, shee-it. You went and stole somethin' from the motherfucker, didn't ya?" His smile vaporized and he leaned forward, bringing his face inches from mine. "Who's the guy? And don't dance around. Tell me or I won't help you with shit."

"Vincent Anaya."

Pit Bull narrowed his eyes, thinking. "I heard that name before. Wasn't he some big player back in the day? Not here, though." He thought some more and then snapped his fingers.

"Sonora. Dude was the head of a bunch of drug-runners—shit—ten years ago? I remember now. I did some work for a couple of assholes out of Obregón. Had to pay a fucking 'toll' to his royal bad-ass-ness before I could finish the job. Damn near took all my profit." His expression hardened. "Heard he was out of the business—sold his assets to some Wall Street type."

"That's the guy."

"How'd a pretty lady like you get mixed up with a jerk-off like him?"

"Long story. Let's just say I made a big mistake a long time ago, and I've been paying for it ever since."

Pit Bull nodded. "Fair 'nough. Since my help'll fuck with Anaya, then I'm in. What do you need from me?"

"Ernesto said you knew how to get in touch with Quinn and his group."

"Oh yeah. Right. My memory ain't the best these days." A smile on his face, he glanced at the half-smoked joint in the ashtray and shrugged.

"How do you know Quinn?" I asked. Quinn had been nothing if not adamant about discipline in his group. This guy acted more like a loose cannon than a commando.

"Did a few jobs for him."

"Why aren't you with him now?"

Pit Bull's upper lip curled into what might have been a smile. "The pay sucked."

I looked around the shack, wondering what constituted good pay.

"Besides," he said, reaching for the joint. "Q don't look kindly on drugs. My current employers do." A silver lighter appeared in his hand, and he lit the end of the spliff, inhaling deeply. Fighting to keep from coughing, he leaned forward and offered me a hit. I declined. He shrugged and exhaled, the sweet-smelling blue cloud swirling between us.

"That reminds me. I gotta do a little somethin' before we go. Won't take long." He rose from the bed and stubbed out the joint in the ashtray, motioning for me to follow him.

I walked behind him out of the shack and over to a copse of vine-covered trees several yards away.

"Stay put," he said and disappeared through an opening in the vines. A few minutes later, an engine caught and turned over, its deep rumble echoing through the surrounding forest.

I leapt to the side as a camouflage-painted Humvee came crashing through the opening with Pit Bull at the wheel. He stopped next to me and rolled down the window.

"Get in."

When I hesitated, the smile on Pit Bull's face died. "Get the fuck in, or you're on your own finding Q."

I climbed in.

25

AFTER WE'D DRIVEN several kilometers, Pit Bull turned left, following an unmarked trail deep into the jungle. A rusty, sprawling Quonset hut came into view, and we slowed to a stop in front of the padlocked doors.

"Gonna need your help with this, if you don't mind," Pit Bull said as he exited the truck. I got out and waited while he opened the lock and swung one of the doors wide.

Inside the hut, flies buzzed near a stack of eight wooden boxes, each about three feet long by two feet wide with Cyrillic lettering stamped on the side and probably holding either AK-47s or some other kind of Russian-made weapons. A few larger boxes lay next to these. Surprised, I scanned the enclosure for more. A few dusty piles of unknown material covered in old tarps looked like they hadn't been disturbed in decades. I'd been expecting a warehouse full of weed, not weapons.

Welcome to Kate's world, I thought.

Pit Bull walked over to the first stack of boxes and looked pointedly at me.

"You gonna grab an end?" he asked.

I lifted one end of the heavy box and helped him carry it to the Humvee. We moved the rest of the cache of weapons, one box at a time, and stacked them in the back of the vehicle.

Yeah. So not what I wanted to be doing with my time when Lauren's and Abby's lives were in danger.

"Is the delivery point very far from here?" I asked, not bothering to keep the tension from my voice.

"Simmer down, lady. It ain't far," Pit Bull replied as the last of the boxes found a home inside the Humvee. He slammed the back shut and locked it, and then closed and locked the Quonset hut. Before I climbed back into the truck, he reached into the console and handed me a semiautomatic. "You know how to use one of these?" he asked.

I nodded.

"Good. Might need it, where we're goin'."

I jacked the slide and checked the chamber, then slipped the gun under the seat.

This couldn't be good.

Pit Bull jumped into the driver's side, and the engine rumbled to life.

"Showtime," he said, and slipped the Hummer into gear.

I drummed my fingers on the armrest as the scenery flowed by, trying to estimate how long it would take to find Q and his guys and convince them to help me. It had to be soon, before Anaya's people contacted Cole and they made their demands. At least, that was what Luis and I assumed would happen. They didn't have a way to contact me since they took the phone they'd originally provided. Cole was all they had.

Unless they weren't going to try.

The sun sank lower in the sky toward an orangey dusk, and the shadows stretched across the roadway as Pit Bull pulled onto a familiar road. My breath caught—I sat up straight and looked through the windshield as we rounded the last curve before the town of Xoc.

My heart raced from the still-fresh memory of my meeting with Hugo Morales' son, Ben, when I'd tried to infiltrate the local cartel for Quinn. I had assumed I'd passed the test and would be working with the lead man himself. Instead, I'd been imprisoned in a cold, dark cell to be used as bait to ambush Salazar.

Sure enough, Pit Bull slowed in his approach to the low-slung cinderblock restaurant that Ben Morales used as an office. This time two SUVs with the same number of armed men were parked out front. We drove around to the back and were greeted by three other gunmen, all dressed in identical black T-shirts, black jeans, black boots. One of them looked familiar and I froze.

"Time to get out," Pit Bull said. "Mr. Morales don't like surprises."

"I think it's best if I stay here," I said. "If somebody asks, tell them I'm afraid of the guns."

Pit Bull shook his head. "Nope. Ain't gonna happen. These guys are suspicious with a capital S. If you stay in the truck, they'll think I'm tryin' to put something over on them." He looked at me. "Shit, lady, you're white as a ghost." He narrowed his eyes and squinted out the window at the gunmen. "You got history with these guys?"

"No. It's like I said. I'm just nervous around all those guns."

"Sure. Whatever you say. Now get the fuck out."

I checked the mirror to make sure the wig was on straight, took a deep breath, and opened the door. Pit

Bull went around to the back and opened the rear door so the gunmen could unload the boxes. I stood in the shade of a large tree and kept my head down, glad for the sunglasses and hat. A couple of the men glanced my way, but their gazes didn't linger.

They'd moved all but the last box when Ben Morales walked out the back door of the restaurant. With a wide grin, he strode over to Pit Bull and engaged him in animated conversation, laughing and slapping him on the back. Morales' expression changed to serious for a moment as Pit Bull said something to him, but soon the laughter resumed. I leaned against the tree and kept my attention on a skinny, free-range chicken strutting by.

Out of the corner of my eye I noticed Morales looking my way. He stepped past Pit Bull and walked toward me. My mouth dry, I took a deep breath and exhaled, anxiety rising in my chest.

"And who have we here?" Ben Morales asked, stopping in front of me. The same gaudy gold watch and rings decorated his fingers and wrist, with the unattractive addition of three gold chains around his neck.

I gave him a tentative smile and was about to tell him some bogus name when Pit Bull joined us.

"Ben Morales, this is Brandy Alexander. Brandy Alexander, meet Ben Morales," Pit Bull said.

Brandy Alexander? Seriously? What the hell did he think I was, a pole dancer? I extended my hand, hoping it wasn't too clammy. Ben Morales took my palm in his hand and bent to kiss the back of my fingers. A cloud of expensive aftershave enveloped me like a coastal fog.

"Pleased to meet you, Mr. Morales," I said.

"The pleasure is all mine, Señorita," he said, a seductive smile on his lips. "Please, call me Ben." He straightened, frowning, and let go of my hand, turning to

Pit Bull. "How is it that a *cabrone* like you is in the company of such a beautiful woman?"

Pit Bull shrugged. "Just lucky, I guess."

"Luck plays no role in such a relationship." He looked at Pit Bull and then to me. He cocked his head and narrowed his eyes. "You like expensive things, yes?" he said to me.

I smiled, hoping I looked flirtatious. "Why do you ask?"

"Because I think you are used to money." His gaze dropped to my boots and moved slowly up my body, lingering at my breasts before returning to my face. "Isn't that right?"

The breath caught in my throat as my mind raced for context. *Why would he say that? I'm not dressed in expensive clothes. Does he recognize me?* If he did, then he'd remember I'd been Salazar's woman, once.

Before I could answer, he reached over and felt my hair. My heart leapt to my throat. "You are familiar to me, but I can't place where. Tell me, how long have you been in the Yucatán?"

"Not long," I replied, barely able to keep my voice steady. I ignored the cascade of sweat running down my back.

"Take off your sunglasses. I want to see your eyes."

Fear lanced through me, but I managed to keep my expression impassive.

"I—I'm sorry, but the sun is too bright. I have an eye condition that prohibits me from removing my glasses, even indoors." I tried another smile. "Although, I'm certain I would remember meeting you," I said, doing my best to flirt with him.

"Ah. I see." Ben Morales' smile vaporized and his eyes grew cold. He turned to Pit Bull. "We have a saying down here about women like this. It is not so complimentary." I held my breath, waiting for him to call me out as a *puta* for flirting with him. Then he laughed. Pit Bull joined him.

Ben Morales pulled out his phone and wrapped his arm around me, extending his other hand to take a selfie.

"Smile, Brandy Alexander. This is going onto my Facebook page for everyone to see." He smiled and scueezed my shoulder. I did my best to appear relaxed and tipped my head toward him, although I was sweating far more than the heat and stifling humidity warranted.

Ben Morales put his phone back in his pocket and headed for the restaurant, motioning for Pit Bull to accompany him inside. "Stay here," Ben said to me with a smile.

As soon as they left I took a deep breath and exhaled, my shoulders drooping in relief as I watched them disappear into the building. My hands shook and my knees had liquefied, making it difficult to stand.

If he recognized me, I'm dead.

A few minutes later, Pit Bull walked out the door and motioned for me to get in the truck. Once we were inside and closed the doors, he glanced at me and said, "Fucking lucky is what we were."

"What do you mean?"

He started the truck and pulled away from the restaurant, smiling as he waved goodbye to the remaining gunmen. "Keep smiling, motherfuckers," he muttered under his breath.

We hit blacktop, and Pit Bull kept an eye on his rearview mirror as he accelerated. Once the restaurant had disappeared from view he visibly relaxed.

"Damn. That was uncomfortable." Pit Bull opened the ashtray, pulled out another joint and lit it, inhaling the smoke deep into his lungs. The Humvee's interior filled with the sweet, acrid aroma. I cracked the window.

"What happened?"

"Let's just say I had to do a little tap dancin' back there to keep ol' Benjamin happy or you woulda had yourself a new boyfriend." He gave me a sidelong glance. "You sure you two don't have history together? Because it sure looked that way to me."

"I've met him before, yes."

Pit Bull punched the dash. "I *knew* it. Fuck me." He jabbed his finger in the air. "You coulda got us killed back there. Next time you need to tell me when you know somebody."

"I didn't realize I'd have to get out of the truck," I snapped. I leaned back in the seat, working to get a handle on my anxiety. "You insisted on doing the delivery."

Pit Bull took another hit off the joint, and then stubbed it out in the ashtray.

"Fine," he said, exhaling. "Ben's got his toys, I got my money, and we're outta there."

I swiveled around to look out the back window. "You don't think they'll follow us?"

He shook his head. "Nah. Too busy. One of his guys told me they were gearing up for some kind of war. That's why they needed the shipment today." He chuckled. "Like a bunch of babies playing soldier. Except dudes die in this game."

"In my experience, if a cartel's not at war with some kind of enemy they make one up."

"You think they'd figure out they could make way more money if they didn't have all this revenge shit to deal with." Pit Bull shook his head in disbelief. "They already got a sweet deal goin' down here."

"You'd think. I quit trying to make sense of cartel culture a long time ago."

"True dat," he said, and reached for the joint. "Life is good, *mi amiga*."

Sure it was. Then why couldn't I shake the queasy feeling in the pit of my stomach?

26

T HE SUN HAD all but set by the time we stopped for gas at the only Pemex station I'd seen in a while. One thing about a Humvee—they're not known for their fuel efficiency. Pit Bull had one of the attendants fill a pair of gas canisters strapped to the back while another guy attempted to clean the dirt-encrusted windshield. I stayed in the vehicle, behind the tinted windows.

Back on the road, we continued driving as I worried about how I'd get back to my rental and Pit Bull complained about how much Mexico had changed.

"Used to be, a guy could come down here, make a few pesos, then run down to Belize for a little R and R." He shook his head as he worked at rolling another joint, using his knee to steer. "Now, the only way to make a buck is to deal with the cartels." Successful at his task, he lit the joint and offered it to me. Again I declined, wondering if he'd be any good with a gun after smoking so much dope.

Shrugging, Pit Bull took a deep drag, the acrid smell of burning weed floating toward me. I leaned my head against the partially opened window and sucked in fresh air in an attempt to avoid a contact high. If it hadn't been so damned hot outside, I would have rolled the window all the way down.

He continued. "Too easy to get yourself killed, now. If you got any skills, they figure out a way to lure you in, maybe even kidnap you, then blammo—" Pit Bull mimicked an explosion. "You're dead meat. They don't give a rat's ass about nothin' but the cash."

"If that's true, then why haven't they 'lured you in'?" I asked.

Pit Bull smiled and wiggled his joint at me. "Stoners of my caliber don't get all jacked up and kill people. Too lazy." His laughter ricocheted off the interior of the Humvee, erupting into a hacking cough.

He had a point.

A short time later we arrived at a tiny village, the brightly painted buildings aglow from the disappearing sun. Pit Bull stopped and parked at a small outdoor restaurant with an iron smoker in front. Three sets of mismatched plastic chairs and tables had been placed in a rough semi-circle near the cooking area. Palm trees and other lush vegetation surrounded the courtyard, the encroaching jungle a dark morass beyond. A crumbling, two-story building stood nearby, covered in thick vines and painted white with bright yellow trim. The words *Hotel de Silencio* in faded black lettering peeked through the greenery above the door.

"Time to eat." Pit Bull rubbed his hands together and smacked his lips as he exited the vehicle and headed for the smoker.

I followed him to where a man dressed in a plaid shirt, jeans, and scuffed leather boots tended the smoker. The aroma of smoked pork drifted toward me, and my stomach growled.

"*Buenas tardes*, Señor," Pit Bull said to the man, and proceeded to order two plates.

"Go sit down. I gotta see a man about a horse," Pit Bull said, and disappeared around the side of the hotel. Since we were the only guests I had my pick of tables.

Not long after I'd taken a seat, the man in the western shirt brought two bottles of beer and two Styrofoam plates piled high with shredded pork nestled in a banana leaf, and a side of beans and corn tortillas. A container of three different salsas sat in the middle of the table. I inhaled the spicy-sweet aroma as I poured a generous amount of salsa on top of the pork and dug in.

The meal could have easily been the best barbecue I'd ever eaten in Mexico. Ignoring the sweat pouring down my face from a combination of the wig, the high humidity, and the habañero chilies poking out of the sauce, I wondered briefly if being stuck in a vehicle with an active pot smoker might have something to do with my heightened hunger and lack of anxiety.

I kept an eye on the road while I ate and scanned my surroundings, remembering why we were there. My shoulders tensed as I remembered how much time we didn't have.

"Is this not the best damned *pibil* you've ever had?" Pit Bull asked, grabbing a chair. "Hey, Señor. Bring me some more salsa, will ya?" he called to the cook. "The señora snarfed it all."

The man brought another container of salsa along with a jar of freshly made pico de gallo and set it on the table. He smiled shyly as we congratulated him on the best *Cochinita Pibil* in the Yucatán.

"*Muchas gracias,*" he replied, before returning to the smoker.

Pit Bull turned his attention to the plate of food in front of him. After a couple of bites, he nodded at the hotel. "We're gonna stay here tonight."

I stopped eating, fork halfway to my mouth. "We're what?"

"Staying here. For the night."

"We can't. We don't have time. I thought I explained—"

Pit Bull waved away my concerns. "Don't get your panties in a bunch. Q's not far. If he's still in the area," he added, polishing off a pork-filled tortilla.

"Dead drop?" I asked.

Pit Bull nodded, still concentrating on his food. "Yep. Q or one of his guys checks it twice a day—once in the morning, once at night. Works better than a cell phone out here. Hell of a lot safer, too."

I relaxed and took another bite. "Sorry. I thought—"

"I get it. It's kids. I'll give you some advice, though." Pit Bull leaned back in his chair and wiped sauce off his mouth with a napkin. "If you're gonna get involved with somebody like Vincent Anaya, it's better not to form close ties."

"Believe me, I know." I took a drink of my beer and pushed my plate of half-eaten *pibil* to the side.

Pit Bull nodded and dug into his dinner again. "Just sayin'." He eyed my plate. "You gonna eat that?"

"Help yourself." I shoved it toward him and stood up. "I'm going for a walk."

I stayed on the main road, listening to the insects' evening concerto. The sun had dipped below the horizon and the intense heat had diminished enough so that the sweat only trickled down my back. Alone with my thoughts, doubts raced through my mind like rats on speed. What if Quinn didn't get the message? What if Anaya's people never called? What if they did, and I had to go to wherever he was holding the kids? I could feel the panic take hold, and I sucked in a breath, trying to circumvent the annoying hyperventilation that always seemed to accompany an anxiety attack.

Stop it, Kate. Worrying won't help Lauren and Abby. You need to be calm and breathe. Remember what Sam taught you up north when Angie was trying to kill you?

The thought gave me enough of an anchor to latch onto so I could at least attempt to breathe and remember the mysterious mantra he'd given me in Alaska. I inhaled and closed my eyes, reciting the words in my head. With each repetition I felt the anxiety lessen until my mind became clear and the threat of hyperventilation had passed. Opening my eyes, I shrugged my shoulders to relieve the tension, and turned back toward the hotel. Calm though I might have been, the fear that I wouldn't be able to rescue Lauren and Abby in time played a continuous loop in the back of my head.

What if I couldn't find Quinn?

27

I STRUGGLED THROUGH the fog of sleep, waking in the darkness of the hotel room. As my eyes adjusted, I focused on the mosquito netting surrounding the thin mattress and worn sheets on the bed.

Oh, right. I'm in Mexico. Memories of the last twenty-four hours jostled for position in my brain. Moonlight streamed through the open window at the far end of the small room. The dinner with Pit Bull and the reason I came back to the Yucatán filtered through my mind before the familiar sound of gravel crunching under tires broke through.

I slipped out of bed and approached the window. Two dark-colored SUVs idled in the parking lot below, their running lights on. They didn't look like friends of the chef.

Not seeing Pit Bull among the vehicles, I raced back to the bed and found the gun under my pillow. I grabbed my pants off the chair by the nightstand, making sure my phone was still in the pocket before heading back to the window. Pit Bull had opted for a room on the ground floor at the back of the hotel. I rented one on the top floor facing the road with a good view of the surrounding area.

I studied the vehicles, careful to stay out of their sightline. They were too new for Quinn's group. Not unless they'd had a recent infusion of cash. It was either some locals, or Morales' crew had followed Pit Bull here. I assumed Morales controlled this part of the Yucatán. His forces killed Leonardo Diaz, the head of the cartel Salazar had been working for, during the ambush at the ruins where I'd shot Salazar. When both Diaz and Salazar ended up dead it created a vacuum at the top of *El Castillo* and the group splintered. This left Morales' organization as the main force in the area, although Diaz's son reportedly got away.

That must have been what Pit Bull had overheard earlier when we delivered the weapons to Ben Morales. If I were a betting woman, I'd wager Ben Morales and Diaz's son were going to war.

The son avenges the death of the father. One vendetta against another. That was the way they rolled. But why were they here? I bit my lower lip, wondering if Pit Bull had somehow double-crossed Morales. And, if so, why would he do such a stupid and reckless thing? Even a stoner would realize that was a one-way ticket to dead.

Or he'd double-crossed me.

The events of the previous day floated through my mind as I searched for an explanation for our visitors. My brain decided at that moment to kick into gear, the reason obvious.

Ben Morales had recognized me.

The driver's door opened on one of the SUVs. The dome light didn't come on, so I couldn't get a good look at who was inside the vehicle. Barely breathing, I backed away from the window and crept to the dresser to slip my boots on. Then I tiptoed to the door and leaned against it to listen. Hearing nothing, I turned the lock and eased it open, moved into the hallway, and headed for the stairs.

The hotel's owners didn't believe in keeping a light on for their guests—the hall was pitch black. I slid my hand along the wall to guide me and tiptoed down the stairs. With each step I braced for some kind of giveaway that someone was coming down the stairway to the first floor. My foot hit ground level and I sighed quietly as I moved along the dark hallway toward the back of the hotel.

A small flame flickered and disappeared a short distance away and I stopped.

"Over here," Pit Bull whispered barely loud enough to hear. I followed his voice and met him near his room.

"The back entrance is over here." He flicked the lighter on for another second, shielding it with his hand, and motioned to where the hallway jogged to the right. Then he doused the flame. "But they're watching the Hummer, so we got two choices. Either we fight 'em, which I don't recommend since they probably came with a fucking arsenal, or we run through the jungle and hide, hoping they'll get bored and leave."

"They'll wait us out," I said.

"Then we come out somewhere else, like another road. Somewhere they don't look. They can't be *everywhere*."

Pit Bull's breathing echoed too loud against the walls. I came close to gagging from the smell of sweat in the narrow hallway.

"You got the gun I gave you, right?"

"Yes," I said.

"I can't figure if they're here because of you, or because they want their money back," he whispered. "How the hell do you know these guys?"

"I—"

I clamped my mouth shut as the front door opened. Pit Bull sprinted down the hallway, surprisingly nimble for a big guy. I followed close behind. When we got to the end of the hall, he moved quietly toward the rear entrance and eased the screen door open.

"It's clear," he whispered. A chorus of frogs serenaded us as we slipped outside, ran the few yards to the edge of the property and slid down an embankment behind the hotel. We stayed low and watched to see if anyone followed.

A few minutes later, an outside door to one of the second floor rooms creaked open and a dark figure moved to the edge of the balcony, the outline of an assault rifle clearly visible in the moonlight. A mosquito landed on my cheek, and I resisted the urge to squash it, not daring to move. The figure remained there for a moment, scanning the surroundings, and disappeared inside the hotel. I exhaled and brushed at the mosquito.

"We've got a couple of hours before sun up," Pit Bull said in a low voice. "I bet they wait until then to come looking for us. We can move pretty deep into the jungle—"

Several shots rang out at the front of the hotel, followed by a man yelling in Spanish. Lights on the ground floor of the hotel blinked on as more gunfire erupted. Someone screamed.

"What the fuck?" Pit Bull swore. We reached for our guns at the same time.

The back door banged open, and a man ran out carrying an assault rifle. I couldn't be sure if it was the same gunman we'd seen on the balcony.

He cut left and raced past us to the side of the hotel and disappeared. Two pops of gunfire followed.

"Sounds like somebody else came to the party," Pit Bull muttered.

"Diaz's men?" I asked.

"You mean Leonardo's son? The nerdy little fuck with the glasses?" Pit Bull shook his head. "Nah. Can't be. That guy couldn't find an AK-47 with both hands if it was stuck up his ass."

"That may be, but I'm pretty sure Diaz taught his son how to run the family business, nerd or not," I said.

"Well, if that's who it is, then I say let the bastards kill each other. They're making it easy for us."

"Maybe they're trying to pick off Morales' guys one by one, isolating them from the rest of the group," I said.

"I'm gonna see if I can make it to the Hummer, set off a couple of grenades. I doubt they're looking for us at the moment," Pit Bull said.

"I'll head around to other side." I nodded to my left. "I can create a diversion if they come after you."

My adrenaline had spiked from the gunfire, so being alert wouldn't be a problem. I racked the slide on my pistol and checked the chamber to make myself feel better.

"Wait for a count of five. If you don't hear gunshots, go for it." Pit Bull scrambled up the embankment and, keeping low, darted to the right side of the building. When he reached the corner he paused for a moment, a black slash against the dull white wall of the hotel, and disappeared from view.

I waited a few beats until I was sure no one headed my way. Then I sprinted for the opposite side.

My back to the wall, I slid along the rough concrete to the corner nearest the parking lot and stopped. Bursts of machinegun fire serrated the humid night air in rapid succession, followed by someone yelling, and the successive *pop* of a semiautomatic. I dropped to a crouch to take a quick look around the corner, and then fell back.

There were three gunmen with their backs to me at about twenty yards, using an SUV as cover. It looked like they each had an assault rifle. I couldn't see the others.

I waited to see if Pit Bull had made it to the Hummer for the grenades before attempting anything. Seconds later, a loud explosion cracked through the air and flames lit the night sky. I glanced around the corner.

The SUV nearest to me was in flames. Two bodies lay sprawled on the ground a short distance from the vehicle, their guns nearby. A third man gripped his arm as he staggered to one of the fallen gunmen and reached for his weapon. His face obscured by camouflage paint, yet another man skirted the rear of the burning SUV, gun drawn. He shot the wounded man, who fell to his knees and toppled forward onto his lifeless friend. The shooter looked up, tracking my direction.

I ducked behind the building, but had moved too late. He'd seen me.

28

O N MY FEET in an instant, I raced along the wall past the hotel to the embankment, skidded down the side and took cover under the heavy vegetation. The sound of slow, measured footsteps on gravel echoed against the building. I held my breath and peeked through the leaves.

The man wore night vision goggles and he swept the area, the barrel of his gun leading the way.

I eased backward until the leaves fell into place obscuring my position. I slowly pushed onto my elbows, and aimed my gun. Almost breathing, I waited.

He paused several yards away and scanned the space in front of him. My heart rate skyrocketed as he stepped closer. He took another step.

Then another.

A shrill whistle from the parking area interrupted his advance and he hesitated. With one last look, he turned and jogged back to the front of the hotel. I let out a sigh and relaxed my grip on the gun.

He'd be back.

I climbed to my feet and ran to the other side of the hotel, the same direction that Pit Bull had gone. When I got to the corner, I stopped and peered around the building. When I didn't see anyone, I slid along the wall, eventually reaching the Hummer. I peered inside but didn't notice anything unusual and continued to the front of the building.

Voices floated toward me and I stopped, straining to hear. One of them sounded familiar, so I moved to where I could get a good look at the parking lot.

There were five men altogether, all dressed in jungle fatigues. Four of them had paired up: two dragged the dead gunmen to the non-burning SUV while the other two hoisted the bodies and shoved them into the back. I spotted the man who'd been stalking me among the living. The fifth man wore a boonie hat and stood with his back to me, assault rifle slung over his shoulder.

No sign of Pit Bull.

The guy wearing the boonie hat walked to the driver's door of the SUV and leaned inside.

"Keys are in it," he said, and stepped back. He turned, giving me a glimpse of his profile and my breath caught.

Quinn. I resisted the urge to call his name. I needed to wait, to make sure the danger had passed and I could walk into the open without getting shot. I didn't know what happened to Pit Bull, and I sure as hell didn't want to join him if it wasn't good. I watched as the men finished cleaning up the bodies.

Something moved to my left and Quinn turned. Pit Bull walked out of the shadows, arms up, holding his pistol aloft.

"Got your message," Quinn said to him. "I didn't think we'd have to fight our way in to see you."

Pit Bull lowered his arms and smiled. "Aw, you say the nicest things, Q," he said.

"You say somebody's trying to get in touch with me?"

I took that as my cue and left the safety of the shadows.

"I did."

Quinn turned at the sound of my voice. Surprise lit his eyes, but then disappeared. "Well, hello, Kate."

Pit Bull smiled. "My work here is done, then. Looks like you two know each other, so I'll be on my way."

"Hold on a minute there, Kenny," Quinn said, his voice deceptively calm. "Maybe you can explain why we walked into a shit storm full of Morales' men?"

The four other guys had finished their grisly duties and now stood nearby, rifles trained on Pit Bull/Kenny. A bead of sweat trickled down his face as he grinned and took a step backward.

"Hey now, I didn't have anything to do with this, believe me." He turned to me, an imploring look on his face. "Tell him. I was as surprised as you were when Morales' boys showed up."

Quinn raised an eyebrow as he looked at me for confirmation.

"He insisted on making a delivery to Ben Morales before he brought me here to look for you," I said, by way of explanation.

Quinn's expression sharpened and he narrowed his eyes at Kenny.

"What kind of delivery?"

Kenny smiled wider, obviously nervous. "Nothing. Just some Ruskie shit."

"Ruskie shit?"

"Weapons," I clarified.

Quinn stepped closer to Kenny, and Kenny took another step backward. Though he wasn't much taller than the stoner, Quinn exuded intimidation. Before I knew his name, I'd referred to him as the Rottweiler.

"You did what?" The Rottweiler in full display, Quinn's voice oozed lethality. Kenny put his hands up as though to fend off an attack.

"Now, now." Kenny's voice had developed an appeasing tone. "A guy's gotta make a buck, you know?"

"Yeah." Quinn's jaw pulsed. "*Not by selling weapons to the local cartel.* Are you an idiot?"

Kenny shook his head. Sweat poured down his face.

"Look, you need some money?" Kenny reached into his front pocket but as he did, Quinn's men stepped in, rifles locked on his torso and head. Kenny froze and eyed them warily. Then, very slowly he said, "Just going for some paper, Q. No guns. Tell your men to stand down."

Quinn let him sweat for a second longer, and then gave an almost imperceptible nod. His men relaxed, but kept their weapons aimed at Kenny as he pulled out a wad of hundreds.

"Keep your money, Kenny. I don't need the dirt."

Kenny blinked once and shoved the money back into his pocket.

"I should shoot you now, put you out of your misery before they decide to get rid of you. It'd be more humane." Quinn shook his head. "Get out of here."

Relief evident on his face, Kenny turned to leave, but stopped. "You still gonna check the drop?" he asked.

"What do you think?" Quinn replied, his voice dripping sarcasm. Resigned, Kenny nodded and walked to his Hummer.

"Hey—what about my rental?" I asked.

Kenny waved my question away. "It's not going anywhere. I don't get a lot of visitors."

"We'll get you back to your vehicle," Quinn said, looking at me. "So, what do you need?"

29

QUINN BLINDFOLDED ME before he brought me back to camp. Although I should have been used to it by now, my aversion to not being able to see where I was going was second only to my aversion to death.

Similar to the compound where I'd first met Quinn and his men a couple of months prior, it consisted of several rows of net-covered tents, or hooches, used as living quarters, with a designated chow hall in the middle of the compound. The latrine was at the back, far enough away from the tents so the smell didn't bother anybody. The only difference between this camp and the other I'd seen was the lack of traditional Maya huts. When I asked Quinn about it, he shrugged and said they hadn't had enough time to construct any. I got the impression these were temporary digs.

Quinn led me to his quarters, and I took a seat at a white plastic table that had seen better days. Aries and Artemis, Quinn's German Shepherds, bounded over to greet me despite the heat, their tongues lolling out. They licked my face and neck, obviously happy to see a familiar person. I ruffled their ears and gave them pets, parceling out equal time to scratch their bellies when they rolled onto their backs.

"*Kommen.*" At Quinn's command the dogs snapped to attention and returned to their pads on the far side of the tent. Quinn sat backward on the chair across from me and leaned forward.

"So you think they're in Sonora?" he asked.

"I'm not sure. That's where they saw the girls last. They left on a twin-engine." I took a deep breath and exhaled, slowly. *Please let him want to help me.* "Anaya used to have a compound in the mountains east of Hermosillo that he used whenever he was in the area. I assume the structure is still there."

"Easy enough to find from satellite photos." Quinn sat for a moment, thinking. I could picture his mind sorting through the information I had given him on the way back to camp, creating and discarding scenarios as he worked out first, whether a rescue might be possible; and second, how much of a chance of success there would be.

"My contact at the DEA secured funding for this. He wouldn't say, but I assume it's from the CIA."

Quinn nodded. "Wouldn't be the first time." He rose and walked over to a walkie-talkie sitting on his bedside 'table'—a plastic soft drink crate placed on its narrow end. "*Uno a Dos,*" he said into the transmitter.

"*Si, Uno,*" a familiar voice replied.

"Come down here, will you?"

"Roger that."

Quinn returned to the table and set the walkie-talkie down.

"I don't have to tell you that this will be difficult. If Anaya's holding the girls captive in Sonora, and we're going to assume that he is since he's familiar with the terrain, then he'll have heavy security in place that will tell him somebody's coming."

"Then you'll help?" I asked.

Quinn stared at me for a long moment before he gave a slight nod. "Find out where the exchange is supposed to happen and we'll go from there."

Relief poured through me, and I had to stop myself from throwing my arms around Quinn.

"Thank you," I said.

A moment later, Pascal walked in the door. The wiry Mayan reminded me of a compact version of Sam: long, dark hair pulled back in a ponytail, runner's physique, calm, almost hypnotic brown eyes. They both had an air of the mystic about them, Pascal more so than Sam. I smiled at the surprise on his face when he saw me and stood up to greet him. He grinned as he crossed the distance between us and wrapped me in a bear hug.

"It's good to see you," Pascal said, taking a step back.

"You too, Pascal."

He turned to Quinn. "What's up?"

"Kate needs our help. I'll let her fill you in," Quinn said.

"Vincent Anaya kidnapped two young girls and brought them into Mexico." I said. "He wants to make a trade."

"For what?" Pascal asked.

"For me and the information I have."

"And that is—?"

"A website and a password. The website has several vacation photographs, two of which the FBI have discovered contain sensitive information."

"Only two?"

"That's all they've been able to decipher so far. They're continuing to study the other pictures, but if there is anything more, the information's well hidden. Apparently they haven't found a back door to the program yet."

"She's working with the DEA, too," Quinn added.

"What, no CIA or ICE?"

Quinn smiled. "Rumor has it the Company's bankrolling the operation."

"Ah. Well, in that case, what's the plan?"

"Kate, first you need to find out where the exchange is going to take place," Quinn said. "Once we know that, I'll check sat photos, see if I can get an overflight with a drone to determine how many guys we're going to need and what kind of equipment. Then we head out to do recon."

"One problem," I said, biting my lip. "I think there's a leak in Luis' organization." Quinn's gaze snapped to me and I flinched.

"Luis is DEA, right?" Pascal asked.

"Right. When I first met him, the safe house where they put me before testifying had been rigged with explosives. While Luis and I were on an unsanctioned walk they detonated and demolished the house. Then, right before going into Witness Protection, my former bodyguard was murdered. The only explanation that made sense was an informant in either the DEA or the Mexican government."

"What makes you think they're still active? That was over ten years ago, right?" Quinn asked. "And why the DEA? The government here is riddled with paid informants."

"Because one of Angie's thugs was recently watching Sam's office in Seattle. She sent two men to kill me, and they knew exactly where I was staying. Angie wouldn't have known Sam had moved to the area. Last she'd heard he still lived in Alaska. She had no reason to believe we'd had contact prior to Seattle," I added. "For all she knew, we hadn't spoken since the incident in Alaska." I glanced at my watch. "I need to call Luis to find out if Anaya's people made contact yet. The sooner the better."

"Then we need to figure out what to tell Luis," Quinn said. "If the informant placed a listening device on his phone or in his office, then they'll know what he knows."

"I can tell him I couldn't find you," I said. "But they mentioned if that happened, they had a Plan B and I haven't got a clue what it entails. I'd hate to put more lives at risk by compromising their operation or yours."

"No, you have to let them know we're in play or you're right, we're all screwed. I'd hate to be target practice for a drone." Quinn fell silent for a moment while the rest of us threw out other options.

Quinn held his hand up and everyone fell silent.

"Let's play it this way: Kate, you tell Luis you found me but I'm being difficult and need more information before I commit. Time's running out, and they'll have no other option but to put you in touch with Anaya, whether my team's a go or not. You relay the particulars to me via burner phone, which you will buy when we take you into town to make the call."

"Already taken care of." I patted the phone in my pocket.

"You know where it's been at all times since you purchased it, right?"

"Yes."

"Good. Once the plan's in place, you can call Luis and let him know what's going on, except you'll give him bogus info. Different time, different event, something to throw Anaya off if there is an informant." Quinn cracked his neck from side to side. "A little misinformation can go a long way."

"That works," I said. "If Anaya's keeping the girls in Sonora, then they're probably at his mountain compound. Salazar and I spent some time there. There aren't any roads into or out of the place. It's only accessible by helicopter or small plane."

"There's a runway of sorts?"

"Not much of one. It's a flat spot along a nearby river. I overheard Salazar joking with him about not being able to land his Lear. Although, he could have extended it or changed its location by now. It's been a while."

"Good to know." Quinn nodded at Pascal. "Pascal can drive you into town where reception's better. Call Luis, find out whether they've made contact yet. We'll meet back here and plan the rest."

30

O NCE WE'D REACHED blacktop and I could take off the blindfold, I asked Pascal how things were going.

"In Q's words, it is what it is." Pascal shrugged. "After finding out about One Shot being a Morales plant, Q went on the warpath and put everybody through a meat grinder, trying to ferret out other possible informants."

"And," I prompted.

"And we scored," he said, his tone dry. "This guy was lower level. I don't think you met him. He left for a week about the time you showed up. Some kind of family crisis, he said. Actually, he'd been living large on Morales' dime at some expensive resort on the coast as a way to keep him out of the line of fire while Morales planned the ambush at the ruins."

"What happened to him?"

"We've been feeding him false information, and assume that filters down to Morales. Q promoted him to lead lookout at another 'installation' several kilometers from here." Pascal smiled. "Our current location is unknown to him and will remain so until his value declines. Then we'll cut him loose."

"You can't trust anyone down here," I muttered. It was déjà vu all over again. Paranoia ran rampant. Everybody was an informant as long as the price was right. You couldn't trust the government or law enforcement and certainly not anyone working for the cartels. I doubted you could trust your waiter or your parking attendant. The cartels cast a wide net and threaded through the very fabric of Mexican life. If you had a skill that they needed, you could say goodbye to your job, your family, and your friends. It used to be that they'd offer money, and lots of it, until you finally broke down and got on the payroll. Now, they just kidnapped you and made you work for them either through torture or by threatening your family.

We entered the town of Ná, and Pascal pulled into a grocery store parking lot, busy with shoppers.

"There should be good reception here," he said.

I glanced at the phone. I had three bars—and two missed calls from Sam. I punched in Luis' number.

He picked up on the first ring. "Luis Gonzales."

"It's Kate."

"About time you called. Why the hell weren't you on the flight I booked for you and Sam?"

"Missed it," I replied. I'd never known Luis to get upset. From the tone of his voice, he'd gone way past angry.

"And why the hell isn't Sam with you?"

"I—"

"You've pissed off a lot of people, Kate. Landers is beside herself. She read me the riot act for letting you go without checking with her first. And Sam. I've been fielding calls from him every couple of hours since you left. Why didn't you take him with you?"

"May I speak?" Since he hadn't let me get a word in edgewise, I figured I'd ask.

"Fine. Speak." His clipped tone told me I'd better tread carefully.

"I'm done putting people I love in danger, Luis. I created this problem. I need to fix it."

"By getting yourself killed?" His frustration echoed through the earpiece.

"I'll call him as soon as I get off the phone with you."

"Did you find Quinn?" he asked.

"Yes."

"Is he onboard, or do we go to Plan B?"

"He's not entirely committed yet," I replied. "He wants more information."

"We're running out of time, Kate."

"Did Anaya's people make contact?" I asked.

"Cole got a call early this morning. They want you to fly to Santa Rita, alone. You'll receive further instructions once you're there."

My heart skipped a beat. "When?"

"Cole asked for proof of life, which bought us some time since we didn't know where the hell you were. They uploaded a video of the kids with today's newspaper onto YouTube about an hour ago."

"Are they all right?"

Luis paused. "They're alive. Scared, but alive."

I exhaled in a rush, relief cascading through me. "How did Cole take it?"

"He's fine." Luis' short answer told me Cole was anything but. I let it pass.

"Can you send me the link? I'd like to see it and show it to Quinn. If anything, that could seal the deal on them helping us."

"On its way," he said. "What's the hold up? Either he's going to help us or he isn't."

"Quinn needs to know what kind of support you and your backers are willing to provide."

"Anything he wants, within reason."

"Drone support?"

"Sure."

"Money for weapons?"

"Of course." Luis sighed. "What's going on, Kate?"

"Like I said, he needs more information. Who's the backer?"

Luis hesitated. "I can't tell you that. They want to remain anonymous."

So it wasn't the CIA. Luis wouldn't have a problem telling me if the Central Intelligence Agency were involved. My antennae pricked up and I wondered who it was.

"I got the impression it was the CIA. That's what I told Quinn."

"Does it matter where the money comes from, as long as the operation is funded?" Luis' impatience put me on edge.

"Depends," I answered. "I'll give Quinn the information, see what he thinks."

"When I told you we'd bought some time, I meant twenty-four hours. You need to be in Santa Rita by eleven thirty tomorrow morning. There's one flight a day from Phoenix. Anaya's people didn't get the video uploaded until after eleven. That means they expect you there tomorrow."

I checked my phone. It was close to noon. "Thanks, Luis. I'll call you back after I've spoken with Quinn."

I ended the call and clicked on the message from Luis containing the link to the video. Pascal leaned closer to watch.

Lauren and Abby stood in front of a patterned backdrop. The light source appeared to be from a single floor lamp to Lauren's left. It was one of those old-timey kinds, similar to the type seen in Victorian parlors. It looked like it still had some of the original paint. Lauren held a newspaper, her eyes red and swollen from crying. Abby was next to her, clutching Lauren's nightgown in her little fist. Her white face and red eyes told me she'd been crying, too. I took a deep breath and let it out, trying to calm myself.

From what I could see in the dim light neither of them had bruises or significant injury. The camera zoomed in on the newspaper and focused on today's date, and zoomed back out, revealing more of the room. My attention kept going back to the lamp, tugging at my mind, but I couldn't put my finger on why.

"We're okay, Daddy," Lauren said, her voice shaking. "Please come and get us soon." A dark-haired man entered the picture and walked toward them, his back to the camera. They both shrank away in fear and Abby started to sob as the picture went black.

White-hot fury mixed with fear for the girls rocketed to the surface. I clenched my fists, nails digging into my palms as I fought for control.

"How long do we have?" Pascal asked, his voice measured.

"Less than twenty-four hours." A wave of nausea swept over me at the impossibility of getting a rescue operation off the ground in that short a time. I wasn't even sure Anaya had the girls at his compound.

I froze as the reason for the earlier nagging sensation returned with a jolt. I'd seen the same lamp during the few trips Salazar and I took to Anaya's compound. I turned to Pascal.

"The girls are at his compound. I recognized one of the lamps from before."

Pascal started the engine and shifted the car into gear.

"Then we'd better get moving."

31

W E'RE GOING TO what?" Stunned, I stared at Quinn. We'd just finished watching the video of the girls on his laptop. With the larger picture I'd been able to confirm the floor lamp was the same one I'd remembered from Anaya's compound.

"It's called HALO, or High Altitude, Low Opening. It's like skydiving, but higher." Quinn continued to stuff a pack with the things we were going to need for the reconnaissance mission. I questioned whether we had time, but Quinn insisted we did, even though he'd have liked more time to plan.

"But I've never even been sky diving much less a high altitude jump. Won't we need oxygen?"

"We'll be harnessed together, tandem style. No experience or oxygen required," Quinn said. "We just step out and let gravity do the rest." He finished filling one bag, zipped it closed, and started on another.

"No, seriously, Quinn. I can't just jump out of an airplane at—how high did you say we were going to be?"

"Twenty-one thousand feet, give or take." His gray eyes held mine for a second before he went back to what he was doing. "Piece of cake. Once we're over the compound, we'll exit, pop the chute, and land. When we've finished the recon, you'll exfil, or exfiltrate, and my pilot will take you into Santa Rita. You'll be on your way with Anaya's people being none the wiser. In the meantime, my team will already be at the compound, waiting for you."

"Easy, right?" I said, unable to keep the sarcasm out of my voice. Okay, it was probably more because of plain, unadulterated fear. The thought of jumping out of a perfectly good airplane in the middle of the Sonoran desert and landing somewhere near Anaya's compound seemed risky. Especially when I had zero experience skydiving.

"Can't you do this without me?"

"Nope. You've been there before. I need your eyes, your memory of the place. The recon will be quicker, not to mention safer." He glanced outside the open door as Pascal walked in.

I glared at him, my arms folded across my chest, not sure whether I was more afraid of jumping out of an airplane or making two visits to Anaya's compound. The thought of doing both had my knees shaking, not to mention the annoying heart palpitations.

Calm down, Kate. If Quinn didn't think you'd be able to do it, he wouldn't have even suggested it.

Right?

"You're okay with me going on recon?" I asked Pascal, hoping he'd see my side.

"It's a tandem jump," Pascal replied. "You'll be in good hands."

"What about you? Aren't you coming?" I asked.

"He is," Quinn answered for him.

"Look at it this way, Kate," Pascal said. "We'll be able to plan our actions to get the girls back by looking at the actual location. Plus, you'll know exactly what's going to happen and when, which will help you help us."

"What about the leak? If I call Luis and ask for a plane so you can do recon, then they'll know you're going in early. Anaya's crew will be ready for you."

Quinn straightened. "Luis isn't going to know about the recon. I'm calling in a couple of favors and securing my own transportation. You're going to tell Luis we're tracking you from a distance. As far as he knows, the girls' location hasn't been confirmed, so that'll make sense." Quinn motioned me over to his laptop. "Does this look familiar?" he asked.

The crisp satellite image showed a flat piece of land with a rundown dock half covered by a *palapa* roof reaching into the tributary of a larger river. A rectangular wall surrounded several structures. I looked closer.

"Can you zoom in?" I asked.

Quinn hit a couple of keys and the image enlarged, allowing me to make out what looked like Anaya's compound. I'd already given Quinn as much information as I could remember about the direction we'd flown and how long it had taken when Salazar and I visited so many years ago, as well as briefed him on the general layout. When Salazar and I had been there, there'd been the main house—a two-story, Spanish-style colonial with a two-tiered patio fronted by arched doorways running the length of the front—surrounded by a twelve-foot-high concrete wall, with security and servants quarters scattered around a large courtyard. A grandiose multi-level fountain stood in the middle of the grounds. A swimming pool was to the left. From what I could see, the place hadn't changed much.

"That's got to be it," I said. "The footprint of the buildings looks right. The dock wasn't as run-down back then but I'm sure it's the same one."

"Where do you think he'd keep the kids?" he asked.

"If I were Anaya, I'd probably put them either in or near the safe room he had built on the lower level of the main house in case things went to shit." I pointed to the northwest corner of the compound. "His office was here, near the safe room. He'll probably take me there to verify the password. He also built an escape tunnel here." I traced a line on the screen outside of the compound to the west. He'd been proud of the room with its adjoining tunnel and made sure Salazar knew about it. Totally self-contained and able to withstand a heavy assault, there were enough supplies inside to survive a nuclear winter.

"Does the tunnel have an exit?" Quinn asked.

"Yes. There's an escape hatch."

"Think you can find it again?"

"I can try."

"Good." Quinn nodded. "When you ask for proof of life, try to get them to bring the girls to you. That way, you'll be able to help them when we breach." He ran his finger north of the area along a light-colored ribbon of land.

"This is an intermittent river that comes in from the north, currently dry, except for where it flows past the compound on its way to the Yaqui River." He traced a line north past Anaya's place and stopped. "Drop Zone One, or DZ One, will be approximately eight-hundred meters north of the compound. Time on target will be fifteen minutes after Nautical Twilight with two elements: recon via HALO, and the main body by static line three hours later. That way, the recon element should be in place and can observe whether the plane causes an increase in activity when the main element drops. Obviously you'll be on recon, Kate, as will Pascal, myself, and seven others. See this white patch here?" he asked.

I nodded.

"That will be our ORP."

"ORP?"

"Objective rally point. We'll leave two men there to secure the site, then conduct the recon. While that's happening, the main body will infil, or infiltrate, two klicks northwest of the compound at DZ Two." Quinn tapped his finger on the screen, indicating a large open field. "This will also be where we exfil, once the mission is complete."

"Okay, but how will I get back in time to make it to Santa Rita? They're expecting me there tomorrow morning." The mission felt like trying to accomplish too much in too little time. I *had* to be at the airport by eleven thirty the next day.

"The main element will leave four men to secure the second DZ and then move south to secure your pickup zone. After the recon, four of our team will stay near the compound for eyes on: two will be west on a hillside to cover the west and south, and two on a hill to the east to cover the entrance and east side. I'll take you back to the pickup zone where you'll leave via helicopter before dawn." He pointed at a fork in the streambed north of the original drop zone. "My guy will fly you to Santa Rita in plenty of time to meet Anaya's contingent. Once you're on your way, I'll brief the rest of the main force. We will then move to the ORP and wait to set up until you return with Anaya's people."

At least that part sounded easy enough. Jumping *into* a helicopter I could do.

"Put this on." Quinn handed me what looked like a halter made of heavy webbing that smelled like mildew.

"What's this for?" I asked.

"STABO exfil."

"I'm sorry—what?"

"Stabilized body harness. For when you exfil from the site," he said, his tone matter-of-fact.

"Why does my body need to be stabilized? Don't I just open the door and get inside the helo? You never said anything about having to freaking *stabilize my body.* Seriously?"

"You put the harness over your shoulders like this," he said, the epitome of patience as he demonstrated on himself with a second harness. "Secure the chest belt and then bring each of these straps between your legs and snap the hooks to the rings at the hip."

"You haven't told me why I need to wear this thing." I crossed my arms.

"There's no place secure enough near the objective to put a chopper down without wasting valuable time. This is the fastest and least compromising way to exfil you. It means you and the helo will be less of a target than if the pilot landed nearby, waited for you to board, and then lifted off. The bird will come in and hover above us, and then drop a line which I will attach to you using these." Quinn pointed to two metal carabineers, one on each shoulder of the harness. "The chopper will lift you up, fly to DZ Two and land. That's when you get onboard and take off for Santa Rita."

"Let me get this straight. Not only do I get to jump out of an airplane at twenty-one thousand feet—which I've never done before and it sure as hell isn't on my bucket list—and then sneak into my worst enemy's ultra-secure compound to take a look around without getting discovered or killed, but I also get to dangle under a helicopter as target practice for cartel snipers. Did I get that right?"

Quinn watched me, his expression unreadable. "If things go as planned, nobody in the compound is going to know you were even there, so no, you won't be target practice. Remember, Kate," he said, unbuckling his harness. "You came to me for help."

I took a deep breath and nodded. "I'm sorry. You're right."

No matter his assurances, I was petrified. This was worse than when I infiltrated Morales' compound. At least then I never left the ground.

"You'll need to dress in multiple layers. It's going to be cold up there," Pascal said, handing me a Gore-Tex shell, a polypropylene shirt, matching leggings, and a pair of gloves. "We may be in a desert environment, but at that altitude the temperature is well below freezing."

I took the clothes and looked around for a place to put them on. Pascal tapped Quinn on the shoulder to get his attention. Quinn looked up and Pascal nodded at the door.

"We should let her change."

"Oh. Right. Gear's ready to go," Quinn said, and picked up one of the bags, swinging it over his shoulder. Pascal grabbed another one and they walked outside.

I changed quickly and was ready to go by the time Quinn returned. Hector, my training partner when I'd first joined up with Quinn's commandos, walked in behind him.

A tall, powerfully built guy, Hector had joined Quinn's group after his wife, Claudia, had been gunned down on their honeymoon by cartel thugs in a drive-by shooting. Hatred for the cartels burned hot in Hector's blood, and he'd sworn to avenge her death. He was pretty good at hand-to-hand combat, too.

"Are you coming?" I asked him.

"Recon," he answered with a nod.

"When Hector found out you were involved, he insisted," Quinn said.

"I couldn't let my training partner go into enemy territory alone, now, could I?" Hector smiled.

"Thank you, Hector. I owe you guys," I said.

"You owe us nothing, *chica*. It's what we do."

"Enough with the old home week. Ready?" Quinn turned to me.

"Not really," I replied.

"You can give Luis a call on the way to the plane," he said, ignoring my comment. He handed me a pad of paper and a pen. "Tell him we'll need reimbursement for two data pushers, two data loggers, and cell phone tracker software. Then ask them to do a flyover with a drone at these coordinates." Quinn recited what I assumed to be a decoy location, which I jotted on the notepad. "That should give them the impression that we're guessing where Anaya's got the girls and that we're tracking you rather than doing recon."

"Got it," I said.

I also wanted to call Sam one more time. Our last conversation hadn't gone well. After a stony silence, he'd finally shown some emotion and yelled at me for taking off without him and only leaving a note. I told him I knew he wouldn't have let me go if I'd told him. He saw the logic but was still angry.

We both knew my odds of survival weren't good. I had to convince Anaya to let the girls go. I didn't expect to make it out alive. Now that Quinn and his group were onboard, part of me wanted to believe maybe we had a fighting chance.

But I didn't have much faith in fairytales.

Hopefully, Anaya would see my life as fair trade for theirs. The man had wanted me dead for so long I was banking on his need for closure.

And vengeance.

32

THE SHIFT IN RPMs yanked me out of a fitful sleep. I'd been lying on a blanket on the floor of the C-123, trying to get some rest, which was difficult considering we were flying at twenty-one-thousand feet in a cavernous, pregnant tin can of an airplane that was loud, freezing cold, and smelled like jet fuel.

The stripped-down Fairchild C-123 Provider sported what looked like an exoskeleton covering its ribbed walls. With two propellers, a distinctive tail that swept up in a modified V, and the capacity to carry heavy loads, the plane had a unique profile and was used extensively in Mexico for transporting equipment and personnel. The ride wasn't exactly smooth—more like riding in an old Model T with worn out shocks on a dirt back road full of pot-holes.

As the flip-down canvas seats wouldn't accommodate a horizontal human, and with only an acre of hard metal surface to lie on, my idea of catching a few Zs before we'd made it to Anaya's compound may have been a tad optimistic. Even with the poly underclothes and Gore-Tex, my muscles cramped from the cold as well as the long, bumpy flight. The nauseating smell of jet fuel mixed with hydraulic fluid didn't help. I was thankful the Provider didn't have to follow a 'nap of the earth', or NOE flight plan for the HALO jump. Pascal had explained that after our drop the main body would return a few hours later, flying just above treetop level, or above the 'nap of the earth', contouring the terrain to make their jump. Apparently, everyone puked on an NOE flight.

Flying in the 123 was uncomfortable enough without having to barf into a bucket.

The main element had taken seats near the front of the plane, since they were going to jump after we did. I counted twelve in the larger group and eight plus Artemis, Quinn's German Shepherd, in recon. When Quinn told me she would make the jump with us, I'd calmed down to the point that I could actually form a coherent thought. I figured if Artemis didn't have a problem jumping with Quinn, neither did I.

Half of the commandos Quinn selected for recon were familiar to me from when I first met up with Quinn's little army: in addition to Hector and Pascal, I'd worked with Buck and Lalo. The three I hadn't met were Fernando, Carlos, and Daria.

Lalo had been a faithful soldier for Leonardo Diaz, the head of *El Castillo,* before he jumped ship and joined Quinn's group. In his early thirties, he had dark, spiky hair, tats everywhere you could see, and probably more where you couldn't, stood no more than five-foot-six, and dripped attitude.

To say Diaz had been unhappy when Lalo went AWOL to attend his younger sister's wedding would have been an understatement. As payback, Diaz dispatched a hit man to Lalo's hometown and murdered his entire family, including a young cousin. It was then that Lalo decided he had nothing to lose and everything to gain by working against the cartels. If I had to guess, I'd say that alone made Lalo the most lethal in the group. He had the distinct advantage of having been privy to the inner workings of one of the more notorious cartels and knew how to think like them. He was also a crack marksman.

I'd learned earlier that Fernando, a younger version of Lalo, had worked for Hugo Morales as a runner, and soon afterward had been promoted to security. When Morales knowingly sacrificed a large contingent of his men during the fight at the ruins, Fernando had given himself up to Quinn and offered his services. I'd been surprised Quinn had included him in the operation, but Pascal had assured me he was well trained and trustworthy. Apparently, Fernando had a way with explosives. The other men referred to him as the "virtuoso of boom."

Then there was Buck. A compact bulldog of a man, Buck was Quinn's main combat trainer and one of the most sadistic men I'd ever met. I was sure death had been imminent when I first began to train with the rest of the recruits. The heat and humidity were brutal, yes, but the sixty-pound packs and three-mile runs in the middle of the day were what almost killed me.

Off the job, though, you couldn't find a more interesting person to talk to. Buck had been around the world many times over working "security" in most known hot spots, as well as some unknown. He'd met Quinn in a bar in Mérida, and they'd hit it off instantly. Other than Quinn's brother-in-law, Pascal, Buck was the only other person in the group who had known Quinn's wife, Maria, before she was murdered.

In the rush of planning and Quinn's insistence on my learning the group's Standard Operating Procedures, I hadn't had a chance to speak with Carlos or Daria. Since my life and the lives of Lauren and Abby would be directly affected by their actions, I decided to remedy the situation. Carlos sat near the front of the aircraft and appeared to be asleep, so I grabbed the blanket and stood up, wrapping it around me as I made my way toward the rear of the plane to the seat next to Daria. She watched me in silence, wariness evident on her face.

"Hi. I'm Kate. I thought I should introduce myself since we hadn't met yet." Smiling, I held out my hand. Her expression guarded, she obliged.

"Daria," she said and withdrew her hand, placing it in her lap.

"Good to meet you, Daria."

She averted her gaze, looking at everything except me. Her glossy black hair had been pulled back in a tight bun, matching the seriousness of her desert fatigues and utility boots. A suppressed MP5 machinegun lay next to her, and a nine-millimeter Sig Sauer rested against her thigh in a holster. Her expression could only be called stoic—unusual for a woman so young. Not sure how to proceed, I thought about asking what a nice woman like her was doing in a place like this but decided against it. Something about her told me not to try too hard—that she wasn't the kind of woman who appreciated instant friendships, or bad one-liners.

"I have to tell you," I said, leaning in with a glance toward the front of the plane where everyone else was sitting. "I wasn't completely sold on this whole HALO thing at first."

Daria looked at me, her expression indecipherable. "And now?" she asked.

"Even though Quinn assures me it's the best way to go in, I'm still nervous. I've never jumped out of a plane, much less at high altitude."

"Quinn knows what he's doing," she said. Where had I heard that before?

"How long have you been with the group?" I asked.

"Couple of months."

"Obviously, he trusts you," I replied. The thought that he'd included not one but two new recruits on the operation made me nervous, but I realized she was right. Quinn knew what he was doing. I needed to remember that. I glanced at the MP5. "You must be good."

A flicker of pride crossed her face, and she inclined her chin. "I've used one before."

"How did you meet Quinn?" I asked.

"Through Fernando."

"Did you both work for Morales?"

She crossed her arms, her expression hardening. "You could say that."

I sensed potent emotions simmering beneath the surface. Though curious, I decided not to pursue it further. Her past was none of my business. If she wanted to talk, she'd talk. I'd ask Quinn about her later.

"It's good you found Quinn, then," was all I said.

As though hearing his name, Quinn broke from the larger group and headed to where we were sitting. Artemis followed at his side, tongue lolling out.

"I see you two have met." Quinn nodded at Daria, and turned to me. "How are you doing, Kate?"

"Good," I lied. Quinn's presence reminded me of the impending jump and my anxiety level spiked.

Daria got up to leave. "Nice to meet you, Kate" she said, and, holding on to the seat frames with her free hand, went forward to join the other HALO jumpers who were putting their chutes on.

"Time to chute up," he said, handing me the harness. "Remember the five points of contact?"

I nodded. "Balls of my feet, calves, thigh, butt, push muscle."

To my relief, Quinn had insisted on all of us performing several parachute landing falls prior to take off and had explained to me how both the reserve and the main chutes worked. I would be attached to the front of Quinn with a harness, and Artemis would be attached to me the same way. The idea of moving to the rear of the aircraft all connected together sounded difficult, but Quinn explained we wouldn't clip together until we were at the ramp, prior to the jump.

"Remember: arch hard at the waist, head up. Keep your arms around Artemis. I'll do the rest."

"Sounds easy," I said, my sarcasm obvious.

"When we're about to land, look at the horizon and don't reach for the ground. Let it come to you."

"Will I even be able to see it?" I asked.

"If you keep your eyes open," he replied, handing me a pair of night vision goggles.

"NVGs?"

"Yep. When you put them on everything will look green, but you'll have good visual acuity once we land." He held up an earpiece. "Remember the fight at the ruins?" he asked. I nodded. "Same gear. Wireless transmitter/receiver. Everyone on the team will be wearing one. Lalo's manning the radio." He handed it to me. "Put it in a side pouch where it'll be safe for the jump."

Already wearing the dreaded STABO harness with two canteens, several pouches of ammunition, a first-aid kit, and a fanny pack, I did as he instructed and then stepped into the harness that would be connected to Quinn's. I pulled the straps over my shoulders and snapped the buckles closed across my chest and legs. Not that I was looking forward to flying through the air under a helicopter. Quinn handed me a helmet and then stooped to secure Artemis' harness.

"If you don't mind me asking, what's Daria's story?" I asked, hoping to delay any more talk about the jump. "I know she and Fernando met when they were both with Morales. She seems like a woman on a mission."

"You could say that." Quinn glanced near the front where Daria sat next to Fernando, their heads bowed in conversation. "She'd been taught to shoot at a young age and earned a reputation with the locals. Morales' men kidnapped her when she was fifteen. At first, they trained her as a sniper, but the better she got, the more the men in Morales' security complained. One night, a group of them gang raped her and left her for dead. Morales found out and decided she'd be more useful in another capacity." Quinn shook his head in disgust.

"He kept her locked in a room on one meal a day, abusing her repeatedly until he got bored. Then he parceled her out to his top guns. When Morales offered her to Fernando, he pretended to take him up on his 'gift.' Instead, he used their time together to teach her how to fight. When he left, he helped her escape and eventually they came to me. They were a package deal. No Daria, no Fernando."

"My god. I can understand her anger." I'd read the file Quinn had compiled on Morales before I tried to infiltrate his organization. Usually interested in younger girls, his sexual proclivities were well known in the cartel world.

"So you helped her direct that anger into fighting the cartels," I said. He'd done the same with my hatred for Roberto Salazar. Daria would have a good chance at revenge now that she'd hooked up with Quinn's group. I hoped it would be enough.

"Twenty minutes," the jumpmaster called out, and flashed ten fingers twice. The lights in the aircraft blinked off and changed to red. The recon unit gave the thumbs up sign, acknowledging the command. I stabbed my thumb in the air, even though I was far from ready. Quinn handed me a pair of wrap-around goggles and I put them on.

The HALO gods, as the main group referred to the recon element, stepped through the shoulder straps of their rucksacks, positioned them behind their legs, and hooked them to their harnesses. Since I would be holding on to Artemis, I didn't get a pack. All of us wore side arms with extra magazines, or mags, and fragmentation grenades, or frags, in our harnesses. Mags and frags. Easy to remember.

The guys had used duct tape to create "pull tabs" on the magazines to make it easier to pull the ammunition out of their pouches. They'd also taped anything metal to cut down on reflective surfaces as well as to keep the equipment quiet.

In addition to Daria's MP5 and Lalo's sniper rifle, Quinn carried a modified, suppressed MP5, and Pascal had an M-203—a 40mm grenade launcher mounted below an M-16. The others were well armed with frags, bayonets, and automatics with suppressors, and Fernando wore a rucksack that I assumed carried explosives. The main element had some serious firepower, including a belt-fed machinegun, shotguns, and suppressed submachine guns.

Yeah, now I was getting nervous.

"Ten minutes."

My shoulders tensed at the jumpmaster's warning.

Ten minutes until I fall out of this airplane and plummet twenty-one thousand feet to the earth with a dog in my arms and a man strapped to my back.

Into enemy territory.

The operation we were about to embark on could certainly be construed as war. I wondered how many other operations were going on in the world. Small ones just like this, and larger ones, too, where soldiers had to parachute into enemy territory on their way to carrying out a dangerous mission. My respect for the people who did these kinds of things for a living skyrocketed. I couldn't imagine going through it again, much less on a regular basis.

A couple of minutes later the jumpmaster patted his head with both hands, the command for all of us to put on our helmets. The commandos gave the thumbs up and put them on. Quinn helped me on with mine and secured the chin strap. The jumpmaster motioned us toward the rear of the aircraft.

Quinn leaned down and spoke directly into my ear. "Time to move to the ramp, Kate." He placed his hand on my back and pushed me toward the jumpmaster. It was hard to walk straight as the plane bucked and jostled, and I put a hand out to steady myself. Despite the cold, a trickle of sweat slid down my neck.

The jumpmaster lowered the ramp, and the noise from the wind increased dramatically. Panic rose in my chest, and I sucked in air to calm my racing heart. Artemis sauntered ahead of me, apparently unconcerned.

Concentrating on Artemis, I made it to the ramp where Quinn lifted her into my arms. I held on to her while he secured her harness to mine. Then, he stepped behind me, and I heard him snap our harnesses together at the shoulder. Surprisingly, Artemis didn't struggle.

The relief must have shown on my face, because the jumpmaster smiled as he leaned close to me and said, "Don't worry, Kate. Dogs don't perceive heights. It'll be just like sticking her head out the window of a car, and you know how much dogs love to do that."

"If that's the case, then this is gonna be the best car ride she's ever had," I replied.

He laughed and went back to his position next to the ramp.

"Stand up," he called, motioning with his arm. The rest of the recon team struggled to their feet and checked each other's packs as they waited for the next command. Quinn and the jumpmaster had gone over everyone's gear before boarding but in this case redundancy was good.

"Move to the rear."

The rest of the recon element staggered to the rear of the plane to join us. They waddled under the weight of their equipment toward the ramp like a group of oversized pregnant women with large bags hanging between their legs. Pascal tried to make me laugh by pulling faces at me, but I ignored his attempts and stared straight ahead.

I stuffed the NVGs into my Gore-Tex jacket, making sure the lanyard was secure around my neck, and glanced out the opening at the rapidly darkening sky. I didn't dare look at the ground.

It was a long way down.

The jumpmaster knelt on the side of the ramp, held onto the aircraft, and stuck his head outside, searching for the drop zone.

What if the parachute doesn't open? I thought.

Then Quinn will deploy the reserve chute, I told myself. *You'll be fine.*

But what if that one doesn't work? I argued.

Then you'll be dead, so stop worrying.

I kept my gaze trained on the light above us. Red meant wait, green meant go. At this point I wished it would change to green already. Obviously, I had committed to the jump, since I was strapped to Quinn and Artemis.

Okay, committed might be too strong a word. Maybe trapped or forced to jump would be more appropriate. Either way, I couldn't turn back now.

I took a deep breath and closed my eyes, reminding myself I was doing it for Lauren and Abby. Maybe if I thought of it as a dream, I'd be better able to function. Yeah, that was it. A dream.

"One minute!"

My eyes flew open. The jumpmaster held up one finger. Panic raced up my spine.

Maybe this wasn't such a great idea.

"Thirty seconds!"

No. Definitely not a good idea. My body froze as the voice in my head screamed at me to turn back.

The light turned green. The jumpmaster struggled to his feet under the weight of his gear, thrust out his arm and pointed off the ramp. It was time to go.

Quinn muscled me forward.

Oh, Jesus God. I'm going to be the first one out.

I looked down as my feet reached the edge of the ramp. The wind howled past me through the gaping maw of the opening. It was dark. And cold.

And terrifying.

Every fiber of my being wanted to dig in my heels and throw myself backward onto the plane.

"Can't we rethink this, Quinn? I can't—I really don't want to go." The panic in my voice was annoying.

"Too late, Kate," Quinn yelled into my ear as he prodded me toward empty space. "Just fall forward."

"But—"

The wind tore the rest of the words from my mouth.

33

WE PLUNGED EARTHWARD, dropping fast. Quinn immediately released a drogue chute in order to stabilize our descent.

I squeezed my eyes shut, refusing to watch.

The sound of the wind as it rushed past and the manic fluttering of everything we wore that wasn't taped down told me we were hurtling through space faster than two people should.

Or, it might have been the flapping sound my cheeks made when I opened my mouth to scream.

I had to give Artemis credit. She didn't even wiggle as we plummeted to earth. Although it could have been because I had her fur in a death grip.

Minutes ticked by like hours. When nothing horrible happened, and I'd moved past the whole paralyzed with fear part, I felt myself relax. Sort of. Unable to take a deep breath because of the panic cowering in my chest, I tentatively opened my eyes to slits, not wanting to miss anything important.

Through the deep blue of twilight, the breathtaking curve of the earth splayed across the horizon. Lights indicating a settlement of some kind twinkled like terrestrial stars far to the west. I glanced below me once but decided against it when I realized how far we were from the ground.

A long damn way.

The wind sheared past us. As long as I didn't think about landing, I found I retained some semblance of intelligible thought. Carefully, I let go of Artemis with one hand to pinch my nose and blew into my ears, trying to release the pressure.

Before I knew it, Quinn's arm came up as he checked his altimeter.

Are we at three thousand feet already? I thought. *I was just getting used to this.*

The rest of the team had grouped close by as we fell, their faint outlines barely visible in the darkness. Quinn mentioned in the briefing that the others would "form" on us until we reached three thousand feet, and would fall away to keep from getting tangled in our chute when Quinn pulled the rip cord. At a hundred feet, he'd release his rucksack and we'd land.

Fine. I'm ready. The sooner we land, the sooner we get this over with.

Quinn waved the others off. I tensed for the release. He popped the rectangular chute and we stopped in midair, hesitating for a second before we resumed our descent, this time at a much slower rate of speed. The roar of the wind changed to a gentle breeze as we floated toward the earth, the chute fluttering above our heads.

It didn't take long before I noticed a welcome change in temperature. The lower we drifted, the warmer it became. Quinn maneuvered the chute toward the drop zone, and when we hit one hundred feet, lowered his rucksack. I felt a tug as it hit the end of the lowering line and we prepared to land.

"Balls of feet, calves, thigh, butt…" I murmured to myself as the ground rushed up to meet us. Quinn flared the chute and we landed. On our feet.

Talk about an anticlimax. The parachute billowed to the ground as Quinn disconnected from me and Artemis.

"Stay low," Quinn said in a quiet voice.

I sank to my knees, relieved to be on the ground. Artemis whined softly to let me know she wanted her freedom. I disconnected the clips holding her, and she ran to where Quinn crouched with his gun, scanning the area through his NVGs. I sank onto my ass and slid the wraparound goggles off and the night vision goggles on. The rest of the team had landed close by and were doing the same. I pulled out my sidearm and slipped the wireless transmitter over my ear as I waited for Quinn's signal.

He raised his hand, and the team pulled in their chutes and rolled them up, daisy-chaining the suspension lines so they'd fit inside their kit bags. I removed the harness that had attached me to Quinn and slid off the Gore-Tex shell, tying the arms around my waist under the STABO harness. Then I peeled off the gloves and shoved them into the side pockets. Tempted to remove the polypropylene underclothes, I realized I wouldn't have enough time before we headed for the predetermined rally point. Good thing we'd arrived when we did. The day's heat still radiated off the desert floor, raising the temperature, but we didn't have to contend with the sun's ferocious rays. The trek to the compound wouldn't be easy, but infinitely more comfortable—and safer—than in daylight.

Quinn motioned for me to follow him. I climbed to my feet and we moved several yards to the right of the drop zone, where he broke a chem light for the others to see. The rest of the group joined us, and he did a quick head count while they consolidated the chutes and cached them in a copse of trees.

Once everyone had been accounted for, Quinn gave the signal to move out. Quinn and Artemis took the lead position, with Lalo and Pascal next: one to the left, the other offset and to the right. Daria and I followed behind them in the same formation, then Hector and Carlos, with Buck at the rear. The objective rallying point, or ORP, lay a little over half a kilometer from where we stood.

My hand sweaty, I repositioned my grip on the gun. The "Ranger Eyes" secured to the backs of the others' packs jiggled and glowed like meth-addicted fireflies, lending a bizarre, dream-like quality to the already surreal situation.

As I stared through the NVGs, everything appeared to move, and I continually double-checked each shape and shadow while I struggled to quash a full-on anxiety attack.

It's just an illusion, Kate. Calm down.

Artemis ran ahead of us on a long leash, nose to the ground, searching for explosives. Anaya had more than likely booby-trapped the area near the compound, although Quinn didn't think he would have bothered this far out. Even so, we proceeded carefully, halting every hundred yards for a security check, where we all dropped to one knee and faced outward to listen.

Half a kilometer didn't sound very far, but creeping along while expecting to get blown to pieces with every step sure made the time drag. The night vision goggles turned the scrubby brush and surrounding landscape a sickly green. Other than the annoying hammering in my chest, the only discernible sounds were our footsteps and the occasional ghostly hoot of an owl. The hot, dry environment of the Sonoran desert turned out to be easier to hike than the stifling damp and humidity of the Yucatán, but not by much. The vegetation, however, turned out to be a lot less demanding, especially when we stuck to the dry riverbed.

Artemis sensed everyone's mood and slowed her pace as she searched. A few minutes after the third security halt, she stopped and dropped to her belly. Everyone froze. She whined softly as Quinn inched toward her.

"What'd you find, girl?" he murmured as he eased into a squat. He scanned the ground around him and picked up a twig to probe the area next to her. Not finding anything in the immediate vicinity, he crept along an imaginary line, balancing the stick between his thumb and index finger, letting one end drop gently to the ground every few inches, and then rise back up. I held my breath as we waited. He continued checking for mines for several excruciating minutes until he paused halfway into the middle of the dry bed.

"Trip wire," he murmured. He reached inside a pouch and pulled out a roll of tape that glinted. I slid the NVGs off but couldn't see the tape.

"The wire ends two meters to your left," he said into his mic. He peeled off two pieces of the infrared reflective tape and carefully draped them over the wire, and then peeled off four more and marked a large X about a foot from either end. We gave the wire a wide berth and continued on.

At the five-hundred meter mark, Quinn signaled for everyone to halt, and motioned to Lalo and Hector to move forward to secure the ORP while we waited for their signal. Several minutes ticked by before Hector called back with an all clear.

We walked the remaining one hundred yards before Hector emerged from the bushes.

"Code?" he asked, his weapon pointed at us.

"Beyoncé," Quinn replied. He'd used the same code word during the fight at the ruins. Hector lowered his weapon and we proceeded. I tried to keep my mind off the fact that we were now only a few minutes from where Anaya had the girls. With each step, my fear for Abby and Lauren's wellbeing grew along with the fear of discovery.

Hector and Lalo had set up the radio base and were in the process of securing the rest of the area. Artemis would stay with them to make sure the site wouldn't be compromised. The rest would continue to the compound.

Quinn glanced at me. "Ready?"

Nodding, I tried to swallow. My mouth tasted like the surrounding desert.

"Let's go."

Further on, the dry creek bed turned damp and we hit water. Buck and Fernando broke west toward high ground behind the compound, and Carlos and Pascal headed east across the tributary toward a hilltop overlook. Quinn, Daria, and I waited in the darkness until both teams were in position. Both Quinn and Daria appeared calm and weren't even breathing hard from the exertion. I couldn't say the same.

Buck signaled first by breaking squelch twice on his radio. A few minutes later, Pascal followed suit. My shoulders inched away from my ears, knowing they were above us, watching, and I managed to convince myself recon wasn't so scary.

I'd always been good at denial.

Quinn acknowledged their positions, and we moved toward the compound.

The terrain had begun to feel and look familiar, and I mentioned it to Quinn. He nodded and moved me closer to the front. The ghostly outline of the old dock came into view.

What if I'm wrong? What if this isn't where the girls are? The panic returned, and I had to pause for a moment and catch my breath, fighting to remain calm. Quinn and Daria waited patiently until I'd taken a couple of deep breaths before we continued.

We'd walked several more yards when Quinn brought his fist up, motioning for us to freeze. He pointed at the entrance, his thumb down. I pulled out my binoculars and scanned to the right of the dock.

A high wall with two large doors loomed several yards to the west. I thought I saw something near the entrance, but it was gone an instant later. I blinked, not even sure I'd seen anything. Quinn had warned me that everything would appear to move in the dark. I thought I'd gotten used to it.

"Gunman at entry," Quinn murmured.

"Copy east," Pascal answered.

I looked through my binoculars again. At that moment, a man with an AK-47 slung over his shoulder stepped from behind a doorway. A match flared as he lit a cigarette.

"Sure doesn't look like they're expecting company," Daria whispered.

"Yeah," Quinn replied. "Just like we planned."

A couple of minutes passed. There didn't appear to be anyone other than the lone gunman. Then another man with the same kind of weapon joined him.

"Make that two," Quinn breathed into the mic.

"Copy west," Buck answered.

The three of us waited, watching the guards chat with each other in front of the building.

The radio squelched. "Another one. Making rounds." I tensed at Buck's clipped tone.

Quinn keyed the mic twice to acknowledge.

Several minutes passed before the gunman passed by, walking east toward the front entrance. As soon as he disappeared from view, we turned west, following parallel to the wall. Quinn stopped and motioned me forward.

"Show me the tunnel," Quinn whispered.

I shrugged off the tension in my shoulders and took a deep breath before continuing. What if I couldn't find it? What if Anaya had changed the entry point?

I walked due west in a straight line, remembering to stop every so often to listen. Warm perspiration slid between my shoulder blades, turning wet and cold in the desert night air. Quinn and Daria stayed close, scanning the area, alert for more of Anaya's men.

Fifteen minutes later, I caught a glimpse of what I'd been looking for and self-corrected, coming to a stop next to a gnarled old mesquite. Its thick, contorted trunk brought back memories I'd prefer stayed buried.

I could almost hear Salazar's laughter when Anaya explained what it had taken to build the tunnel and how he'd stocked the safe room with a months' worth of provisions in case of attack. Roberto had liked the idea of the safe room but scoffed at the amount of supplies, thinking it overly paranoid and unnecessary. Even though they'd been drinking heavily that evening, I'd been surprised Anaya had shown us the tunnel. Although, once I thought about it, I realized it had been his way of telling Salazar how much forethought he'd put into his own survival. I didn't doubt there were more escape routes than he'd indicated, and had mentioned my concerns to Quinn.

"This looks like the tree. The entrance should be over here," I said. My heart in my throat, I moved to the right, searching for signs of the trap door. I knelt and ran my hand along the ground until I came to an indentation. It took a couple of passes to brush the dirt away before I could make out a section of the hatch. With a smile of relief, I leaned my head back and looked at Quinn. He squatted beside me, and we brushed the rest of the earth away, revealing a metal trap door. About a meter square, the opening would easily accommodate a person with gear.

"Metal rungs lead down the shaft into the tunnel. The tunnel itself is made of concrete with lights every meter or so. If I remember correctly, the door into the safe room is made of metal with sliding locks."

Quinn nodded and marked the spot with a strip of glint tape while Daria and I pushed dirt back over the hatch.

"How do you intend to get inside?" I asked.

"Cutting torch," Quinn replied. "Once you come back with Anaya's people, we'll move into position near the interior door of the safe room, observing the meet with a fiber optic camera under the door. When they bring the kids to see you, move the three of you to the corner of the room. That'll be our cue to breach, so be ready. You need to secure Lauren and Abby immediately. It's going to be loud and scary and confusing. Get them into the safe room as quickly as you can. We'll exit through the tunnel."

"What if they come after us? There's only one way out of there." My stomach twisted at the thought of being trapped in the tunnel as Anaya's men mowed us down from either end.

"If everything goes right, the only people who will know what happened will be the gunmen in the room with you. The rest of Anaya's forces won't have a clue until it's too late. Fernando's going to booby-trap the tunnel and the ground near the hatch. We'll do the same along the riverbed when we retreat. We've got surprise on our side, Kate. It's going to work."

"Then let's hope everything goes right," I said. The far-off muffled drone of the 123 echoed through the valley, signifying its return for the main body drop. Alarmed, I glanced at Quinn. "What if they hear that?" I asked.

"Then we'll see some activity," he replied.

I looked behind me, expecting Anaya's forces to come running out of the compound like a stream of agitated ants. Nothing happened. *Maybe it's far enough away,* I thought.

Quinn finished marking the hatch, and we headed south, parallel to the compound. We'd covered several meters before Buck's voice came over the radio.

"Guard."

Motionless, we waited. A few minutes later the gunman who'd made the rounds earlier appeared, walking along the perimeter of the compound. We waited until he disappeared around the far corner of the wall before we continued.

We crested a rise with a clear view of the rear of the compound and stopped. Quinn placed his hand on my arm.

"Stay here," he whispered. I nodded and slipped behind a bush while he and Daria melted into the trees and headed down the hill to investigate the back wall.

The night insects buzzed, accompanied by the occasional chirp of a frog, and I closed my eyes, thinking back to more carefree days before I'd met Salazar. It felt like another lifetime. Fresh out of college and on one last vacation in Mexico before heading back to Minnesota to take a fast-track job at an investment bank, I'd learned how one seemingly innocent decision could morph into something terrible, where the only way out involved murder.

I'd probably be married with two-point-four children and a house in the burbs, looking forward to my three-week vacation at some tourist destination. I would never have met Cole, or Lauren, or Abby, or Sam. My breath caught at the memory of Sam, heart aching at the thought of never seeing him again. *Stop it, Kate,* I scolded myself. Cole and the girls were counting on me. I doubted I'd make it out of Anaya's compound alive, but I'd be damn sure the girls did.

I opened my eyes and glanced at the wall of the compound. Something moved. I raised my binoculars and peered through them at the spot where I thought I'd seen something. Nothing. I scanned right and found Daria near the wall, and continued further west to where Quinn stood in the shadow of a tree, covering her.

Again, I caught movement in my periphery. I brought the binoculars back to where I'd first seen something. This time, a shadowy figure slipped around the northwest corner of the compound, hugging the wall. I blinked to make sure I wasn't seeing things, but the figure moved again. My adrenaline spiked and I hit the squelch two times on my radio as I kept my eyes on what now appeared to be a man running along the wall in a crouch.

"Someone's coming at you from the north," I warned, hoping I'd said it loud enough. One of the team broke squelch twice, indicating that somebody heard me. I stood rooted to the ground, riveted to my binoculars, watching as Quinn melted into the tree line and Daria dropped to a crouch next to a bush.

The gunman slowed as he neared Daria's hiding place. I held my breath as he stepped closer. Daria eased her semiautomatic out of its holder and waited. I couldn't see Quinn.

Gun first, the guard tracked several yards one way and then the other, carefully scanning the area. Apparently not seeing anything, he brought his radio to his lips. A few seconds later, he continued around the far corner of the compound. My shoulders sagged, and I released my breath with a sigh. A low whistle made its way over the radio.

Quinn and Daria left the area by the wall and moved up the incline, walking toward me along the ridge, staying near the trees.

"That was close," I whispered to Daria.

"No shit," she replied.

"We've got what we need," Quinn said. "Time to get you out of here, Kate."

We'd made it through the first leg of the mission. Now for the hard part.

With Quinn in the lead, we turned and headed back to the dry riverbed and my date with Anaya's people.

34

AS WE APPROACHED the objective rallying point where Lalo, Hector, and Artemis waited, Lalo emerged from the shadows and issued a challenge. Quinn answered with another predetermined code and we continued into the secured area before heading for the pickup zone.

I took a drink of water from my canteen and tried to relax, but my fear of flying through the air in the dark attached to the underbelly of a helicopter trumped any thought of unwinding from the recon. I didn't want to think about what I'd have to do later, either, once I'd made it to Santa Rita. My nerves were frayed enough.

"It's almost over," Daria said with an encouraging smile. She sat down next to me and offered me a Chiclet. Her concern was touching. I must have looked as worried as I felt.

"Thanks," I said, accepting the gum. "I'm definitely ready to be done with this."

As if he'd heard me, Quinn signaled that it was time to go. Daria stood and offered me a hand up. With a weary sigh, I grabbed her forearm and got to my feet. I said a heartfelt goodbye to Lalo and Hector, and then bent down to give Artemis a final pet, not sure I'd see any of them again. Then I followed Quinn and Daria up the dry riverbed to the pickup zone.

The glint tape Quinn had placed on either side of the trip wire glowed eerily through the NVGs as we passed by the booby trap. A few hundred yards later, as we neared the pickup zone, a commando materialized from the bushes.

"Code," he asked.

"Disneyland," Quinn answered.

The commando lowered his gun and moved aside to let us pass. Four of Quinn's men met us when we reached the PZ. All were dressed in desert fatigues similar to Quinn's.

"Call in the bird," Quinn told a tall, wiry guy I didn't recognize. He nodded and spoke into his mic. Quinn told the others to set up the landing area.

They immediately spread out, setting three infrared strobes in a V formation around the pickup zone to guide the helicopter in.

"Let's get you prepped," Quinn said, leading me to an area in the center of the PZ. "You'll want to put your coat and gloves back on. It's going to be cold."

I untied my jacket and put it on, followed by the gloves. "What do I do once the helo picks me up?"

"When the bird's in position over you, they'll drop a rope, which I'll attach to your rig by these snap links." He pointed to two metal carabineers on the harness. "There'll be a pretty good rotor wash coming down from the blades, so be prepared for that. Once you're connected, the bird will pull you straight up. As you're lifted into the air, extend your arms and legs in a spread-eagle position, otherwise you'll wobble. You'll be flying fast, so it'll be over before you know it."

"Easy for you to say," I shot back. Apparently my nerves were showing.

"I'm not going to lie to you," he said. "It'll feel like your crotch is being pulled into your chest. As soon as you've cleared the trees, the helo will move forward and pick up speed. The sensation's going to be different than the HALO because you're vertical. You'll also be able to see the terrain rushing by below you."

"Sounds awesome." It was possible I meant to be that sarcastic.

"Just before you reach the drop zone," he continued, ignoring my remark, "the bird will slow down and terminate at a hover, gradually descending until you're on the ground. As soon as you touch down, run out to one side so the helo can land. Don't worry about the rope. One of my guys will be there to unhook you, and you can board the aircraft."

And end up at Anaya's compound, where I would probably be killed for sure, instead of just scared to death.

After checking my harness connections and running through the instructions one more time, Quinn dug into a pocket and pulled out two energy bars, offering one to me.

"Thanks," I said, peeling the wrapper off. We each ate a bar in silence, watching the other commandos attend to their tasks as we waited for the helicopter.

"Can I ask you something?" I said. Quinn nodded. "What's your next move? After this, I mean. Are you going to stay in the Yucatán and continue to fight Morales?"

"Yeah. It's what I do. Why?"

"I don't know. I'm just curious. I read an article not long ago about some homegrown vigilantes doing the same thing as you and your group, and thought you'd be a great candidate to train some of them. You've got the experience. You're fluent in Spanish. You understand the dynamics of the situation." I paused, searching for the right words. "A lot of these groups have had a hard time defending themselves from the government not to mention being infiltrated by the local cartels. If you trained them like you've trained these guys, just think how effective that movement could be—how far it could reach. Instead of just you and these guys—" I glanced at the others. "It would be you and your guys, and then more and more groups. It could grow exponentially."

Quinn watched me with a look of wry amusement. "What makes you think that isn't already happening?"

"Oh." I arched an eyebrow. "You're already way ahead of me, huh?"

Quinn gave me an enigmatic smile. "You sound kind of excited by the prospect." He gazed into the distance before turning his attention back to me. "Why don't you stay?"

His eyes burned with an intensity I hadn't seen before. Uncomfortable with his scrutiny, I shifted my position, not sure how to respond. *Say something, Kate. He's not one to put himself out there like that.*

"If I get out of this alive I might just take you up on that."

A mask slipped across his face as he nodded.

Before I could say anything else, the sound of the helicopter broke through the still night air. A speck of light appeared in the distance, growing larger.

"Ready?" Quinn asked.

"You keep asking me that, and I'm gonna keep telling you no," I said, annoyed at the thought of having to leave the safety of the commandos.

A few minutes later, the helo flew overhead, hovered above us, and then rotated 180 degrees. Quinn hadn't been kidding—the rotors kicked up a lot of dust and sand. I kept my lips clamped shut so I wouldn't eat dirt.

"You'll be fine," Quinn yelled into my ear. He signaled the pilot and the rope snaked down, and he and another guy and I ran forward to meet it. Quinn grabbed the end and connected the rope to my harness. Both Quinn and the other commando backed away and motioned to the pilot. I leaned my head back and watched as the chopper rose and the rope straightened out, growing taut. The harness squeezed my legs as I stood on tiptoe and danced along the ground. The next thing I knew, both feet left terra firma and I'd levitated above Quinn and the others.

Adrenaline shot through me. My heart beat faster the higher I climbed, and my breath came in short bursts.

I closed my eyes.

Relax, Kate. Lots of people have done this before. Quinn wouldn't have suggested you do this if it weren't safe. The rope will hold.

I opened my eyes to slits and glanced down. The strobes at the pickup zone resembled blinking lights on a video game. *Holy crap.* How high did we have to go?

I must have been telepathically connected to the pilot, because the helicopter paused in its ascent and then moved forward. We picked up speed, and soon I felt like I was flying down a freeway at ninety miles an hour without a car.

The riverbed rushed by beneath me and I took a quick peek below, sending me into a wobble where I came close to losing control. Terrified that I'd finish the flight upside down, I tried to straighten out with no success before I remembered to spread my arms and legs. Within seconds my body stabilized.

What if I hit something? Heart in my throat, I tried to calm myself by imagining Mary Poppins. But this wasn't a beloved Disney movie, and I sure as hell wasn't a magic nanny. Give me a gunman with an AK-47 any day.

And oh, holy Jesus, it was cold. Teeth-chatteringly, mind-numbingly, January-in-Northern-Minnesota cold. You'd think flying above the desert floor the air would be balmy.

Not so much.

We left the riverbed and turned northwest. The rocks and trees rushing by below freaked me out, so I closed my eyes, opening them again a second later. Apparently, I'd rather see what I was going to hit.

After what seemed like an hour but was probably more like five minutes, the helicopter slowed as we approached the blinking lights of the second drop zone. My teeth chattering as much from fear as the cold, I reminded myself to get out of the way as soon as my feet hit the ground.

How the hell am I even going to be able to walk? If my knees hadn't turned to pudding from fear, then I assumed my circulation had been cut off by the boa constrictor death squeeze the harness had on my thighs.

Well, then you'll have to crawl, Kate.

I really hated the smartass who lived in my head.

The pilot hovered above the blinking strobe lights for a moment and then began to descend. I watched the ground come closer, and sighed with relief as my feet hit dirt. One of the commandos rushed to my side, grabbed my arm, and helped me out of the way of the descending helo. Two more guys waved the pilot in and the aircraft landed. They ran to the open side door and unhooked the rope.

Out of breath, I mouthed "thanks" to the commando who had now unclipped my harness.

He guided me back to the helicopter and helped me climb in. "Good luck, Kate," he yelled.

I was going to need it.

35

WE TOUCHED DOWN a few kilometers south of the Santa Rita airport with a little over two hours to spare. I didn't know how I'd get inside the terminal without Anaya's people seeing me, but I'd figure that out when I got there. Hopefully, I'd be earlier than they were.

The pilot and the other commando gave me a thumbs up through the windshield and then lifted off in a flurry of dust. I lowered my head and closed my eyes against the downdraft of the helicopter blades, the fear returning as I watched them leave.

I was on my own.

With a deep breath I shook it off and struck out for town on foot. The day hung hot and dry, the slight breeze not quite brisk enough to keep the annoying flies at bay. *Better dry than soaking wet from the cloying humidity,* I thought. Besides, I knew the desert—knew the dangers of not taking water along, of uncovered arms or legs or scalp blistering in the searing hot sun, of heat stroke hitting when you least expected it.

Of deadly snakes and stinging scorpions.

Maybe it wasn't comfortable, but it was familiar.

For the first time since Angie had tracked me to Seattle it looked like things might work out. The possibility of discovery had kept me wary, and I hadn't dared hope for a positive outcome. Now that our group had successfully made it back to the ORP without detection and I was almost to the airport, I finally allowed myself a spark of hope.

Twenty minutes later I reached the road leading to the main terminal. A woman walking alone, especially an American, would stick out, so I skirted the roadway, hiding behind creosote bushes and straggly mesquite trees. I'd still be more than an hour and a half early for the flight from Phoenix. I assumed Anaya's people weren't interested in sitting around for an hour or two, waiting for my plane to land.

The whitewashed concrete terminal looked as worn as the dehydrated plantings that surrounded it. An empty grocery bag struggled to break free of the sharp branches of a brittlebush, the hot, gentle breeze teasing it one way, then another. There were few cars parked in the lot. I imagined most belonged to employees, as there didn't appear to be many travelers around.

After loitering outside and checking to make sure no one lurked in any of the vehicles in the lot, I slipped inside the terminal.

A dark-haired man dressed in a tan work shirt and pants pushed a wheeled rubber garbage can across the floor. Two attractive young women wearing identical navy blue blazers with matching yellow and blue neck scarves chatted with each other behind a counter. A bored security guard leaned into the conversation, flirting with the women. No one gave me a second look. I glanced at the schedule to make sure the flight from Phoenix was on time. It was.

Canned elevator music floated through the air-conditioned space as I headed for the rear of the terminal. Immigration and customs were concealed behind a divider and not immediately visible from the lobby, making my job easier. The sign to the ladies' room hung behind me and to my left, next to a duty-free store with half-empty shelves. I still had over an hour until the flight from Phoenix arrived. Fearing discovery in case one of Anaya's thugs showed up early, I walked to the women's bathroom and went inside.

With a sigh, I stepped up to the sink and checked myself in the mirror. The effect of the STABO ride under the belly of the helicopter wasn't a good look for me. Windswept would have been too tame a word to describe the bird's nest my hair had become. Finger combing helped, sort of. But then I wondered why I cared. Who did I want to impress? Anaya's gunmen?

I washed the grime from my face and arms and used paper towels to dry off. I'd removed the polypropylene underclothes onboard the chopper and left them with the pilot. Anaya's people would probably question my attire if I showed up overdressed.

The probability of their restraining me for the flight to the compound was high. And, there wouldn't be a lot of time once we touched down. Anaya would have his minions extract the website address and password as soon as possible, then kill me. The look on Quinn's face as we planned my actions told me my hope that Anaya would let the kids go was pure fantasy. Deep down I'd known but hadn't wanted to face the possibility. Lying to myself came easily. My default when things got scary.

I couldn't lie anymore.

If Quinn's men weren't able to breach the compound or Anaya's people got the drop on them, Anaya could conceivably keep Lauren and Abby alive and sell them to sex traffickers or traffick them himself. That was the best-case scenario. Worst-case—again, I stopped myself from going down that road. Neither situation involved me staying alive.

This is going to work, Kate. It has to. There's too much at stake.

Unable to suppress a feeling of impending doom, I walked into one of the stalls, closed the door behind me, and sat down to wait.

"Am I ever glad to be on the ground." The young woman in the bathroom sounded relieved.

"I'd never been on a plane with so much turbulence before," her friend answered. "I would have stayed in Phoenix."

I walked out of the stall, smiling at the one waiting to use the toilet as I stopped at the sink to wash my hands.

"Was the flight very full?" I asked in Spanish.

The woman laughed as she nodded. "With only one a day from the US the flight is almost always full."

Just what I needed to hear.

With clammy palms, I slipped out the door and scanned the lobby for one of Anaya's gunmen.

He wasn't hard to spot.

Dressed in all black with dark sunglasses and a dark attitude, the man waited near the door, arms crossed, looking over the crowd. Somewhere around six feet tall, he had on a loose, short-sleeved shirt, perfect for concealing a gun. Tattoos covered both forearms, and he had what looked like a knife scar on his left cheek. The stream of travelers parted and flowed past on either side, giving the *narco* a wide berth.

Ignoring the other passengers and my shaking hands, I walked up to him and said, "I'm Kate. I believe you're my ride?" He looked much scarier up close.

If I'd surprised him, he didn't let on. He nodded and we headed through the door and out to the parking lot. After the air-conditioned terminal, being outside felt like walking into a furnace. Curious onlookers watched us with covert stares, but no one got too close. I didn't blame them.

"Aren't we flying?" I asked, knowing full well I wouldn't receive an answer but wanting to establish some kind of rapport.

It might come in handy later, when he tried to kill me.

As we neared a white SUV with darkened windows, two more men dressed in black materialized and grouped nearby, observing the parking lot as they moved toward the vehicle. Scary Face handed me off to a different man with a heavy gold chain around his neck, and climbed in the driver's seat. The third man wore a bulky jacket, which looked odd considering the temperature hovered somewhere between blisteringly hot and hellfire. With one last glance at the lot, he slid into the front passenger seat while Gold Chain and I got in the back.

As soon as the doors closed, Gold Chain grabbed my wrist, pulling it toward him. "Turn around," he grunted. I did and he lassoed both my hands with a plastic zip tie, cinching it tight.

"Does it have to be that tight? Remember, I came here on my own. It's not like I'm going to try to overpower the three of you. I'm not that stupid. Or strong."

Gold Chain ignored me.

The gunman in the front removed his jacket and set it aside, revealing a shoulder holster with a semiautomatic. A submachine gun, modified to fit underneath his coat, and a wicked-looking knife rounded out his private arsenal.

We drove out of the airport and along the main highway, passing by dozens of rusty corrugated steel shacks along the side of the road, crisscrossed by clotheslines heavy with laundry. A malnourished mule, its ribs poking through dun-colored skin, munched lazily on brown grass, separated from the roadway by a rickety wooden fence. A man wearing huaraches on a bicycle and carrying a large bundle on his handlebars trundled along the side of the road, his clothes dark with sweat.

I leaned back, trying to get comfortable, and wondered at the gaping financial divide between the *narcos* and regular Mexican citizens. Choices weighed heavily in these parts. As if to underscore my thoughts, we passed a bright yellow shrine filled with colorful silk flowers and a painting of a saint, designating the spot where someone had been taken from this world too soon.

A few kilometers later, the driver slowed and turned onto a dirt road. We continued for another kilometer or so, and turned into what appeared to be a driveway.

A large, corrugated metal building loomed in the distance, although this one didn't look rusty. In fact, it was downright pristine. A red and white Cessna stood next to the hangar. We parked in front and both Scary Face and Arsenal Guy got out and walked over to the airplane.

"I'd have expected Vincent to send his personal jet," I said to Gold Chain. "I mean, we *are* old friends."

Gold Chain snorted as he exited the vehicle, walked around to my side, and opened the door. "Get out, *puta*."

"Never heard *that* before," I mumbled, unable to keep the sarcasm from my voice. You'd think he'd come up with something a little more original than *puta*. But, maybe I was giving him too much credit. I doubted a strong vocabulary had been a requirement when applying for a job with Anaya. I climbed out of the SUV, and he took me by the arm, guiding me into the hangar. We stopped next to a bench with a pile of clothes.

"Put these on. Leave what you're wearing here," he ordered.

I looked around the hangar for some place to change.

"Do it now, *puta*. You think I'm gonna find you a fucking changing room?" His laughter reminded me of the donkey by the side of the road.

He cut the tie around my wrists. I kicked off my boots, stripped out of my T-shirt and jeans, and reached for the clothes. Gold Chain shook his head.

"Not so fast. I'm supposed to make sure you're not wearing a wire. Take it all off."

Inwardly cringing, I unhooked my bra and stepped out of my panties as he watched. His gaze dropped as he stared at my breasts and traveled lower. I resisted the urge to cover myself and turned, hands on hips, so he could get the full view. I wasn't about to give him the satisfaction of humiliating me.

"Can I get dressed now?" I asked. He took his time answering.

"Hurry up, man," Arsenal Guy called to him, pointing at his watch. With a grunt, Gold Chain backed off, and I

quickly donned the clothes, glad I'd left my jaguar necklace with the helicopter pilot.

The sweatpants were a men's large, and I had to cinch up the cord. I swam in the extra-large, long-sleeved shirt and had to push the sleeves to my elbows so they didn't completely cover my hands. A pair of cheap, hot-pink flip-flops completed the ensemble.

"Turn around," Gold Chain ordered. I did as instructed and he viciously cinched another zip tie around my wrists.

Scary Face climbed into the Cessna while Arsenal Guy did a walk-around. Gold Chain grabbed my elbow and led me to the open door of the plane.

"Get in."

I climbed into the back and took one of the seats in the middle row. Arsenal Guy got in the front passenger seat. Gold Chain boarded last and closed the door, sitting in the seat next to mine. The three gunmen took up most of the space in the small aircraft. I was surprised when we easily lifted off the dirt runway. They weren't svelte.

The plane smelled of fuel, but was otherwise clean. I gazed out the window at the bleak landscape and wondered what Quinn and his commandos were doing now.

This has to work, I thought. The girls had to get away safely and go back home to Cole. They deserved to live good lives, with school, and friends, and dates, and first jobs. A chance to meet the special people who made their hearts flutter with excitement. Their last memories couldn't be of Anaya and his thugs.

Gold Chain sat next to me and stared, his intent obvious. Uneasy, I tried to ignore him by watching the dry, unforgiving desert fall away as the Cessna climbed higher.

And wondered if I'd be coming back.

36

WE FLEW OVER an expanse of uninhabited, rocky desert and the rugged mountains of the Sierra Madre, turned north and followed what I assumed to be the Yaqui River. By the position of the sun I estimated the time to be close to three in the afternoon. I hoped Quinn and his men had been able to get some rest.

I also hoped they hadn't run into any trouble. Quinn had assured me he'd planned for every contingency, calling the worst-case scenario his ETS plan, or Everything goes To Shit plan. It didn't do much for the anxiety roiling in my stomach, but I doubted anything short of being back in the US with Cole's kids would alleviate that.

Neither of the gunmen was very talkative. Arsenal Man kept nodding off and Gold Chain poked him awake with his foot more than once. It would have been comical, except the closer we got to Anaya's the more anxious I became.

Stay calm, Kate. Quinn has everything under control. The girls are going to be fine.

I stared out the window, trying not to think. Inevitably, the landscape began to look familiar. Dread pooled in my stomach as I recognized the section of river below us. The plane dropped in altitude, flying low over the rocky terrain as Scary Face set up for his approach. The ersatz runway stretched along the river to our left. To our right, the compound slid into view. In daylight, it looked remarkably similar to when I'd been there a decade before: same two-story hacienda with matching verandas on the upper and lower floors, same servant's quarters, same fountain.

We dropped again and landed, taxiing to a stop a few minutes later. Arsenal Guy snorted awake after Gold Chain jabbed him in the ribs with the toe of his boot. He shook his head, rubbing his face with his hand, and then exited via the passenger door. Gold Chain opened the side door and climbed out next.

"Get out," he ordered.

Hands still tied behind me and completely numb, I scuttled forward and jumped onto the shore. The high humidity near the river stood in direct contrast to the dry sand and gravel beneath my feet. Late afternoon shadows provided little shade, and a ferocious sun beat down on my neck and head. My mouth tasted like someone had stuffed flannel in my cheeks, although I wasn't sure if that was because I was dehydrated or just terrified.

Scary Face hopped out of the cockpit and walked to an inflatable boat beached on the shore.

"Let's go." Gold Chain pushed me toward the boat and everyone but Arsenal Guy climbed aboard. He gave his MP5 to Scary Face and threw his considerable girth against the hull, shoving the boat into the waterway. He jumped in at the last minute and took a seat near the stern. Scary Face started the outboard and steered us into the middle of the river. The current appeared strong but was no match for the motor. A few minutes later we crossed the Yaqui and entered the mouth of the intermittent river, headed for the dock.

A man with an AK-47 slung over his shoulder met us as we docked. He caught the mooring line Arsenal Guy threw him and tied it off to a metal cleat. Gold Chain told me to stand and pushed me toward the metal ladder.

"Listen, I've tried climbing up ladders with my hands tied behind my back. It doesn't work well. If you don't want me to fall in and drown, I suggest you cut my hands free."

Without a word, Gold Chain bent over, grabbed me by the back of the legs and threw me over his shoulder. He climbed up the ladder, depositing me onto the dock like I weighed nothing.

I'd have to figure out another way to get them to cut my hands free.

Scary Face led the way through the large double doors, escorting us into the compound. Another gunman swung the doors closed behind us, slamming them shut with the finality of a prison cell. The enormous fountain in the middle of the courtyard gurgled and splashed, echoing against the stucco walls. A beetle crawled by us on the ground, oblivious to the drama being played out overhead. Birds called to each other. Everything appeared calm and serene.

A stark contrast to my erratic heartbeat and cold fear.

"Where's Anaya?" I asked, wondering if he was even in Mexico. "I thought he'd at least grace us with his presence."

I didn't get a reply. They'd avoided any kind of dialogue other than commands and instructions. It would be so much easier to kill someone you didn't think of as a person.

As we neared the hacienda, another man carrying a machinegun and a surly attitude appeared. Gold Chain handed me over to him. Before letting me go, he leaned in close to my ear.

"See you later, *puta.*"

"Not if I'm dead, *cabrone,*" I whispered back.

"Especially then," he answered, a sadistic grin on his face.

"This way," the surly one said, practically wrenching my arm from its socket. The tiny beetle scuttled away, narrowly missing death by snakeskin boot as the gunman dragged me past the gaudy, gold-plated fountain into the hacienda.

The thick walls absorbed most of the scorching hot rays of the sun, providing welcome relief from the oppressive heat. As my eyes adjusted to the dimly lit interior, I recognized many of the paintings on the wall from my earlier visits over a decade before: a formal portrait of Anaya, complete with parade sash and the helmet of a Spanish conquistador in the crook of his arm; a dramatic study of a magnificent horse with Anaya sitting astride in jodhpurs and knee boots; a formidable oil of his mother, a wholly unhandsome woman wearing a black lace dress and a Machiavellian smile. Stately banners of purple and white hung draped between paintings, each with a gold crest stamped in the center. An imposing wrought iron chandelier dangled overhead; on the floor, thick carpets covered the Saltillo tile. A sweeping stairway led to the second level, its risers faced in colorful Talavera tiles.

"I see Vincent is still a man of Napoleonic taste," I quipped, trying to hide my growing fear.

Don't start, Kate. You're in some serious shit right now. I bit the inside of my cheek to keep myself from saying something sarcastic before I screwed up my chances of ever seeing the kids.

Or staying alive.

The surly guard pushed me toward the staircase. "*Vamanos,*" he grunted.

I balked. This wasn't according to plan. The safe room was on the main floor. *How is Quinn going to know where we are?* Surly prodded me with his gun. I had no choice but to move.

We hit the first step, and I could feel my chest constrict and my throat close as I began to hyperventilate. Asking to relocate would raise the alarm. I had to calm down and play along. I willed myself to relax and breathe normally. Quinn and the rest of the commandos would have to be able to work things out on the fly. I trusted them. I had to.

We reached the second level and turned right, heading north down a long, dark hallway. At least we were moving in the right direction. The occasional wall sconce cast a dim glow as we passed by a number of dramatic landscape paintings, most depicting dark, angry clouds over stormy, windswept seas. We passed by a Rococo period hall table with an enormous flower arrangement against the wall to our left and several closed doors. Surly stopped at the second to last one, opened the door, and shoved me inside.

The richly appointed room boasted heavy, masculine furniture and yet another humongous portrait of Anaya—in this one he leaned against a red Ferrari in the shade of a massive tree, smoking a cigar. A buxom brunette wearing a clingy dress, huge diamonds, and way too much makeup clung to his bicep. The painting occupied most of the back wall.

"Sit." Surly pushed me toward one of two leather chairs in front of a massive wood desk.

Panicked, my mind spun in circles, trying to figure out a way to signal Fernando or Buck. Flanked by velvet curtains, the room's lone window faced west. The setting sun cast an orange glow across the red tile floor. *Would they see me if I stood at the window?*

"What a view," I said as I changed direction and headed for it, but Surly grabbed my arm and dragged me back to the desk.

"You're not here for the view." He sneered as he thrust me into the nearest chair.

Two cameras had been mounted near the ceiling on each side of the desk and were pointed at the chairs. I assumed Anaya would view the meeting remotely. An iPad with a separate keyboard sat in the center of the desk.

"Where are the girls?" I asked. "I won't give you any information until I know that they're still alive."

He didn't reply.

"Would you mind cutting my hands free? I can't feel my fingers."

Again, no answer.

The odor of dead vermin wafted past me and I turned in the chair to see what the hell the guard had let into the room. My heart dropped to my stomach when I saw Toothless Bob standing in the doorway, an evil grin splitting his obnoxious face. Actually, evil may have been a misnomer. He reminded me of one of those jack-o-lanterns kids carve at Halloween. The ones with three teeth.

"Nice to see you, Bob," I said. "I wondered where you were. I've missed you so."

Bob walked up to me and, closing his fist, punched me so hard on the side of the head I saw stars.

"That's for the yacht, bitch," he said, his face contorted in what might have passed for a satisfied smile.

"Damn, Bob. That hurt." I squeezed my eyes shut and shook my head to stop the ringing, but abandoned the idea when the nausea hit. Thankfully, I didn't feel any blood on the side of my face.

"Good. That's just the beginning."

Can't wait, I thought. Going mute would probably be advisable. No sense pissing him off more than he already was.

"You'd better leave her alone or you'll be sorry, *cabrone*," the other one mumbled to Bob.

Yeah. You tell him, Surly. Although, I'd like to have seen Bob on the sharp end of sorry.

The minutes ticked by in silence, and when I began to wonder what was taking so long, the door opened behind us.

"I thought you were dead." Anaya's smooth, cultured voice preceded him. "Apparently, my sources were wrong."

He walked to the desk and sat down facing me. Aware that my mouth was open, I snapped it closed.

"I see you weren't expecting me." His broad smile revealed a gold incisor. He sighed and shook his head. "Never send a lackey for such important things. What is that old saying? Good help is always so hard to find."

The smell of expensive aftershave permeated the room. It almost made up for Toothless Bob. Anaya looked tan and fit, as though he'd just come back from a restful vacation. Apparently, he'd been dying his hair jet black. The last time I'd seen him, there'd been a touch of gray at the temples. Now, not so much.

He wore a shoulder holster with a semiautomatic over an expensive-looking button-down shirt, and either he'd eaten a lot of tamales since I'd last seen him, or he was wearing body armor.

"Where are the girls, Anaya?" I asked. The determination in my voice surprised me.

"Not so fast." He leaned back, hands behind his head. "I want to enjoy this. You're such a slippery target. It's nice to know I'll be able to tie up loose ends. Unlike *some* people I know," he added, annoyance thick in his voice.

"Angie?" I asked. If he'd gotten rid of her, that would be one less worry for Quinn and the others.

He waved his hand in the air, dismissing the assassin. "She went back to whatever hell-hole she came from. Some godforsaken part of the US, I think." He sniffed. "She had her chance to redeem herself for letting you get away in Alaska and failed. I would have killed her, but for some reason she came highly recommended and they wanted her back. I can't imagine why. Although," he said as he brought his gaze to mine, "she did have particularly good taste in clothing."

"May I remind you, Vincent, that you dressed me for the occasion."

The faux-conviviality vanished, replaced by a malicious smile. "What you're wearing hardly matters." His meaning wasn't lost on me.

"Where are the girls?" I asked again, hoping he hadn't noticed the tremor in my voice.

"Give me the website address and the password first. Then you can see the girls."

I smiled, surprised my lips slid over my teeth so easily, what with the dearth of saliva in my mouth. "Not until I see Lauren and Abby. I need your word that you'll let them go free—and not in the desert to die of exposure. I want your promise that you'll take them somewhere safe so they can go back to their father in Arizona." Not that his word meant a lot.

Anaya's face darkened. People didn't dictate to Vincent Anaya. Scared though I might have been, I had nothing to lose and everything to gain by affecting a tough stance. He'd keep me alive until my value dropped, which would be a split-second after I told him the information. Plus, I had to prolong the conversation to give Quinn and the others more time.

If they were coming.

His face split into a grin. "I know what you're doing, you sneaky little *puta*," he said, wagging his finger at me. "You believe you're going to die anyway, so why not hold out for whatever concessions you can, eh?" The smile vanished. He glanced at Surly. "Bring them here."

Surly left the room, and another gunman stepped in to take his place. An awkward silence yawned between us. Anaya drummed his fingers on the desk as we waited.

"Since you're going to kill me anyway, mind if I ask what the big deal is with the website? I mean, I'm going to lose my life over it. I think I deserve an explanation." Couldn't hurt to ask, right?

That made him laugh. Not the response I was looking for.

When he'd finished wiping the tears from his eyes, he shook his head. "You haven't changed, have you? I remember Roberto—" His eyes grew cold at the mention of his old business partner, and he flexed his hand, curling it into a fist.

He's still angry because Salazar betrayed him, I thought. I doubted word of my killing Roberto had filtered back to him yet. No one knew except Luis, Quinn, and Pascal.

"Roberto used to joke about your impertinent American attitude," he continued. "He quite enjoyed it, at first. But by the end he found it tiresome. I'd never seen him so angry as when you left him and took the money. Still, he loved you, which he demonstrated by not sending someone to kill you while he rotted in prison. Only women we care for can make us show such restraint."

I was about to add my thoughts on Salazar's twisted idea of love but thought it prudent to keep them to myself.

"I take it you're not going to tell me," I said. Anaya cracked a smile at the droll delivery.

"See? There you go again. Such sarcasm. I'm almost sorry you'll be dead soon. I might like to have you around to keep my spirits up. My security detail is sorely lacking in that regard." He shot a dark look at the guard holding a gun to my head.

Just what I needed—a job as a comedian to a vicious psychopath. Didn't court jesters wind up dead if they failed to please the king?

"Then again, I'm not sure I could trust you." Anaya's eyes once again grew cold, and his voice dripped menace. "If you can murder a man you once loved, you're capable of anything."

37

W HAT ARE YOU talking about?" Cold fear snaked up the back of my neck, nestling just behind my skull.

How does he know? Before I could process the information, something moved behind me. Anaya's gaze shifted to the hallway.

"Ah. Here they are. And they're doing just fine, aren't you, my little puppies?" he said, his voice sickly sweet.

"Kate!" Abby's plaintive wail pierced my heart as I swiveled in my chair. Lauren's hopeful expression faded when she saw my hands tied behind my back. *Smart kid,* I thought.

They both looked pale and wan and thinner than I remembered, even though it had only been days since I'd seen them last. No longer wearing their nightgowns, they had on brightly colored T-shirts and shorts and each wore a pair of sparkly pink jelly shoes. Dark circles ringed their eyes and their hair hadn't been properly brushed, but otherwise they appeared unhurt.

I turned back to Anaya. Affecting a conciliatory tone, I asked, "One last request? Cut my hands free so I can hug them." He glanced at the girls and back at me. I had to get to that window. "Please," I added.

"I don't think so," he replied.

"Then you're going to have to kill me. Cut my hands free, or you'll never get the information." The voice inside my head screamed that I shouldn't demand anything from Vincent-freaking-Anaya, but my tongue wouldn't listen. I stared back at him, defiant. *What the hell*, I thought. I'd be dead soon.

The air in the room stilled. The guards grew quiet.

Would he kill me right here, in front of Lauren and Abby?

He slammed his fist on the desk and I winced. Abby started to cry. Anaya's eyes bulged with anger as he stood up from his chair and took a step toward me, breathing hard.

You may have gone too far this time, Kate. It seemed to be a pattern. I braced myself for whatever came next. Part of me watched, fascinated, as Anaya tried to wrestle himself under control. His face had turned a deep shade of red and his hands shook. After a few moments, he closed his eyes, took a deep breath, and let it go. With a curt nod at the gunman he said, "Cut her free, but keep your gun handy."

The gunman cut the plastic tie and I leapt out of the chair and ran to the girls, wrapping them in as big a hug as I could manage. They both melted into the embrace, hugging me back and crying, their tears soaking my shirt.

I pressed my mouth to Lauren's ear and whispered, "Take your sister and go stand by the window." *Buck and Fernando have to see them*, I thought. It was the only way.

"Enough," Anaya snarled.

Reluctantly, I released my hold on them and stood, angling my body so that Anaya couldn't see Lauren's gaze dart from the window back to me. I lifted my chin a fraction of an inch, praying she'd do what I asked. With a protective arm around Abby, she took a tentative step toward the window. I pivoted to face Anaya and wiped at the tears on my cheeks, obscuring his view of the girls.

"Give me the information. *Now.*" Anaya's gaze pierced through me. I had to keep stalling, give Quinn's people time to find us.

I paused, pretending to search my memory.

"Your commandos aren't coming," he said.

Startled, I stared at the grim triumph on his face, not understanding. *How did he know about Quinn?* My brain slowed as I came to grips with what he'd said. Luis had promised to keep things quiet, assuring me he wouldn't let anyone under his command know. Had Quinn and his team been caught? How could it have happened? I closed my eyes.

"That's right. I know about them tracking you."

He doesn't know they're here. I opened my eyes. My despair vanished, replaced by determination.

"You really shouldn't have enlisted their help. Now, you'll be responsible for their deaths, too." He shook his head. "You're just a walking disaster, aren't you? Everyone you come into contact with dies, don't they?" A lethal glint flared in his eyes. "*Give me the information,*" he repeated through clenched teeth.

"I'm trying to remember."

Fury contorting his face, Anaya yanked the gun from his shoulder holster, vaulted out of his chair and crossed to the window in two strides. He seized Abby by the hair and dragged her away from Lauren, shoving the barrel against her temple. Lauren screamed. Little Abby's face blanched white and her lips trembled as she hiccupped between sobs.

My god. No.

"Stop!" My voice cracked as I recited the web address and password from memory, tears streaming down my cheeks.

"Write it down," Anaya commanded over the girls' wails.

My hand shook as I picked up a pen from the desk and proceeded to write the information on a notepad.

"There." I slid the paper toward him and straightened. White-hot anger mixed with terror for the girls boiled in my stomach. The voice in my head screamed at me to do something, anything to stop him.

Anaya released Abby and lowered his gun. Lauren ran to her little sister and threw her arms around her. I released my breath in a whoosh and leaned over, gripping the edge of the desk.

He walked back as if nothing had happened and opened a side drawer to retrieve a pair of reading glasses, which he calmly put on. He sat down, reached into his shirt pocket, and removed a business card, placing it next to the pad of paper. Hands on the keyboard and eyes focused on the notepad and card, he typed the information into the tablet and waited. A few seconds later, the screen populated with columns of data, followed by several paragraphs of text.

My position only allowed a partial view of the screen, and I couldn't make out the details. Anaya scanned the information, scrolling down as he read. His expression morphed from intense focus to a puzzled frown and then surprise. He leaned back, staring at the screen.

I didn't move, didn't speak, didn't dare breathe, hoping he'd forgotten I was there. My mind screamed at me to go to the girls, but I remained where I was. He'd kill me next. I didn't want to be near them when he did. They'd been through enough. At least for the moment, my death had taken a back seat to the information on the screen.

"You asked me earlier what was so important about the information you had." He faced me, his eyes dark. "You have no idea what this means. I'd never have suspected." He swiveled back to the screen, shaking his head. "They will all answer to Vincent Anaya when I'm finished," he muttered to himself.

At that moment, a muffled *pop!* came from outside the hallway. The guard nearest to me grunted, dropped his weapon, and crumpled to the floor. At the same time, a metal canister flew into the room, detonating in midair with a blinding flash. The girls screamed and I lunged, pulling them to me as the stun grenade went off. Less than a split-second later, two more *pops* came in rapid succession and Toothless fell, his head a gory mess. Anaya disappeared under the desk, clutching the iPad.

Ears ringing and eyes closed against the smoke, I hugged the girls tight as the commandos swarmed the room.

"Hold on to me." Quinn's muffled voice broke through the chaos. He guided my hand to his belt as he hoisted Lauren into his arms. Abby had her hands over her ears and her little eyes squeezed tight as I lifted her and held her to me.

Quinn led me to the doorway and stopped. Barely able to see, I narrowed my eyes to slits and watched as he peered around the jamb, and indicated the hall was clear.

"Hawk coming out!" he yelled. With Lauren in his arms, he slipped out of the office. Abby and I followed close behind as we raced down the hall.

Daria and another commando ran in front of us to clear the way. We reached the second floor landing and froze. Several of Anaya's gunmen had made it halfway up the stairs. Daria and Quinn's other guy raised their weapons and fired, dropping the men where they stood. Abby lifted her head to see what was going on, but I covered her eyes with my hand.

"Don't look, honey. It'll be over soon," I murmured in her ear. She burrowed her face into my neck, her cheeks wet with tears.

We raced down the stairs, picking our way over the bodies, and paused at the bottom until Daria gave us the all-clear.

The two commandos followed us down the dark hallway to the larger office where Anaya had installed the safe room. Quinn reached the door first and flung it open. I sprinted past with Abby and entered the closet-sized room. Quinn and Lauren followed close behind.

The entrance to the tunnel lay at the far end of the space. The sound of gunfire erupted in the hallway behind us.

"Kate," Quinn called out. I turned. He set Lauren down and pushed her toward me.

"Go!" he shouted as he slid his sidearm free and turned back toward the fight.

Holding Abby with one arm, I grabbed Lauren's hand with the other, and the three of us raced into the concrete tunnel.

The murky passage stretched before us. Every few yards a cage light glowed, guiding our steps through the musty-smelling concrete walkway. I sighed with relief when I caught sight of Buck standing at the end near the section leading up to the hatch. We sprinted toward his outstretched arms.

"Climb the ladder, Lauren," I said, breathless.

Buck lifted her onto the first rung. Another of Quinn's men peered down from above, arms extended. Lauren nodded and scrambled up the rungs where he took her by the arms and lifted her out.

"You got it?" Buck asked.

"Yeah," I answered. Abby had her arms wrapped around my neck with her face pressed into my chest.

"Abby, honey, you need to hold on tight, okay?" I said. She nodded, her face never leaving my chest. I grabbed the nearest rung and stepped onto the ladder, hoisting us up, one step at a time. As we neared the top, the commando reached down and lifted Abby out while I climbed the rest of the way.

Several of Quinn's team were in position outside the hatch, pulling security while waiting for the others to emerge. Fernando smiled at Abby and Lauren, climbed through the hatch, and disappeared, on his way to booby-trap the tunnel. Abby ran over and threw her arms around my legs. Gently, I pried her free and swung her up into my arms. Buck's head appeared at the hatch opening a minute later. He climbed out and walked to where the girls and I stood.

"I'll take you to the rallying point," Buck said, his eyes on Lauren. "Young lady, are you ready to go on a hike?" he asked.

Lauren nodded. "Yes," she said, her voice small.

Buck's expression softened even more. He'd morphed into someone I wasn't familiar with. I tried to think of a name to describe him. *Uncle Buck? Mr. Nice Guy?*

"If you get tired, you just let me know, okay? It's kind of a long way."

"Okay," Lauren replied.

Tears coursed down Abby's face and dripped from her chin.

"Don't cry," Buck soothed. "You'll be with your daddy soon." Abby pulled in a ragged breath and hiccupped.

"Hand her to me when your adrenaline crashes," Buck said in a low voice. I nodded, giving him a grateful smile. The way I was feeling, it wouldn't be long.

With Buck in the lead, we ran along the small rise toward the dry riverbed, on our way to safety.

38

WE REACHED THE rallying point without incident. The sound of intermittent gunfire behind us in the distance reminded me we'd left several of the assault team behind. Buck answered Lalo's challenge and he let us pass. Artemis padded over to greet us, tongue lolling from the heat. Lauren glanced at me to see if it was all right to pet her. I nodded. She put out a tentative hand, and Artemis moved closer and licked her face. Abby squirmed in my arms, and I set her down so she could pet the German Shepherd, too. Loaded up and ready to go, Lalo and Hector joined us, anxious to find out how things went.

"Anaya put me in the wrong room, but Quinn and the others found it." I searched the shadows behind me. Darkness had fallen and I couldn't see much.

"Did anybody smoke Anaya?" Lalo asked.

"I didn't see his body, so I can't say for sure." I'd learned the hard way to never assume a person was dead unless you had verification.

Buck suggested we rest before continuing. I sat down on a rock near the dry riverbank with Abby in my lap. Lauren sat beside me. The sound of fighting became less pronounced as the minutes ticked by. The sun disappeared below the horizon and dusk turned into night.

Even though she had to be exhausted, Abby grew restless in my arms. I ran my hand through her hair and murmured in her ear, hoping to calm her. Buck noticed and walked over.

"How you doin', Abby?" he asked, squatting so he could look her in the eye.

Abby took a deep breath. "I want to go home," she said, a stern expression on her face.

"We're almost there, sweetie. But first, you get to go on a helicopter ride."

Lauren and Abby both perked up at the mention of the helicopter. Distracted for the moment, Abby gasped. She turned to me, her mouth a small O.

"We're going on a hellacopper?" she asked, her eyes wide.

"We are," I answered. I didn't think her little heart could beat any faster, but with the anticipation of seeing her father again, coupled with a ride in a helicopter and all the excitement she'd just been through, it galloped.

The two sisters looked at each other in surprise. I felt my shoulders inch away from my ears at the picture of two safe little girls.

Moments later, the distant clack of the belt-fed machinegun erupted behind us. Alarmed, I glanced at Buck. He shot to his feet. With Abby in my arms, I struggled to my feet, my heart pounding. Both the girls were quiet.

"Shit," Buck muttered. "The M-60. That means they're coming after us. Hector—" he called out. Hector sprinted over to see what he wanted. "Take Kate and the girls to the pickup zone. Call the bird when you get there." He turned to me. "Go with Hector. We'll be right behind you." He handed me a pair of NVGs, which I slid on.

Hector reached for Abby and, grateful, I handed her to him. Hector was stronger and well rested. His taking Abby would make it easier to cover more ground. I took Lauren by the hand and the four of us set off at a run toward the pickup zone.

"Trip wire," Hector warned and we approached the double Xs Quinn had used to mark the wire. We carefully skirted the trap and continued on. Someone would remove the markers on the way back in the off chance Anaya's gunmen forgot the mine was there.

"If his men are aware Anaya had been killed, why are they coming after us?"

"Too much confusion, probably. Word hasn't gotten back to them yet," Hector replied.

Or he's not dead, I thought.

Hector veered northwest, and we left the dry riverbed behind, heading up a small rise marked by a piece of glint tape. The terrain changed to scrub and desert trees and we picked our way through, careful to avoid holes in the ground where an ankle could twist.

We reached the perimeter of the pickup zone a short while later. One of the commandos from the security team materialized from behind a rock and issued a security challenge. Hector answered him and he stood aside.

Two commandos met us as we made our way to the center of the zone. Hector handed Abby to me and spoke into his headset, calling the pilot. The other two commandos set up the strobes in a Y pattern, separated by several yards. The five infrared lights pulsed in the darkness, ready to guide the helicopter in for a landing. I could see why Quinn had chosen the site: devoid of trees, the flat expanse of desert had a large area for landing the group of commandos as well as an aircraft.

Lauren and Abby stood next to me and we watched the others as they prepared for the pickup. I kept looking back the way we'd come, hoping to see the rest of the group, but saw only scrub.

I wondered what Anaya had meant when he'd told me I had no idea what the information signified. He'd grabbed the computer when the commandos showed up, but if he'd been killed then the information didn't matter anymore. Part of me wished I could have seen it. He'd been so surprised. The other part never wanted to have anything to do with Anaya, the cartels, or even Mexico, again.

One of the guys came over and handed me a radio transmitter. Thanking him, I slipped it over my ear in time to hear Quinn say, "ETA five mikes." I breathed a sigh of relief. He made it.

Several commandos came toward us from the southeast, with Quinn in front. I counted fourteen. With the three that were here, that left two unaccounted for. I scanned the group, trying to figure out who hadn't made it back yet. The only ones I didn't see were Buck and Fernando.

Quinn stopped and spoke to two of his men before he headed our way.

"What happened? Where are Buck and Fernando?" I asked.

"Anaya's forces came after us. Pascal and Carlos opened up on the compound, launching grenades and delaying them with sniper fire until we were able to move the M-60 to the ORP. Anaya's men followed, but we cut them down mid-assault. Buck stayed behind to cover Fernando while he booby-trapped the riverbed to catch anybody coming after us. They should be here in a few minutes."

"And Anaya? Why did his gunmen follow you? If they knew he'd been killed, they wouldn't have."

"They know now." Quinn scanned the rest of the group, found Daria, and got her attention. She ran over to see what he wanted.

"Daria confirmed the kill." Quinn nodded at her.

"Back of the head," Daria said. "I thought you might want a memento." She smiled as she reached in her ruck and pulled out Anaya's iPad, handing it to me. It looked intact. I stared at her, and at the tablet, speechless.

"Thank you," I managed.

"Any time, Kate. I'm glad we got the bastard."

"Thanks, Daria. That's all for now," Quinn said. Daria nodded and left to join the others.

I stared at the tablet in my hands. "Whatever it was that he accessed on the computer, it must have been huge. He doesn't surprise easily."

"Aren't you going to boot it up? The information is probably still on there. I doubt he had time to shut it down."

"How long until the chopper gets here?" I asked.

"A few minutes," he said. "You have time. I'll be over here if you need me." He walked away to join the group. Catching sight of Buck and Fernando, I waved, relieved they'd returned.

I pressed the button and the iPad flickered to life. A spreadsheet with account numbers in one column, dollar amounts, dates, and names in the others appeared on the screen. I doubted that would have surprised Anaya. So what? A bunch of old bank accounts from a decade ago. The owners had probably changed banks and account numbers by now. I looked more closely at the names listed in the far left column. Several of them were familiar: known leaders of each of the drug cartels active in Mexico at the time.

I still didn't get why Anaya had been so surprised. I scrolled back to the top of the page. Fulcrum Industries' familiar gray and white logo had been embedded in the spreadsheet.

Why would an international mining company worth billions be listed on the same page as dozens of Mexican drug lords? Did they have their fingers in cartel business, too?

The *thwap thwap* of the rotor blades broke the silence as the helicopter approached the pickup zone. My questions would have to wait. Lauren squeezed my hand and I squeezed back. Abby leaned against my legs, watching the big bird flare above the strobes, hover for a moment and land.

Pascal motioned for us to come forward and board the aircraft. I picked Abby up and turned toward Pascal. Lauren slipped her hand in mine and we ran to the chopper, ducking our heads at the rotor wash.

We were going home.

39

COLE AND HIS ex-wife, Lorna, were waiting for us at Sky Harbor airport. So was Agent Landers. I didn't see Sam anywhere, and my mood took a nosedive. *He's probably back in Seattle, trying to forget me,* I thought.

The relieved look on Cole's and Lorna's faces as Lauren and Abby ran toward them through the exit gate said it all. His face a portrait of raw emotion, Cole knelt on one knee with his arms stretched wide as the girls descended on him, enveloping him in a mammoth hug. Lauren broke away first and ran to her mother, with Abby following a few seconds later. I kept my distance and watched the tearful homecoming, grateful to see them together.

Agent Landers walked up to me and held out her hand.

"Welcome back, Kate. Good to have you home," she said. "Although, I'm not happy you did this on your own. A lot of things could have gone wrong."

"Yeah. I know." I set my backpack down, opened the main compartment, and rummaged around for the iPad, which I handed to her. "The information Anaya wanted is on the tablet. I'd describe him as surprised when he saw it."

Landers turned it over in her hands. "Did you look at it?" she asked. We both knew I had.

I nodded. "It's a spreadsheet with a list of the cartel bosses who were active at the time it was created," I said. "Along with dollar amounts by month. The only thing I could think of is that it signifies a payment from each of them to someone specific. The amounts are pretty large."

Landers clicked open the latches on her briefcase and placed the tablet inside. "Payments to whom? It couldn't have been Anaya if he was surprised at the information. Salazar?"

I shook my head. "No. Both Salazar and Anaya were on the list. The logo for Fulcrum Industries is embedded near the top of the page."

"The mining company?"

"Yep. Looks like they've had their fingers in the cookie jar."

Agent Landers whistled. "There've been rumors of a big boss—known as *El Jefe*—but so far there's been no evidence. None of the DEA's informants have been able to pinpoint who, or even if, *El Jefe* exists. If Fulcrum Industries is somehow involved, then that's a hell of a lead."

"Glad I could help."

"Why are you giving this to me and not Luis?"

I hesitated, unsure I should say anything. It's not like I had proof. *Screw it,* I thought. Someone leaked Quinn's involvement. It had to be from Luis' camp since no one else knew the bogus information.

"Anaya knew about the commandos tracking me." Her expression didn't change as I continued. "Quinn had me give Luis bad information in case there was an informant in the DEA. Chance Goodeve, Luis' boss back when I testified against Salazar and Anaya, had thought as much and kept a tight rein on the information going into and out of his office. When Chance retired, Luis took over that same team. Eventually, the wrong people found me—first in Alaska, then in Arizona. When I finally met with Anaya yesterday at his compound, he'd been aware of the false information. That would also explain how he knew about the FBI tracking me to the meet."

"Good to know." Landers took a moment to digest the information. "Any ideas who it might be?"

"I think it's Luis." On the surface it looked as though he'd been helping me, but when I thought about it, I realized he'd actually been keeping tabs on me for Anaya. The betrayal hit me hard, as all betrayals do. Yet another person I shouldn't have trusted. I'd been confusing Salazar's personal vendetta against me with Anaya's lack of one. Until I told Anaya I'd lost all the money. Then he'd tried to kill me.

If the information had surprised Landers, she didn't show it.

"But how do you explain Salazar and Anaya not being able to find you for so many years?"

"Anaya knew exactly where I was. He mentioned it when I saw him in the Caribbean. He thought I'd hidden something that belonged to him and patiently waited until I went back to find it."

Landers lifted her chin. "The card with the website and password."

"That was part of it, yes." I watched as Cole broke away from the reunion with Lauren and Abby and walked toward me. "That's everything I know. If I can help you with anything, you have my number."

Her glance flicked to Cole, and back to me. "Sure. Good luck, Kate." She held out her hand.

"Thanks. You too. And thank you for your help." I shook her hand, picked up my backpack, and walked toward Cole, meeting him in the middle of the busy corridor. We looked at each other for a long moment as travelers pushed by on the way to their flights. Cole spoke first.

"You risked your life to get my kids back. Thank you."

"I'm sorry, Cole. I never meant for any of it to happen. You have to believe that."

"I do. I'm sorry too. But they're here now. That's all that matters. We can begin to put our lives back together." He looked at Lorna and the girls. "The possibility of losing them helped Lorna and I come to a better understanding. We're going to try to work together more—for the sake of the kids."

"That's great, Cole. I'm happy for you."

"Did you want to come and say goodbye? We're taking the girls back to Lorna's for the night. We'll be heading to Durm in the morning."

I shook my head. "We already said our goodbyes on the plane. I gave Lauren my email address. I hope that's all right. If it's not, I'll understand."

"No. That's fine. They really love you, Kate. I just wish—" He shook his head. "For what it's worth, I'm sorry I don't remember you. According to them, we were happy." The look in his eyes told me he meant what he said.

"We were," I said. "But things change. People change." I held out my hand. "Good luck, Cole. Take care of yourself and those two precious kids."

Cole smiled. "I'll do that. Good luck to you, too, Kate."

I'm going to need it, I thought.

He broke contact first and returned to Lauren and Abby, who were both vying for Lorna's attention. Cole leaned down and said something to them. The two girls turned and waved. I raised my hand and watched as they left the airport: Abby on Cole's shoulders and Lauren by his side. Lorna walked a couple of paces apart from them.

With a sigh, I looked at the crowd of people rushing by me: families, couples, business men and women with somewhere to go. I never felt so alone. Shrugging on the pack, I walked through the airport, not sure what to do next.

Well, Kate. It's time to start over. Again. I'd been disappointed when Sam didn't show up, but not surprised. Even though I had my reasons for going to Mexico without him, I didn't expect him to wait around for me. It's not like I expected to come back. He knew that. Why would he want to be with a woman who didn't listen to reason? I felt for the onyx jaguar on the chain around my neck. Maybe now that Anaya was dead I'd have a chance at a new life. Maybe the bad spirits would finally leave me alone. Yes, I wanted to spend whatever life I had left with Sam, but that obviously wasn't going to happen.

As I neared the glass doors leading outside to the city buses and cabs, someone fell into step beside me. My shoulders stiffened at the intrusion and I glanced up.

And smiled.

Sam.

THE END

ACKNOWLEDGEMENTS

I'd like to thank the following people for their generous help in writing A ONE WAY TICKET TO DEAD: Laurie Boris, TSODA134, Sgt. J.G. Vineyard (Retired) Dallas DEA Task Force, Steve Miller (Det., Retired), Melinda Case, Ruth Ross, Ali Mosa, Jennifer Conner, Darlene Panzera, Sharon Kleve, Brian Yelland, Michelle Yelland, Bev Van Berkom, Larry Van Berkom, and last, but certainly not least, my first reader, Mark Lindstrom. All errors and omissions are entirely the fault of the author.

ABOUT THE AUTHOR

 **DV Berkom** is the USA Today bestselling author of two action-packed thriller series featuring strong female leads **Leine Basso** and **Kate Jones**. Her love of creating resilient, kick-ass women characters stems from a lifelong addiction to reading spy novels, mysteries, and thrillers, and longing to find the female equivalent within those pages.

Raised in the Midwest, she earned a BA in political science from the University of Minnesota and promptly moved to Mexico to live on a sailboat. Several years and many of adventures later, she wrote her first novel and was hooked. ***Bad Spirits,*** the first Kate Jones thriller, was published as an online serial in 2010 and was immediately popular with eBook fans. ***Dead of Winter, Death Rites***, and ***Touring for Death*** soon followed before she began the far grittier Leine Basso series in early 2012 with ***Serial Date***.

D.V. currently lives in the Pacific Northwest with her husband, Mark, and several imaginary characters who like to tell her what to do. Her most recent books include ***Shadow of the Jaguar, Dakota Burn, Absolution, Dark Return, The Last Deception, A Killing Truth,*** and ***Vigilante Dead.*** She's currently working on her next thriller.

For more information, visit her website at www.dvberkom.com.

NOTE FROM THE AUTHOR:

Thank you for reading A ONE WAY TICKET TO DEAD. If you would like to find out more about Kate or my other novels, see the links below:

Facebook: facebook.com/DvBerkomAuthor
Twitter: twitter.com/dvberkom
Website: dvberkom.com
Pinterest: pinterest.com/dvberkom/
Instagram: instagram.com/dvberkom
***Sign up for my free newsletter and be the first to find out about new releases: **http://bit.ly/DVB_RL**

Other books by D.V. Berkom
Kate Jones Thriller Series:
Kate Jones Thriller Series Vol. 1 Books 1-4
(Bad Spirits, Dead of Winter, Death Rites, Touring for Death.)
Cruising for Death (#5)
Yucatán Dead (#6)
Vigilante Dead (#8)

Leine Basso Crime Thriller Series
A Killing Truth
Serial Date
Bad Traffick
The Body Market
Cargo
The Last Deception
Dark Return
Absolution
Dakota Burn
Shadow of the Jaguar

The next page-turning thriller in the Kate Jones Thriller Series, *Vigilante Dead,* available now.